"YOU'RE GOING TO KILL HIM."

■ ━━━━━ ■

"Count on it."

"You won't get close enough without help."

"I'll get close enough to do the job." There was no doubt in her voice.

"But will you get *safely* out again, when you've done it?"

"I found out where he is, without outside help. I do have my own . . . channels, General. I'll get out."

"I'm sure you've got your channels. I expect you to. You were in this business long before I even knew you existed. But those same channels can be compromised. There are long memories out there. Don't go getting yourself killed, Mac. I'd hate that."

Books by Julian Jay Savarin

MacAllister's Task
MacAllister's Run
Pale Flyer
Trophy
Target Down!
Wolf Run
Windshear
Naja
The Quiraing List
Villiger
Water Hole
The Queensland File

Published by
HarperPaperbacks

MacAllister's Task

JULIAN JAY SAVARIN

HarperPaperbacks
A Division of HarperCollinsPublishers

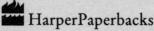

HarperPaperbacks
A Division of HarperCollins*Publishers*
10 East 53rd Street, New York, N.Y. 10022-5299

This is a work of fiction. The characters, incidents, and
dialogues are products of the author's imagination and are not to
be construed as real. Any resemblance to actual events or
persons, living or dead, is entirely coincidental.

Copyright © 1997 by Julian Jay Savarin
All rights reserved. No part of this book may be used or
reproduced in any manner whatsoever without written
permission of the publisher, except in the case of brief
quotations embodied in critical articles and reviews.
For information address HarperCollins*Publishers*,
10 East 53rd Street, New York, N.Y. 10022-5299.

ISBN 0-06-101059-6

HarperCollins®, ▟®, and HarperPaperbacks™
are trademarks of HarperCollins*Publishers* Inc.

Cover illustration by Edwin Herder

First printing: April 1997

Printed in the United States of America

Visit HarperPaperbacks on the World Wide Web at
http://www.harpercollins.com

❖ 10 9 8 7 6 5 4 3 2 1

THIS ONE'S FOR SIMON, HENRIETTE, MAGNUS,
PETRA, AND NOT FORGETTING,
THE ONE AND ONLY . . .
LARS!

Hohendorf listened to the muted sounds of the aircraft. It was almost as if it knew and understood what had happened. He looked about him, noting the silhouettes of the others in the red-gold splash of the setting sun: Selby and Flacht to his left; Bagni and Stockmann, his right; and holding station behind the tail, Cottingham and Christiansen.

He had to remind himself that this was not a permanently recurring sunset as they flew westwards, the sky itself appearing to be pay homage to McCann.

The other aircraft were tucked in close, an honor guard to escort their fallen comrade home. They moved slightly up and down as they kept station, their control surfaces constantly shifting as the computers made ceaseless, minute adjustments, keeping the powerful machines in stable flight. Within the aircraft, the advanced technology ensured the crews enjoyed a smooth ride.

No one had spoken for some time. It was as if everyone had decided to keep a respectful silence. There was a terrible sense of shock too. McCann gone! They found the thought hard to assimilate. The Kansas City Dude dead? It did not seem possible. Other people died. Not Elmer Lee McCann.

Alive, he drove them crazy. Dead . . . They didn't want to think of him dead.

Flying with the finely honed alertness that marked them out as the elite of an already elite unit, each was nonetheless deep within his own thoughts; and the pilots were almost startled out of their reveries when their respective backseaters called the new course.

"Right, three-three-zero," the navigators advised the pilots at precisely the same instant.

As if in chorus, the pilots acknowledged, "Roger. Three-three-zero." Then the relative silence descended once more.

At forty-five thousand feet and wings at mid-sweep, the four Tornados—three ASVs and Hohendorf's IDS(E)—wheeled in a tight, neat package onto the changed course, each aircraft holding station perfectly. They were now on the last leg to the November base, on Scotland's Moray coast.

Elmer Lee was nearly home.

The four aircraft flew in a tight diamond formation—the IDS(E) leading—directly along the length of the main runway, at an altitude of a hundred feet. Eight mighty engines roared their salute to McCann as the Tornados swept along to bank hard in a left break, still in formation.

On the ground, it appeared as if the entire November base had come out to watch. The news had already come through that McCann was dead. No one spoke. A pilot, who had once only half-jokingly replied to

McCann's plea on a wet day for something to do by suggesting that he stop breathing, now felt hugely guilty and somehow responsible for what had happened to Elmer Lee. All who watched the wheeling aircraft felt a distinct sense of loss they could not quite explain. Many did not know McCann personally; but everyone knew of him. And while he was not the unit's first casualty, he was the first mortal loss in air combat. That fact concentrated all minds.

In the control tower, Flying Officer Karen Lomax, the object of McCann's relentless but unrequited desires, felt hot tears come to her eyes as an unexpected pain seemed to have taken up residence near her heart. This surprised her, and she turned quickly away from the sympathetic glances of the others in the tower. They all knew that McCann—treading where even maddened angels would balk before attempting—had pursued her vainly. The fact that her boyfriend—a formidable rugby player who loved hurting people on the playing field—not only outranked him but was at least twice his size, had not deterred him for a single moment. McCann was like that.

Wise counsel from those who knew of his obsession and felt duty bound to remind him of self-preservation had spectacularly failed to deflect him from his determined pursuit of her. He was either completely insane, they'd thought, or so hopelessly in love, he might as well be. With McCann, it had been hard to tell which was which.

But he was an exceptional navigator; many thought the best on the unit. Modesty not being his strongest suit, McCann himself certainly thought so. Normally crewed with Selby, he had been paired with Hohendorf for the special mission over Bosnia. He had returned from the successful mission, but no longer alive.

Like virtually everyone else on the base, Karen Lomax was finding it hard to accept he was gone. She stared wide-eyed at the four Tornados as they broke into pairs for the landing, wondering at the strange ache that now seemed to have gripped her.

"But I didn't love him," she whispered to herself.

Yet, there was a question in the words even as she spoke them.

"Did I?" she added softly.

"Not long now, Elmer Lee," Hohendorf said quietly to the body in the rear cockpit as he brought the Tornado over the runway threshold.

"Hey! What's going on? Where are we?"

The suddenness of it nearly made Hohendorf jump out of his skin, and only his consummate discipline and skill enabled him to put the aircraft down safely.

"Lieber Gott!" he heard himself exclaim involuntarily. His heart was thumping as he eased the Tornado onto the runway, the aircraft wavering slightly as he did so.

It was not one of his better landings.

I'm hallucinating, he thought as the thrust reversers came on, slowing the aircraft. *I'm hearing things. I just thought I heard Elmer Lee!*

Just beyond his left shoulder and slightly behind, Selby's aircraft had touched down at precisely the same moment. He had the distinct impression that Flacht, in the backseat of Selby's Tornado, was staring at him.

I'm not surprised, he thought grimly. *That was a lousy landing, and I'm hearing things.*

"That was one hell of a rough thump-down, Axel," came McCann's critical tones. "They do that kind of aerobics on carriers. You sure you're okay out there?"

Hohendorf felt his hands grip the controls, more to steady himself than the aircraft.

He can't be alive, he thought. *He can't be! I'm imagining it. As soon as I get out of here I'm going to see the Doc.*

"Elmer Lee?" he began tentatively, feeling extremely foolish. Now he was talking to the dead. Was McCann's ghost still occupying the backseat?

Everyone knew aircrew ghosts haunted their old aircraft and bases, though no one would openly admit such a thing. Was that happening on this particular Tornado?

Pull yourself together, Hohendorf! You're an officer in the Marineflieger. *You're one of the best Tornado pilots around, and you're flying with an elite international unit. You don't hear or speak to ghosts; even McCann's.*

But the "dead" voice was saying, "Yeah, it's me. Who do you think's going to be back here? You sound kind of funny. You okay?" McCann repeated. Then came a sharp gasp. "Jesus! Something in me sure hurts!" He seemed totally unaware that he'd been unconscious.

Hohendorf heard himself breathing rapidly in his oxygen mask and said nothing; but in his mind, one thought was continuous.

It's not possible! he kept thinking.

In the other aircraft, Flacht was staring over at Hohendorf's Tornado.

"Mark," he began hesitantly to Selby, interrupting the taxiing instructions from the tower.

"Yes?"

"That was not a good landing from Axel," Flacht commented in his precise English.

"I thought so too. Just didn't want to mention it."

There was a pause.

"I was looking at his Tornado," Flacht continued, "after he touched down. I saw Elmer Lee's head moving."

A deep silence followed.

"What do you mean 'moving'? Must have been that landing. It rattled his body around."

"Perhaps."

Flacht said nothing more, not wanting to startle Selby while the aircraft was still moving, and so close to the other.

There was still plenty of light from the sunset, enabling him to see clearly both the front and rear cockpits of Hohendorf's aircraft. He didn't want to tell Selby that McCann's head was turned towards them.

Besides, he wasn't sure it wasn't his mind making him see what he wanted to. Just like everybody else, he didn't want to believe McCann was really dead.

The Tornados taxied off the runway and headed for their hardened shelters.

In the lead aircraft, Hohendorf was trying to come to terms with the fact that the man he had thought dead was indeed alive, in the back cockpit.

He said nothing to the others. They would know soon enough.

The Pentagon, June the following year.

Major General Abraham Bowmaker, USAF, sat at his desk staring at a photograph. It had been taken during the past year. A series of emotions rushed through him: anger, rage, despair, shame, and finally contempt, both for those whose direct actions had produced the situation that had led to the incident, and for those whose unforgivable inaction had allowed it to happen.

He put the photograph down slowly and continued to stare at it.

"You were somebody's child, once," he said to the hanging corpse in the photograph.

The Billie Holiday song, "Strange Fruit," came powerfully to him, the words tolling like funereal bells in his mind.

But this had not been the result of a lynching party;

nor had it taken place during the bad old days in the South; nor was the body that of a black male.

The body in the much-copied photograph, which had been seen on TV screens and the pages of newsprint around the world, was that of a young woman. The pink of her sweater seemed closer to crimson, and the tree she hung from was somewhere in what used to be called Yugoslavia.

She had not been lynched.

Overcome by the shame of the sexual and physical abuse she had experienced at the hands of those who had captured her, she had been unable to live with it and had taken her own life.

To Bowmaker, it was a metaphor for the obscenity of what had been allowed to happen to Bosnia. That photograph, he decided, should shame the international community. The gross ineptitude that had resulted in this and other atrocities during that terrible conflict should have caused them to ruthlessly examine their own motives. But long years of experience had sharpened his cynicism. He knew they wouldn't.

What had once been normal life for the victims of that war had been lost for good. New, centuries-long scars had been laid to join those of previous centuries. And there'd always be, he was certain, new demagogues who would be only too happy to employ their own perversion of history, to suit their own ends. And they would find willing hearts and minds in new generations. People, it would appear, were clearly unable to learn the lessons of history and possess the wit to ignore those malevolent, siren voices.

"If they did," he said aloud, "there'd be no need for people like me."

It was an idea that over the years he'd found attractive though he knew that, realistically, it would never happen.

Ever since he'd been a green and eager young officer candidate, he'd wondered if, by the time he'd made it to general rank—if at all—the world would have civilized itself.

"You'd think they'd have got smart by now," he growled. "Fat chance."

Bowmaker again felt the disgust build within him, as he looked at the photograph once more.

There was supposed to be peace over there now, but he was highly sceptical of its chances of lasting. As soon as the NATO troops had cleared the dust of that wretched country from their heels, the cycle of revenge would continue. Pockmarked here and there in the devastated country, it was still continuing. There was never going to be any peace in that place, unless the international community sat heavily upon those who would seek to destroy it.

"But they haven't got the guts," he muttered contemptuously. "And so, the barbarians are on the loose." He tapped at the photograph. "But someone's going to pay for this, girl." A hard edge had come into his voice as he made a vow to the dead young woman. "And I'm going to make sure we get at least one of the bastards."

He'd been thinking about that for months. Now it was time to put his plan into action. A lot of people owed him favors.

He picked up one of his three phones, to begin the process of collecting on some of them.

The Hallingdal, Norway, between Nesbyen and Geilo, a week later.

Bowmaker, in civilian clothes, drove the blue self-drive Saab he'd hired in Oslo along the spectacular narrow

road, heading towards Kinsarvik. He glanced in his
rear-view mirror. The white Volvo 840TR was still
there. The powerful, turbo-charged estate had been on
his tail since the Bromma junction, a few kilometers
ago. There was hardly any traffic, but the Volvo had
made no move to pass him. The Norwegian standard,
non-motorway speed limit on the open road was eighty
kph. Perhaps the Volvo driver was being good.

Bowmaker had seen it slip into position behind him,
having come via the mountain road from Åmot nearly
a hundred kilometers away on the edge of the
Hardangervidda, the great high plateau of south central
Norway. The arrangement that had been relayed to him
via the British intelligence agent, Charles Buntline, was
that a car would join the road at the Bromma junction,
although the make of the vehicle had itself not been
specified. He hoped it *was* the car he expected.

They were nearing the sweeping bend that would
take them towards the resort of Gol, still some distance from Geilo, when the Volvo flashed its lights. He
saw the turning he'd been told about on his right—a
narrow, country road—almost on the apex of the bend,
and turned into it.

The Volvo trailed him.

"You'd better be the right one," he murmured to
himself, "or I could be in trouble." He was not carrying
a weapon.

He'd traveled for about a kilometer, when he noted
the small clearing just off the road. He pulled into it,
and stopped. There was no other traffic, and it
appeared as if there hadn't been for some time. The
feeling of isolation was palpable, despite the beauty of
the scenery, which at that moment was the last thing
on his mind.

The Volvo drew up behind the Saab.

Bowmaker remained in his car, watching the rear-view mirror.

For some moments the driver of the Volvo, just as Bowmaker had done, remained within the estate car. Then the driver's door opened. Female ankles appeared, attached to long slim legs, as she got out and shut the door.

She was an incredible chameleon, he thought, watching closely as she approached the Saab. Today, dressed in a smart business suit of pale olive green and a white blouse, she looked every inch the successful, high-flying executive.

Bowmaker heaved a sigh of relief then beamed as he too climbed out.

"Good to see you again, Colonel," he greeted as Sian MacAllister, U.S. Marine sergeant, Russian Army lieutenant-colonel, and many other things besides, came up to him with a smile that he remembered well. "The hair's different."

"General." She briefly touched the golden brown, jaw-length tresses. "I got rid of the blond Marine crop some time ago." She gave him a quick hug and a kiss on the cheek.

"Well, that beats being smacked in the mouth any day," he said approvingly.

Once, in her guise as the Marine sergeant—complete with the severely cropped hair—a senior officer had made the serious mistake of fondling her. Her response had been so swift and hard, the officer had been knocked cold. No charges were ever pressed; but Mac, as she liked to be called—though it was not her real name—had been rapidly posted out, ending up at the Pentagon where she'd met Bowmaker for the first time. Since then she had sometimes worked with him, and thus with the November unit.

Bowmaker was still not sure where her true loyalties lay, despite the first-rate jobs she'd carried out since he'd known her. Hell, she'd worked *in* the Pentagon, and he'd never known then that she was Russian. He had no idea who really sanctioned her orders and wondered what she'd say if he asked about that and her loyalties. Not the sort of questions to ask, he decided.

"Look at you," he went on. "You're looking pretty good, Mac. When I saw you last, after you'd got out of Bosnia . . ."

"I wasn't looking so hot. Don't I know it!" She gave him another of her quick smiles.

"Well, you had been in there for some time, and on the run." Bowmaker glanced at the magnificent landscape about him. "The wilds of Norway. No one can hear you yell," he added drily. "Good choice of location."

"I'm always careful where survival is concerned. There are more spies around now, I believe, than during the Cold War." She said that with a straight face. "Everyone's gearing up for something," she went on. "But no one seems to know exactly what it's supposed to be. It's a game that gets more complex by the day."

"Some game."

She nodded slowly, and just as Bowmaker had recently done, looked calmly around. "I also took a route that would confuse anyone who might have tried to follow us," she said, still surveying the scenery about her. "Can't be too careful."

She had left the main road at Hønefoss to head for Åmot, before going right to cut across the mountain, making for the junction at Bromma. She seemed satisfied by her scan of the area.

"During this month, festivals and golf tournaments get into their stride in this area," she informed him, "especially up the road in Gol. The traffic grows correspondingly. But no one's followed," she added. "We're clean."

Bowmaker smiled at her, impressed, as he'd always been, by her complete professionalism. "I didn't expect to find you in Norway, when I asked the well-bred thug to make contact for me."

"The well-bred thug. You mean Charles Buntline?"

"The man himself. He owes me some favors. The air vice-marshal once described him that way. Good family, went to one of the best British private schools . . ."

"Public school. They call their best private schools public . . ."

"That's the Brits for you."

She smiled thinly. "He's good at what he does. He did get me out of Bosnia. You made him."

"He came to me for help," Bowmaker corrected. "I roped in the November boys and hey presto . . . we had a rescue mission."

"McCann nearly died," she remarked soberly.

"Yeah. How do you figure that kid? Stubborn as hell. Just refused to give up, even when the Doc believed he'd had it. Everyone was shocked, of course. I've heard even Wing Commander Jason, who felt plagued by McCann, had watery eyes when he got the news. Then the planes returned to base and McCann, in true Kansas City Dude style, comes awake just as Hohendorf is about to land. Gave the poor guy the fright of his life.

"They reckoned a rookie pilot couldn't have made a worse landing. Exaggeration, of course . . . but you know what I'm saying. Then McCann went straight out again, and Hohendorf thought he'd been hearing things. After they took the body out of the aircraft, the Kansas boy comes awake for good."

She grinned. "Wouldn't be McCann otherwise."

"It certainly wouldn't. According to the base doctor," Bowmaker continued, "when Hohendorf spotted the doll's eye for the backseater's oxygen flow—that's a gizmo on the instrument panel that blinks when you're still breathing—when he saw it wasn't doing its stuff, he made a rapid descent to lower altitudes to allow McCann to breathe without the mask. But, of course, the kid was out of it.

"At the base in Italy where they first landed, the detachment doctor misdiagnosed. It happens. Recently, a woman in Britain was pronounced dead; but she woke up days later. She'd had an epileptic fit, only no one seemed to have spotted that at the time." Bowmaker gave an expressive shiver. "Talk about a premature burial.

"In McCann's case," he went on, "the spent bullet that hit him knocked him out but didn't actually touch his heart, although it came as close as hell. That same bullet, passing through the aircraft, damaged not only the oxygen flow warning system, but also prevented the warning light from coming on. Hohendorf thought McCann had also suffered oxygen starvation; but the kid was actually receiving oxygen all the time. That's what really saved his life. And, of course, there was no brain damage." Bowmaker shook his head in wonder. "You need the luck sometimes, flying fast jets. But McCann's got a whole parcel of it, all to himself."

A silence fell between them.

Then Mac said, "You didn't come all the way up here to talk about Elmer Lee, General."

He gave her a sideways look. "No. I didn't. Eager to get right to it?"

"I want to know what could be so important to make you search me out *in person*, all the way up here in Norway."

"I'd have gone to the Antarctic, if necessary."

He still didn't get immediately to the point, studying instead the clothes she was wearing. "Buntline says you run a language training school for some local airline company." The quotation marks over "training" could almost be seen. "Good time to position up here . . . given that life could start getting exciting again in this part of the world, from the Baltics to North Cape and the Murmansk region."

"It's never really stopped," she said. "Things have just moved up a gear."

"Speak the Scandinavian languages, do you? Even the crazy one that doesn't sound Scandinavian?"

"I speak all of them. And if by 'crazy' you mean Finnish . . . the answer is yes. I speak some Sami dialects too."

"You mean the Lapps."

"They prefer 'Sami.'" She wondered whether he knew she'd had a Finnish mother.

"I bow to your knowledge. Just how many languages do you speak, Mac?"

"Enough." She also had command of a wide spectrum of accents, in English. She could sound very American when she wanted to, even picking a particular state accent to suit the occasion.

He gave her a tight smile. "Seems I still haven't learned not to ask the wrong question."

"You'll just have to trust me on that, General."

"Don't *you* trust *me?*"

"It depends. I had a very good friend, once—not a lover—a truly good friend. He was in the business, and very good at what he did. Like Buntline, only better . . . "

"Better than you?"

"At some things. I'm better at others." She didn't specify which, but there was no boastfulness in her voice. "He stayed alive," she went on, "by being very careful about whom he gave his trust to. One day, he fell in love, quit, and got married. He trusted her enough to tell her certain things. He believed it was forever, you see. He thought he could depend on her, and thought she was the best thing that had ever happened to him." Mac paused. "She was the worst. When she'd got really close to him, she walked. She must have been incredibly selfish."

She paused again, remembering. "She used the things he'd told her," Mac continued, "against him. It totally wrecked him. Every time he saw a woman with hair like hers, or who walked like her, or even was approximately shaped like her, he'd *think* it was her. She was inside his head. He was so traumatized, he was seeing her everywhere. Such a waste of a good man. General, she did more damage to him than all his years in the field."

She paused for a third time. "Sometimes, I wonder about people, and why we bother putting our necks on the line for them. It's not as if they really give a damn. They'll always follow the next maniac who wraps himself in a flag, or warps a religion, and comes along to sweet-talk them on the way to hell."

"Like Yugoslavia?"

"Our doorstep nightmare. But it happens in other countries too. No country is immune, and on occasion, it can happen on a personal level. Love is blind, they say." She shook her head slowly. "You'd think that, by now, I'd no longer be surprised by what human beings can do; but just when you think you've seen it all there's always one more stupid, or more brutal, than the last. And then there'll be the others, even more stupid, ready to march to the beat of his drum. I'm mixing everything together, but they're really all linked."

Bowmaker watched her, fascinated, realizing she'd been deeply affected by whatever had become of her un-named friend. He wondered at whom, and at what, her contempt was directed. At the country that used to be Yugoslavia? Or at her friend for sacrificing his sanity in the name of a dubious love?

"I got a card from him," she said. "The only one . . . and that was some time ago. All it said was, 'Love sucks.'"

"He's an *American?*"

She didn't say anything to that. "For a long time after," she continued, as if Bowmaker had not spoken, "he used to check out the feet of any woman he dated . . ."

"Their *feet?*"

"Their feet. Can you believe it? But feet are supposed to tell you plenty. She had small feet and short toes, you see, and in his mind, he equated that with being a mean bitch. So if he met a woman with short toes he was off in the opposite direction, as if she had some kind of contagious disease. It didn't matter how attractive he'd found her." She gave a brief, humorless chuckle. "Generalizations can be dangerous. I've got longish toes. Well . . . kind of. There are some men who would tell you I'm the original bitch from hell . . . if they were still walking around."

Bowmaker knew precisely what she meant. "You talk about your friend in the past tense. What happened to him? Killed?"

MacAllister shook her head. "He's around. Somewhere. Dating those other women didn't help. He just couldn't get her out of his mind. She'd fucked up his brain. Last I heard, he was getting drunk on a beach they'd been to for the first time together, staring out to sea. I haven't seen him, so I can't say for sure. If it's true, perhaps he's looking for whatever it was he lost when he met her. It's as if she assassinated something inside him and left just a shell. For him, she was pure poison, and he didn't know it. This was a man with the instincts of a jungle cat. Even now, I find it hard to believe he was taken so easily."

"Perhaps he's really looking for whatever it was he lost when she *left*." Happily married himself, Bowmaker could imagine what such a loss could mean.

"Maybe." MacAllister gave Bowmaker a neutral look. "But it's really the same thing, isn't it? She did take something out of him when she left. It doesn't mean she'd brought it to him in the first place. She found it in place, and destroyed it. As I said: the woman's an assassin." She gave a strange smile. "She does emotionally what I do as a profession. He really should have watched his back. That's what trust does when you give it to the wrong person."

"You didn't say love."

"The other side of the same coin . . . sometimes."

"I get the point about your friend's emotional nightmare; but do you put me in her category?"

"No, General. I've got a very different category for you." This time, she gave him one of her special smiles.

Bowmaker leaned against the Saab and pulled slightly at the brightly patterned Norwegian sweater he was wearing. "Shouldn't have put this on. I didn't think it would be quite so warm up here in June. I look like a damn tourist."

"It can get a lot warmer in Norway than outsiders think. On the 'vidda in August, it sometimes gets baking hot. Hotter than farther south in Europe. And the mosquitos go crazy. Whole clouds of them rise like attack squadrons." Mac looked pointedly at the sweater. "Loud for my taste, but you did the right thing. Being a rubber-necking tourist is good cover. But we're not here to talk about the climate either, General. Or your taste in sweaters."

She watched him closely, waiting to hear what he had to say.

"You wearing a gun?" he asked abruptly.

"Of course."

"I can't tell."

"That's the point, General."

"I hear you're planning a private trip."

Her eyes did not waver. "What exactly did you hear?"

"You're wondering if Buntine told me."

"I'm not wondering anything. I'm waiting to hear what you've got to say."

"We could help each other out. I'm not going strictly through channels either."

"I'm still waiting, General."

For reply, Bowmaker heaved himself off the Saab, reached in, and took out an A5 envelope. With care, he pulled out a photograph, which he lay flat on the roof of the car. It was the picture of the hanging girl.

MacAllister drew closer to study it. She was silent for a long time as she looked at the image and appeared to be willing herself, by the strength of her gaze, into the place where the tragedy had occurred.

Bowmaker watched interestedly as the planes of her cheeks gradually tightened.

"I want at least one of the bastards who made this happen," he said to her, as she continued to study the photo. "Forget the one or two who may have surrendered themselves in the hopes of plea-bargaining with the international court. I want one of the high-ranking bastards, and I want him where we can put him before the cameras. Then I want him punished for all to see. I've had this on my mind for months. I think the so-called peace that's been brokered hasn't got much longer to go. Those people out there are itching to get back at each other's throats."

Long moments passed before she at last turned away from the picture to look at him with eyes that had gone so cold, he had to restrain an involountary shiver.

"What did Buntline tell you?"

"Not much. When he'd heard what I'd got in mind, he thought I should talk to you. 'She may be able to help you.' I quote him directly. 'She's got some plan that might fit in with yours.'"

"He said that?"

"Exactly as you've just heard it. I've got to say I'm surprised you're wanting to go back in there. Bound to be people who remember you in an . . . unfriendly way. You took out plenty of their guys, especially those snipers, and the soldiers who were sent to capture you . . ."

"I gutted one of the bastards." She said that so brutally, it shook him. "Psychopathic, murdering, raping, fat shit of a militiaman. He was in command of a small district. He raped a young girl I knew, who worked in one of those cafés that the militiamen frequented. I'd met her just the once. Before they started killing each other in that sick country, he was a petty criminal. He tried to rape me too. It was the last mistake he ever made. He was trying to feed his guts back into himself as he died."

MacAllister's entire face was a frozen mask as she spoke, despite the warmth of the day. Bowmaker, listening to her chilling remarks, could only wonder at the many facets to this woman with the elusive identity. Mac trod a path that was both solitary and highly dangerous. In the days of the Old West, she would probably have been a scout. Out there, alone, surviving by wit and skill, every shadow a possible enemy; and life even more dangerous because she was a woman.

"From what I hear," he began quietly, "you also took out some of the best special troops around. What were those boys called?"

"Omegas. They too were after me."

"And commanded by a Russian major doing his own Bosnian thing, under very special orders . . ."

"The omegas are their own people. No one except another omega really commands them, even someone like the major, who was KGB."

"Old KGB?"

"Old KGB, new KGB . . . it's all the same. That part of things hasn't changed, whatever fancy names they give themselves. Same wine, new bottle."

"Could be very risky for you out there, Mac. Plenty of people with old scores to settle. Plenty who would be happy as a wino locked in a liquor store to find you exposed and on your own. You need some real backup. I'll come right out and tell you, I'd no idea how you'd react to what I had to say; but hearing you were going in anyway, I thought I'd give it a try. This is a request, Mac. Not an order. Assuming I can give you orders . . ."

"You can't. Not unless I'm assigned to you."

"Which you're not."

"Which I'm not. But I'm willing to listen."

"Good enough," Bowmaker said.

He paused as he heard a truck, unseen in the far distance, grind its way up a steeply sloping road. The solitary noise echoed about the surrounding mountains. The sound came to him as a strangely haunting cry, reaching, it seemed, into his very soul. For the briefest of moments, the beautiful landscape about him was alien and primeval. It was as if he'd suddenly been transported back in time and was once again a puny human being, fearful of unimaginable terrors beyond the distant ramparts.

That's the permanent state of the world, he thought. *We're always fearful of what lies beyond the next slice of time.*

"That truck sounds lonely," he observed softly.

They both listened, each remaining silent; each interpreting the sound according to the way it affected them.

Bowmaker waited until the wail of the laboring truck had become a barely perceptible background noise that gradually faded into the mountains, before deciding to continue.

"From the little that Buntline was prepared to tell me," he said, "it looks like you're going in to settle your own score. Not what I'd have expected of Mac, the consummate professional."

"As I said earlier, General . . . it's a private trip. Outside normal channels . . . as *you* said."

"I also said you'll need some real backup. We can help each other. We're after the same thing. This . . . person you're hunting out . . . big cheese, is he? Bigger than the militiaman you . . . er . . . gutted?"

Her eyes were steady upon his. "Much bigger. The NATO implementation force would love to get their hands on him, if they could get their act together."

"But you can."

"I know where he is."

"And you won't let IFOR know."

"Not a chance in hell," Mac said in a harsh voice. "I *want* that piece of offal. That militia commander I told you about? He had a room at the back of the café. Normally, he took whores in there. But he'd long had a fancy for the young girl, and for me. The dogshit."

She paused, lips briefly tightening.

"I used to call at the café sometimes," she went on, "for a coffee and a light bite, whenever I came down from the mountains. It was also a good place to pick up intelligence, just by observation. They used to raid the UN convoys in those days. Still do, in some areas, except it's IFOR stuff they take now. Sometimes, I had real French coffee—taken by the militia, in ambush."

She studied his expression closely, as if checking to see whether he disapproved.

"He knew me as a Russian volunteer," she said, continuing as Bowmaker remained silent and impassive, "whose job it was to take out the snipers. I took all the snipers I could find, irrespective of which side they were on. He never knew that at the time. I met the girl during one of my visits, and she looked on me as some kind of hero. She kept asking me about getting into the fighting. I did my best to stop her. There were enough damaged people around without my creating another one of my very own, and adding to the number.

"When my cover was blown, he used her as his first act of revenge. He raped her right there in the little room back of the café, while the pigs he called bodyguards stood watch outside. He abused her for hours, until they and the bodyguards were the only people left in the place. The others, even the soldiers, were so scared of this man and his thugs, they never tried to help her. They just left her with them. It was well into the night by then. Then he sent her to a special combat unit, run by another psycho called Serenic.

"In a land that seems to have bred more psychos per head of population than it's possible to believe, Serenic is even worse than that man ever was. The combat unit call themselves the Black Lynxes. Their reputation stinks with the blood of many, many innocents. It was to that . . . bunch the commander sent the girl; then feeling like a macho man after what he'd done to her, he decided to come after me. While he was trying to rape me, he boasted about what he'd done to her. I'm glad I killed him the way I did. Couldn't have happened to a nicer person."

Her mouth became so hard as she remembered, the skin about her lips whitened. She paused and took a deep breath, as if trying to cool whatever was burning away within her.

Bowmaker watched and continued to listen.

She noted this and said, wryly, "I'm the one who's supposed to be listening to what you have to say. Not so cool, huh?"

"What *you've* got to say is just as important. It's tough about your young friend. We can't help her now; but we can avenge her. So please . . . go on, Mac. Let's hear more about this Serenic and see what we can do about him."

"*I* know what I can do about him." She sounded uncompromising. "He's become quite a power in his own little piece of real estate; but his group also travels round the country, doing nasty jobs for the other warlords. Nothing he'd like more than to see the peace break down. He'd be back to spilling even more blood, and enjoying it.

"When the girl got to Serenic's unit he sampled her first—for *days*, almost without pause—before turning her over to his men. He'd kept her locked in an ammunition store when he wasn't using her. When others found her body, she'd been mutilated and discarded in the snow like so much garbage. She was barely recognizable. Of course, they all deny she was ever with them."

MacAllister's expression had changed again, a savage contempt stamped upon features that were normally quite unexpectedly beautiful.

A continuingly fascinated Bowmaker kept his silence.

"The miserable cowards," she went on harshly. "She must have died in so much pain, General. I owe it to her to get him. I owe it to *me*. The West will never prize him out of there and he'll get away with his butchery, just like so many of the others. My way will ensure at least *one* gets paid in full."

"You're going to kill him."

"Count on it."

"You won't get close enough without help."

"I'll get close enough to do the job." There was no doubt in her voice.

"But will you get safely *out* again, when you've done it?"

"I found out where he is, without outside help. I do have my own . . . channels, General. I'll get out."

"I'm sure you've got your channels. I expect you to. You were in this business long before I even knew you existed. But those same channels can be compromised. There are long memories out there. Don't go getting yourself killed, Mac. I'd hate that."

At his words, a reluctant smile came slowly to her lips.

"I've got a good idea of how you feel," Bowmaker pressed on, hoping it was an advantage. He reasoned gently with her. "I feel it too. We're both looking for some kind of restitution out of this horror, so let's join forces. As you'll be going in, whatever I say or do, why not let me help? I have this nightmare, Mac. If you go in alone—even with your channels in place—you're not going to get out again.

"Don't kill him out there. Make him pay for your young waitress, sure, and . . . for her." Bowmaker tapped at the photograph of the hanging girl. "And for all those like her. Bring him out. Let the world see the monster's face. Let the world see him being made to pay. Send an unequivocal message to all those who are like him. Let *them* know they're not safe.

"If you kill him on some mountainside, *you'll* know he's gone. The world won't. Another shot, another body in a forest somewhere. So what? Let's bring him out together," Bowmaker urged. "Let's do this for all those poor people out there who think the world's deserted them. What do you say?"

She said nothing for a long time. She walked a little distance away from the cars and stared up at the high plateau of the Hardanger.

MacAllister had an unusual presence. A man seeing her for the first time would think she was okay to look at, but would feel no immediate rush of blood through his veins. A smarter man would look again and realize he'd nearly dismissed an outstanding beauty. This hidden aspect tended to serve her very well in the sometimes exceedingly dangerous pursuit of her work. She could blend into any surrounding.

She kept herself very fit and her tough body was slim, but without the excess muscling with which fanatical gym addicts inevitably cursed their own bodies. Priming her physique to just the right level had bestowed a softness upon her that had gradually captivated the one man for whom she cared deeply, but could see only infrequently. Some men, she knew, would have preferred a fuller, more curvaceous body; but Morton wanted her as she was. That was all that mattered.

A gentle, rounded prominence to her cheekbones and the hint of an almond shape to her blue-gray eyes betrayed the touch of Sami blood in her, to those who would know what to look for. The people with such information could be counted on the fingers of one hand. The true color of her hair was white blond. But she hadn't worn it like that in years.

She strode slowly back towards Bowmaker.

"I'll have to think about this, General," she said at last.

"Fine by me."

Her expression softened. "How's Chuck?"

"I wondered when you'd ask about him. The good major's doing fine. He seems to be making it okay in his new posting as a pilot with the November boys. Still sending him a card now and then? No postal origin, as usual?"

She nodded. "For now, that's how it's got to be. I hope he understands."

"I'm sure he does. But it's bound to be tough on him."

Again, she nodded. "He must know that I care."

"He does."

"All these things I do," she said in a thoughtful voice. Her eyes seemed to be looking at something deep within herself. "MacAllister's Task," she continued wryly. "Like the Labors of Heracles ... Hercules, if you prefer ..." She paused. "But I've long passed my twelfth. This is a hell of a job sometimes, General."

"I know," he told her gently.

She gave him a quick, impulsive kiss on the cheek then walked back to her car.

"I'll be in touch," she said, and got in.

"Okay," he said.

He stood watching as she turned the Volvo round, to head back towards the main road.

They did not wave to each other.

He remained where he was for some minutes, giving her plenty of time. She'd be heading back towards Oslo. He'd be continuing towards Kinsarvik, where he'd hand the car over. From there, he'd take one of the coastal boats to Bergen, then catch a flight out on a scheduled airline.

It would be as if they'd never met.

2

Major Chuck Morton, USAF, was very pleased with himself. After fuel mismanagement in an F-16 had caused him to be grounded and slotted into a dead-end job at the Pentagon—despite a superb display of airmanship by safely landing the bird dead-stick—he'd tried every desperate plea in the book to get back into flying, with a singular lack of success. Without power, the supremely agile F-16 had become little more than a gliding brick. But he'd bought down the taxpayers' expensive flying hot-rod in one piece, on a once-only chance.

Everybody had said it had been a fantastic piece of airmanship. Everybody had expressed the view that most pilots would have ejected, or died. Everybody, except the powers-that-be, who'd taken a very dim view, indeed, of majors who committed the sort of flying crime that even a rookie shouldn't have. He'd thus found himself staring into a very bleak career future.

But one of life's crazy twists had saved him.

Mac had been posted to the same cubbyhole office, deep within the bowels of the Pentagon, as his assistant. *Her* offense had been that now-famous right hook to the jaw of the officer with the exploring hands. The unofficial nickname of the senior officer in question was Glassjaw, and it seemed that every rank in every service now knew that name. Interestingly, only a very few people knew that Mac was the reason for this uncomplimentary tag. The officer in question was not among those. It was as if she had vanished. The name she'd been using then was not the one she used now, wherever she was. She had also looked very different at the time, the epitome of a crop-haired Marine.

Morton had long resigned himself to the fact that he had fallen in love with a woman who was never going to fully belong to him. At least, not until she was ready to quit that strange job of hers. Which identity would she be carrying then? But he felt privileged to know her and to be allowed to share in the very little of what was known of her, outside her own highly classified, professional circle.

From time to time, he got postcards from her. They mainly carried nothing more than cryptic little messages that only he understood. Their postmarks were from all over the world, but he knew that, sometimes, they were not posted from where she might have been at the time. Most, he was certain, though written by her, had been passed on to be posted from somewhere well away from where she'd written them. She could have been in the very next town a few miles from him, and he wouldn't have known it. Unless she'd wanted him to.

It was Mac who had spotted a secret radar in the

African desert, leading eventually to a clandestine strike by the November squadrons, initiated by General Bowmaker.

The successful mission had brought Morton some valuable kudos. It had so pleased the general that Morton's desperate request to be returned to flying had been favorably considered, the general's considerable influence going a long way to making that happen. And while the USAF had still not totally forgiven him for nearly losing one of its precious aircraft, he'd got what he considered to be *the* best prize of all: flying the fantastic Super Tornado ASV, with the November squadrons. Hot ship, hot missions. He knew a lot of guys who would sell their very souls to get into the unit.

But here he was, sitting in one of the marvelous aircraft, preparing for takeoff. All this and Mac too. Sometimes, a guy got really lucky.

On this warm day on the Moray coast, he sat in air-conditioned comfort in the front cockpit of the two-seat ASV and went through his final checks. From his position at the threshold of the main runway, he stared beyond the wide-angle head-up display at the great tarmac slab of the main runway, as it speared its way towards the waters of the Moray Firth. Beyond *that* was the northern vastness of the Norwegian Sea.

It had been a long haul. Coming from the F-16 Falcon, the all-singing, all-dancing electric jet itself, he'd thought he'd known all there was to know about flying fighters. After all, he'd put one back on the ground without power, hadn't he? But he'd soon stopped thinking he was an ace pilot, when he saw what the November boys *really* got up to on a average day. It had been like going back to school, and the experience had been humbling.

In the early days, he'd been anxious about making the

grade, certain he never would. The November squadrons flew on the edge, *and* beyond. The boss and father of the whole November idea, Wing Commander Jason, demanded and expected it. There were no passengers.

When Chuck had been a younger, eager, and green pilot wanting more than anything to get into the cockpit of the F-16, he'd thought he'd at last reached the pinnacle of his expectations when he'd finally been passed fit to fly one of those aerial masterpieces. Walking out to the aircraft on the very first solo, he'd scarcely been able to believe his good fortune.

It hadn't mattered how many times he'd been up with an instructor. That first solo had been the *real* thing. That was when the fledgling had been turned into a hawk. Then had come the awful humiliation— well into his career—of running out of the vital juice on a simple training mission. Running out of fuel was a virtual kill for the enemy. Had it been a combat situation, he'd have had it, one way or the other. At the very least, he'd have had to eject. It still caused him acute embarrassment, just thinking about it. Majors didn't run out of fuel.

But he had.

Starting again at the November base had been a lot tougher than the time first spent coming to grips with the F-16, an aircraft he would always have plenty of time for. But it was all over. No more F-16s for him. There was the bittersweet sense of loss to remind him of what flying it had been like; but, it had been time to move on.

Going from the single-engine lightweight to the awesome power of the twin-engined Super Tornado had been like leaping from a skittish mustang onto the back of a ferociously wild but sleek racehorse that would as soon kill you as look at you. Until you began to understand and appreciate the potency of the sophisticated, high-tech machine, and what it placed at your finger-tips.

"*Never* . . . never allow yourself to get behind the power curve," one of his instructors had drummed into him. "Stay with her, and she'll do your bidding. Become one with her, and you'll find her easy to fly. If you let her master you, you're in deep trouble. Let her know you're right there with her, and she'll take you into the jaws of hell and bring you back. Lose that control, and you won't come back at all. If that scares you . . . good. Scared students are smart. They live to become smart pilots. I can do many things. Teaching dead, stupid pilots isn't one of them."

Morton sensed a faint smile in his oxygen mask as he remembered the instuctor's dry words.

He'd done it. He'd become one of the smart pilots. He was now one of the elite, in *the* elite unit. The embar-rassing incident with the fuel was now just a sharp memory to keep him aware; a lesson learned for good.

A guy could certainly get lucky sometimes.

"Sparrowhawk Two-Six," the female voice from the control tower was saying. "Clear to take off."

"Sparrowhawk. Roger."

"Bye, Mummeee!" came familiar tones from the backseat.

"Sparrowhawk!" admonished Karen Lomax from the tower. "Please observe correct radio procedures!"

"Hear that tremolo in her voice?" McCann said glee-fully. "I make her go weak at the knees. C'mon, Major. Let's get this ship airborne."

What malign sense of humor, Morton wondered, *had persuaded the boss to give him McCann as backseater for today's training mission?*

His feet having swiveled the rudder pedals down-wards to hold the aircraft on the toe brakes, Morton had already pushed the throttles into max dry. He released the brakes, and gave the throttles a firm shove past the detent all the way until they could no longer move. Full afterburning thrust came on, sending an eager tremor through the airframe.

Holding the throttles firmly against the stop, Morton watched as the tarmac streamed towards him. The airspeed numerals on the HUD began to whirl themselves into a blur, counting upwards.

The Super Tornado—officially designated the Air Superiority Variant—was more commonly called the ASV, or the F.35, by its crews. Some also tended to call it the super flick knife, or superflick. Caroline Hamilton-Jones, the November unit's prospective female candidate pilot, the only one so far, had her own private, anatomical variation of the name for it.

Morton's ASV now hurled itself along the runway in a phenomenal burst of acceleration. In keeping with the November practice of constantly upgrading and evolving its aircraft, many of its Tornado ASVs now had engines that produced thirty-eight percent extra thrust above those of the standard Tornado F.3, and eight percent more than the remaining, as-yet-unmodified Super Tornados. The lower-powered ASVs had been allocated to the second November squadron, which was working up to full operational status.

The augmented engines, like those of the lower-powered ASVs, were even more fuel efficient. The aircraft, in comparison with the standard F.3, was longer, with the variable-sweep wings having an appreciably greater area. This expansion of the wing area had been kept within tight limits, so as not to affect the airplane's unrivaled high-speed performance at low level. Together with its enlarged tailerons—with dog-tooth leading edges—the augmented ASV was even more dangerous in a turning fight at *all* levels, from low to medium to high altitudes.

Tangling with it in the hands of a good November pilot was always a bad idea; in the hands of a pilot of the caliber of either Selby or Hohendorf, it was verging on the suicidal. Morton was not there yet.

The ASV's flattened underbelly, which normally carried four extreme long-range Skyray B missiles in recessed housings, was itself a lifting device and perceptibly wider than standard, further generating extra lift. Leading edge extensions blended out from the wing roots to vanish into the sleek nose at points just beneath and ahead of the forward edge of the windscreen.

The usual three-section, braced version of the standard Tornado had been replaced by a one-piece curved screen; and the big canopy had been extended slightly rearwards, giving spectacular all-round vision. The aircraft was also much lighter than the standard variant due to the extensive use of composite, radar-absorbent materials at strategic points throughout the airframe.

With its greatly improved lift capability, and a combined afterburning thrust of 46,920 pounds from the twin engines, the modified ASVs of Zero-One squadron virtually sliced their way through the air at a top speed that approached mach 2.6 at altitude. Their thrust-to-weight ratio far exceeded unity and at 1.9 to 1 bettered the mighty F-15 Eagle, which was itself one of the most potent fighters around.

On full afterburner, even with a complete warload of air-to-air missiles, it was as if the ASV's engines had no weight to push. Its shattering acceleration was complemented by the extra agility given to it by the lifting capability of its LERXes, which was a nasty surprise for any opponent.

The LERXes had been modified too. The metal skinning had been replaced by transparent, non-reflective material that was lighter and more than tough enough to withstand the fierce changes of loading during hard-maneuvering combat. This transparency had two valuable uses: it enabled the crews to "see through" a possible blind spot just beyond the edge of the cockpit and also served to alter the visual aspect of the aircraft during maneuvering. In a turning fight, it was a factor that served to confuse an adversary.

Adding further to this visual confusion was the optical stealth system. A very special coating of paint, whose crystals could be excited via a fine electrical matrix embedded within it, enabled the aircraft to alter its photochromatic aspect in flight. The system could be operated automatically via combined sensors or by the backseater using a dedicated programmable keypad. Nothing about the basic paint scheme, of low-visibility gray with its tinge of the palest blue, outwardly betrayed this capability. The party trick was to make the aircraft become "invisible" over any background, mottled or plain.

The official terminology for this piece of kit was the tongue-twisting **C**amouflaging **H**eat **A**ug**ME**nted crysta**L** **EN**hanced system. To everyone, inevitably, it was the Chameleon.

A favorite with the crews in the system's catalogue was something they called the "white fright." Hohendorf and Selby had once suckered four opposing aircraft from another unit into a cloudbank, whereupon the Tornados had seemed to vanish into the whiteness. They had in fact been skimming the tops of the clouds. When one of the other pilots had seen a ghostly aircraft suddenly appear before him, unable to control his reactions at that moment, he had screamed. The November crews still dined out on that one, and continued to sucker other pilots into cloud.

Before very long, they had also started calling the latest version of the ASV Tornado the super-superflick, or ASV Echo. Officially it was the ASV(E)—for enhanced—and everybody wanted to get his hands on one.

Morton's aircraft was one of the newly enhanced ASVs and the aircraft seemed to fling itself on its way, like a stone from a slingshot. Twin tongues of blue-white flame roared out of expanded engine nozzles, a dancing, transparent haze billowing in their wake. Soon, the nose was lifting; then the entire aircraft was airborne. The wheels were swiftly tucked in and it reefed into a steep climb, pointing its nose skywards, its crisp thunder slamming at the ground as it rapidly diminished in size.

The takeoff had been neatly done.

Watching closely from the control tower, Wing Commander Christopher Tarquin Jason, warrior-scholar, boss and originator of the November project, followed the rocketing Tornado's progress with keen eyes. He allowed a satisfied expression to grace his features and, for the time being, was prepared to ignore McCann's breach of radio procedures.

Standing next to him was one of his two deputy-commanders. *Fregattenkapitän* Dieter Helm, on permanent secondment from Germany's *Marineflieger*, was like the second deputy; *Teniente-Colonello* Mario da Vinci of the *Aeronautica Militare Italiana*, his other deputy-commander, practically a founding member of the unit.

"Morton's handling the aircraft well," Jason said to Helm, eyes still on the vertically ascending ASV. "It's not running away with him; at least, for the moment. He's come a long way."

Helm nodded. "He's had to *un*learn some of his style

of flying," he began in his carefully precise English, "but yes. I agree. He has become a good pilot."

"Thanks to you and the other instructors."

"You picked him, sir," Helm said, "even when some of us were not . . . sure."

Helm had been one of those. He hadn't liked the idea of having on November strength a pilot who'd been careless with his fuel management. It hadn't made the slightest difference to him that Morton had otherwise been an excellent F-16 pilot, or that General Bowmaker himself had backed the application.

Jason's insistence that Morton was good material from which they could fashion a true November pilot had won the day. Helm was honest enough to admit that Jason's instincts were sound. The wing commander would not have picked a lemon, and the results had so far vindicated him. And after all, Helm reasoned, Jason had picked *him* to be one of his deputies.

"If you slavishly agreed with everything I did or said, Dieter . . ." Jason looked away from where the aircraft had now disappeared, towards his second-in-command, ". . . you would not be much of a deputy."

A ghost of a smile flitted across the angular planes of Helm's features. "I guess not."

Jason walked slowly past the concave bank of the controllers' consoles. He did so with a slight limp, the legacy of the horrific crash he'd experienced in a Hawk advanced trainer, piloted by Caroline Hamilton-Jones. Jason was still alive only because of her remarkable flying skills.

An assassination attempt on Jason had resulted in the Hawk being hit by a small, remotely piloted drone missile. There had been no explosive warhead, but the damage caused by the subsequent impact had been enough to bring the aircraft down.

Hamilton-Jones, a flight lieutenant and former fighter controller, had displayed exemplary calm when suddenly faced with the disastrous situation. She had force-landed the Hawk on a patch of ground more suitable for small, propellor-driven light aircraft. She'd nearly made it safely down; but rain the day before had left the surface of the landing site too soft for the small jet. Furthermore, the overgrown end of the clearing had effectively hidden a waiting ditch. The landing gear had collapsed, firing the rear ejection seat in the process. Though the seat had separated cleanly, there had not been sufficient height, and the already badly hurt Jason had landed heavily.

His subsequent injuries had been severe: both legs broken, and his visor had been smashed into his face. He'd been very lucky to escape serious spinal injury, and with the exception of the barely perceptible limp, had made a full recovery. He had pushed himself hard to become fit to fly once more, in record time. But the accident had left its marks, the limp being one of them. The others could be seen on his face, depending on the light.

During the early days of his recovery, the scars had marched across his puffed face in patterns of raw, livid weals, making his butchered skin look like a crazily drawn map. Barely visible now, tiny webbed scars were etched upon those parts of his skin that had been exposed beyond the limits of the visor and the oxygen mask. In time, they would disappear almost completely.

Jason now paused near Karen Lomax. She'd been newly promoted to flight lieutenant, a matter of days before.

"Miss Lomax."

"Sir?" She stood up quickly, brushing a wisp of hair from her forehead.

"Inform Captain McCann when he's back down that I want to see him."

She blushed. "Yes, sir."

"Thank you, Miss Lomax."

"Sir."

Jason went out onto the upper balcony that surrounded the glass house of the tower like a veranda. Helm followed as they walked round, until they were well away from the exit.

"Did you see how she went bright red?" Helm began.

Jason gave a thin smile. "McCann and Lomax. That boy never does anything by halves, does he?"

"He even refuses to die," Helm remarked drily.

"Death-defying Elmer Lee. Must be something in the Kansas City water."

Jason braced his hands on the railing and looked out upon the runway, tracking his gaze along it. Out to sea, two Tornados were making a low approach, positioned accurately for a fast pass.

Helm was looking critically at the rapidly advancing aircraft. Both had chameleoned to the standard paint scheme, always used on approach to base.

"Cottingham and Christiansen," he announced. "The Double-C, leading in new boys from Zero-Two squadron. They have got them well positioned."

"Lamotte and Ilanez?"

Helm nodded and followed the passage of the two ASVs. They roared along the runway, rolled briskly into a snappy fighter break, fanning out as they did so to prepare for the landing.

He nodded again, approvingly. "They are coming along, our Frenchman and his Spanish backseater."

"The Double-C must have given them a hard workout," Jason commented. "That was a well-executed break." He rubbed at his leg reflectively.

Helm noted the gesture and glanced down. "Is the leg a problem?" has asked with concern.

Jason shook his head. "It's fine. I think I rub it now and then just to reassure myself it's still there."

"You were very lucky that day."

"I was lucky Hamilton-Jones is a good pilot."

"Yes," Helm said.

Jason looked a him. "Still worried about having her join us?"

"I'll reserve judgement, sir, if you do not mind. She's a good pilot, yes. But I think I shall wait until she has flown the superflick, *and* learned to use it as a weapon. Then I shall know. But I will not object to letting her try."

"Good enough for me."

They watched as the incoming Tornados landed in tandem.

"What do you think, Dieter? Was I right to pair McCann with Morton today? And in one of the more powerful aircraft?"

A great thunder filled the air as the thrust reversers on the two aircraft now on the ground were deployed, the buckets clamshelling together over the engine nozzles. Opaque hazes boiled astern of the ASVs as they decelerated rapidly, almost coming to a halt well before they were halfway down the runway.

The clamshells re-opened and retracted as the Tornados taxied off, heading for their respective hardened shelters.

"We've put him through all the tests," Helm was saying. "He's had physiotherapy; Doctor Hemelsen has given him a rigorous psychological examination over many months; he has been taken through many hours of simulator work in the backseat—sometimes with myself as the pilot, and sometimes with you.

"He has been given some easy rides in the air, bringing him back up to speed. He has had more tests than we perhaps even normally give a new candidate. He has passed them all. It is as if nothing had happened to him." Helm sounded amazed. He shook his head slowly. "McCann is an original. So, yes. It is okay to put him with Morton at this stage. It is the right time. He will consider himself far superior in skill to Morton, so he will take charge when they get into the fight with the F-16s.

"If he does well today, he will return fully primed and be emotionally ready to climb aboard a plane with Hohendorf. This will be a moment of great importance for him, being again in the air with the man who was the pilot of the aircraft when he was hit and came so close to death. If he makes it through that okay, then he will be ready to pair up with Selby again. He will have regained his old self. As for Morton, the power of the aircraft will not be a problem. He is ready."

Jason was nodding in agreement. "Good enough. It's what I hoped you'd say. Though God knows what a returned-from-the-dead McCann is going to be like. The old one was bad enough." He gave Helm a sideways glance. "Provided, of course, you're not just saying that to please the boss."

Helm's eyes were unblinking. "I'll never say anything just to keep you happy, if I do not believe it."

"As I've just said, that's what makes you a good deputy commander. Mario too is not averse to standing on my toes when he believes it necessary."

Helm grinned. "You picked us."

Jason turned his head to look at the Tornados, which were now on the far side of the airfield, heading for their flight line. "And I picked McCann, God help us all."

"But we were beginning to miss him, when we thought he had died."

"And there, my dear Dieter," Jason began with a sigh, "you have it. For our sins, we did begin to miss the Kansas City pixie. Like the familiar itch that drives you nuts when it's there, and when it isn't . . ."

"You feel as if something important is missing."

"Thank God there's only one of him," Jason said with feeling. "Let's go down the hole to hear how they're doing," he continued. "Go on ahead. I want a word with Doc Hemelsen. They should be in area by the time I join you."

Helm nodded. "Yes, sir."

Jason strode along the spotless corridor of the unit hospital until he came to a door with the legend MAJOR H. HEMELSEN, MD. He gave a soft knock, removed his cap, and entered.

Helle Hemelsen had been the first of Jason's poaches from the Royal Danish Air Force—the second being Lars Christiansen, Cottingham's backseater. She smiled brightly as he entered and got up from behind her desk. The white coat she wore over her uniform flapped gently as she came round to meet him. There were no badges of rank on the coat. Rank was not something that featured seriously in her mind.

"I would like to think," she began, "that you're here to visit me. But, of course, that is not so. My name is not Antonia." Her command of English was virtually perfect.

A brief frown creased his forehead. "Antonia?"

"Ah. Such, such apparent innocence. I'm talking of course about the air vice-marshal's daughter . . . as if you didn't know. When are you going to put the poor child out of her misery?"

"Misery? What misery?"

"You can't run forever," Helle Hemelsen continued as if she'd not heard him. "That girl is going to make an honest man of you some day. She is very determined, and when a woman is determined . . ."

Jason looked at her in mild exasperation. "Helle, I . . . I . . . You're doing it to me again, aren't you? You're playing those mind games before I've barely got a foot in the door."

"You're such a good subject," she said unrepentantly.

"I'm not here to talk about me, as *you* well know. And leave Antonia Thurson out of this. I haven't seen her for ages and, as you've just said, she's a child. There are plenty of younger pilots who . . ."

"You may think she's a child. She's past twenty-one, and has a completely different idea of childhood. She doesn't want the younger pilots. She wants *you*, and she intends to get you. There will be wedding bells one day," Major Hemelsen finished portentously.

"You don't sound very much like a Lutheran Dane. Do you know that?"

· A wickedly amused look came into her eyes. "Never stereotype the Danes."

"I'll do my best."

The doctor's close-cut hair was a beautiful, fine, golden blond that tended to gleam in sunlight. Delicate features and a willow-slim body that was just five and a half feet tall gave the impression she was not yet out of her teens. This effect was enhanced by the glasses she wore, making her pale blue eyes seem even larger. Many men, frequently and erroneously, tended to think she needed their protection from innumerable dangers; a fantasy that existed only in their fevered brains.

There was no lipstick on her pale lips, and that somehow seemed right; for there was a natural golden color to her complexion that would have made lipstick a garish aberration. There were also many who swore that no matter how ill they felt, a smile from the Doc warmed them to the core.

Despite her implied suggestion that next to Antonia Thurson she would come a poor second, there was many a male on the unit whose heart beat faster whenever she came into view. A favorite pastime was trying to work out who was the focus of the Doc's romantic attentions, as no one wanted to believe that someone so aesthetically and intellectually pleasing could remain so determinedly unattached. But Doc Hemelsen was not telling. Neither was the person concerned, if there was such a person.

"All right," she went on. "I shall put you out of your misery. No more teasing, for now. You have come to see me about Elmer Lee. Now that the SMO has cleared him for the first air combat training mission that will expose him to November squadron levels of stress since his recovery, you want my opinion. Am I right?"

"You've hit the bulls-eye," Jason said. He had thoroughly studied the senior medical officer's recommendation, confirming that McCann could be returned to unrestricted operational flying. "The SMO's report is just one of the many aspects I must consider."

She shoved her hands into the deep patch pockets of the coat and walked over to the front of her desk, to lean against it. She drew the coat close, her hands still within the pockets.

"Please. Take a seat. Some coffee? Tea?"

Jason shook his head regretfully. "Much as I like that coffee you give me whenever I'm here ... I must decline. Can't stay long. I'm going down the hole when I'm finished here. I'd like you to come with me ... if you've got some time."

She raised her eyebrows at this.

"First, your comments on McCann," he said to her.

"Ah well ... I could give you enough to fill several textbooks ..."

"An abridged version, please, Helle."

"With Elmer Lee, it is almost as difficult to know where to begin as where to end. Now take someone like you . . ."

"Not *me*, Helle. McCann . . ."

"Take someone like you," she repeated firmly, and continued before he could interrupt further, "because doing so will give us one of the clues to understanding Elmer Lee and . . . most of your personnel."

He stared at her.

"You have no idea what I'm talking about, have you?" she said.

"I'm sure you'll tell me."

"Well, Wing Commander . . ."

"You know you can call me Chris when we're in conference like this, Helle. We've been here before."

"Yes. I know. I sometimes forget. You are a very difficult man to assess. And although you are tight on discipline, you're also a very unconventional wing commander."

"I intended to remain difficult to assess," Jason said unrepentantly, "and uncoventional."

"It works with your personnel . . . with all of us."

"I take discipline very seriously, but not for its own sake. It's only useful when those you command recognize and understand its value so that they, in turn, can impart it to those *they* command. Otherwise, the whole thing falls to pieces. I'm very well aware that some of my peers and superiors see things differently . . ." He shrugged. "For my sins . . . may I be judged later."

"That judgement might come sooner, rather than later." There was no smile upon her face as she continued, "Here's a man—you—who has searched out the best people he could find in the NATO and EU countries, to build a dream. You are right, of course, in what you're trying to do, or I would not be here. Many of us share what you are working for. But . . . that dream has many enemies—as you know—both inside and outside the group of countries of your search. You are trying to kill something that many, many people love to nurture, cherish, and hang on to.

"I am talking about jingoism, about isolationism, and about nationalism. You are creating an evolutionary process, but here we are in the month of the soccer and to read some of your national papers, you would think this country is at war. I believe they have taken leave of their senses. It is like going back in time, and is very embarrassing for anyone who thinks it through for more than two seconds."

She gave an exasperated sigh. "And then, there is this ridiculous BSE business with the beef, which is creating tensions we do not need. We're approaching the twenty-first century and all such idiocy should belong to the past. It is so senseless, so . . . primitive. There are many other things, so much more important and dangerous, that require our urgent attention."

She paused, looking at him with eyes that seemed to have become incredibly larger. But that could have been the effect of her glasses.

"The United Kingdom *is* a great nation," she went on firmly. A hint of mischief sparked briefly in the pale blue eyes. "After all, we did pay you neighborly visits from the eighth century onwards and carved ourselves out a nice piece of real estate—as McCann would say—during the tenth and eleventh centuries; and if Harold had lost to us at Stamford Bridge that September in 1066, instead of in October to the Normans, who knows how history might have turned?"

Then an unexpectedly hard look came and went so quickly, Jason nearly missed it. "But what these foolish . . . people are doing is insulting to the nation itself. It is an insult to the patriotism you possess, which is one of honor. *They* have no honor. It is an insult to your crews, who are multi-national and . . . to what you're trying to do.

"All the nasty and moronic attitudes, which you are trying to fight with what you're building here, are out in the open for all to see. It is like . . . like seeing a mass of pale, ugly worms that have been exposed to the light of day, by the lifting of a rock." She paused. "You think I am out of line."

He shook his head slowly, eyes slightly narrowed. "No. Do go on."

"You are sure?"

"I'm sure."

"You should take courage also," she went on, hesitating briefly as if to reassure herself that it was all right to continue. "The people you have chosen are of good caliber. They understand. You went for the best, and you have got them. Oh, of course, they are fallible. We are all fallible humans. But those you have here with you will work very, very hard not to fail you and . . . this is the most important . . . they will *follow* where you lead. They will go out there, and perhaps die for you . . ."

"Not for me, Helle," Jason said quietly, bemused and touched by the passion he'd never suspected was within her. "For what we're *all* trying to build here. I don't want them to die in the execution of their duty. I want them to *live* doing it. Dead aircrews are no use to me. I am not one of those commanders who sees his personnel as chess pieces, to be sacrificed to some greater plan. My way is maximum damage, for minimum cost."

"They will do so for *you*," she insisted. "You have given them the enthusiasm and the belief. You have given them a taste of what could grow out of this, and they like it. *I* like what I see. Despite the high standards you have set for entry, you are still having to turn volunteers away. Does that not say something encouraging to you? People want things to move on, and to evolve.

"It means that even with the stupid jingoism and the xenophobia, there are those from this country *and* from the other countries who believe as you do. They have realized it is our future you wish to safeguard. You are fortunate that there are also those who are powerful enough to back you, or no funding would have been available for the program. And as for the air vice-marshal and General Bowmaker . . . they protect you whenever they can . . ."

"And use me too."

"Naturally. It is to be expected."

"No free lunch then," Jason commented ruefully.

"That is normal. But you know this. The November project would be useless if it could not be shown to work. You have put yourself on the edge; therefore, you will always be a target. You are not the kind of man who wants to accept the status quo . . ."

"I'm a military man. The status quo runs the system."

"You are talking of the status quo of *rank*. I mean something else entirely. The great ideas and deeds of history have never been brought to us by those who were too frightened to go to the edge. In the end, though we're always afraid to go where the edgeriders live, we all claim their successes as ours.

"Think of all those worthless politicians who wrap themselves in the mantles of the heroes of the past. If those same heroes were around now, doing what they did then, those same politicians would try to *stop* them. Just as they're trying to stop you. Because you are an edgerider, and they cannot stomach it. But as I have just said, your crews will follow you."

"I take it you do not think much of politicians," Jason remarked drily.

"Only a very, very few are of any value. Most are people of straw who steal the deeds of others to enhance their own minute stature. They are in it for what they can get." She spoke with open contempt.

Jason was fascinated by the vehemence of her words. But he could sympathize, having personal experience of one such politician.

"I can think of a politician I wish I'd never met," he told her wryly, unwillingly reminding himself of the person in question.

Unfortunately for the project, the culprit was a minister of the Crown, and one of those who would like to see the November program curtailed. Yet, in a neat confirmation of what she had just said, that same minister was not averse to taking the credit for the successes of the November squadrons' clandestine missions. Jason was well aware that any November disaster making the news would be just as easily disowned by the man. Accountability was something that tended to slide off his well-oiled back, leaving not the slightest trace.

"But don't put one of your heroes' mantles on me," Jason now said. "I'm no hero."

"You have no idea how closely you fit the historical profile," she countered, looking at him as she would an interesting specimen beneath the probing eye of a microscope, "whether you want to or not."

"Have it your own way, Helle. I know better than to get into philosophical arguments with you. But what has all this to do with McCann?"

"Everything," she replied. "McCann wanted to live because he did not want to let you down."

Jason stared at her. *"What?"*

"He told me himself."

"I would have thought Karen Lomax had more to do with that," Jason said. "Isn't that what happens in cases of severe trauma? Isn't it the strong emotional tie that drives you to fight . . ."

"Not necessarily. Strong emotions, yes . . . but this does not always have romantic connections. After your crash, you fought hard to regain your fitness. Why?"

"That's self-evident. The November program . . ." Jason stopped.

Helle Hemelsen raised a triumphant eyebrow at him. "Exactly. Elmer Lee may have found Karen Lomax floating somewhere in his thoughts, but that was not what brought him back. He sat here, in this room, and told me how it happened. It was not what I expected. At the time, I was telling him how impressed I was by his rapid recovery. His emotional state was very stable.

"I will tell you exactly what he said. 'Doc, all the time I was out of it, I think I was dreaming. All I could hear in this dream was a voice saying over and over: *I musn't let the boss down. I must get back.* I reckon it must have been my voice because it was all dark and I could see no one. Crazy, huh?' Those were his exact words."

Jason was stunned.

"I think you will find," Helle Hemelsen went on gently, "that all of them, in their various ways, feel the same. It doesn't mean that everything will be plain sailing. They would not be human otherwise, and would be without the very spirit you need them to have. But they share the same ethos.

"When Elmer Lee was given leave to visit his family in the States during his convalescence, he could barely wait to get back. We all know his father is a rich banker who gives him a brand-new Corvette sportscar *every* year. He wants his son to become a banker. Elmer Lee wants to fly as long as he is able to.

"So what does he do? He runs back—*before* his leave is up—to the person who respects him enough to give him the one job that makes real use of his natural talents, even though he nearly died while doing that job. For Elmer Lee, November base is home. The father's mistake, from the very beginning, was in trying to buy his son. But *you* picked *him*, infuriating as we all sometimes think he is. To Elmer Lee, that means everything. He is like a puppy that's so eager to please, when he wags his tail his whole body moves and, at times, the wagging breaks things. You have a great responsibility, Chris . . . to Elmer Lee, and to all of them."

"Yes," Jason said, finding no real fault with what she had just told him. "I know."

"Don't think this means Elmer Lee's a reformed character."

"Perish the thought. I wouldn't know how to deal with him."

"Have I answered your questions?"

"You appear to have done more of an analysis of me," Jason commented drily, "but yes."

"Oh, I haven't done an analysis of you. But I would love to get the chance."

"You won't," Jason growled.

She smiled at him. "It's the response I expected. The strongest of men are always the most reluctant."

"With good reason. Now if you have got the time, I really would like you to come down the hole with me. We'll be listening in on their transmissions and I would like you to study McCann's voice. See if there are any hints of the trauma . . ."

"A double-check?"

"Yes," Jason replied. "I want to know if he's likely to crack up under pressure. Any chance of that, and he puts at risk anyone he flies with. I cannot afford to have that happen. In running this unit I won't always be able to prevent every accident, nor influence the outcome of any mission that might result in operational casualties. But I'll do my damnedest. First priorities are to see that my crews and their aircraft are in top condition, in every conceivable way.

"Despite what you have just said to me about him, if McCann even looks like he is becoming a danger to himself or to the others, I would have absolutely no qualms about grounding him. I would do the same to any of them. But if they do have what it takes, I will push until they find it for themselves. I have grounded or rejected people who believed they had it, but didn't."

"I have had to deal with, some of those," Helle Hemelsen remarked soberly. "They all take it very hard."

"I can well understand. But I cannot afford the risk. I must have people who I am confident will go to the wire—the edge, if you prefer—when the time comes. In addition, the safety of my crews and their aircraft is paramount. The better they are, the safer they fly—even at the edge in combat—and the better the results we get. As you've already said, there are too many people out there who would like to see us fail. I've also pushed through some candidates who had never realized they did have what it takes. Morton is one of those, and McCann is up with him at this moment. So yes, I do have a responsibility, and I take that very seriously indeed."

She nodded. "Of course. I shall come." She began to remove her coat, then paused. "What you are doing here is very important, Chris, for the coherence of the whole of Europe. I will take an example closer to home to show you what I mean."

She removed the coat and carefully hung it on a coat stand in a corner near her desk.

"This base is here in Scotland," she continued, taking her cap off the stand and putting it on. "What would happen to it if say . . . Scotland separated from England? And to the RAF bases? Would your split be like the Czechs and the Slovaks? *That* will give problems one day. Or perhaps your split will be more like Yugoslavia, which managed to get friends and families killing each other? What would happen to all the families with Scottish names in England, and those with English names up here? And would England and Scotland go to war over the oil in the North Sea?"

Jason was again staring at her, as if she'd suddenly taken leave of her senses. "That nightmare scenario will never happen."

"How do you know?" she asked, as if daring him to prove it never would. "And when the oil is finished? What then?

"What's your point, Helle?"

"Nationalism again, and all the damage it can do. That is my point. My reasons for being here. I want you to succeed because I don't want to see Europe once more divided, nation against nation. We have done it twice this century and once was too much. The price was too high. There are many—too many—who would like to see that again, or are too stupid and complacent to read the signs."

"Helle, you continue to surprise me."

She gave him the tiniest of smiles. "Good. And you are the little Dutch boy."

"The little *Dutch* boy?"

"The one with his finger in the seawall."

"Oh. *That* one."

3

"You see them? *You see them yet?*"

In the front cockpit, Morton's helmeted head was constantly moving as he searched the sky about him.

"I see squat," he replied.

In the backseat, McCann sighed loudly in his mask. "They're here, Major. You should be seeing them!" He sounded exasperated. "I've got them on radar at short range, *and* the threat warner."

They were tasked to fight two F-16s from Belgium, within the North Sea air combat maneuvering and instrumentation range. For the exercise, they would not be using long-range radar, nor the helmet sight. Simulated weaponry was also limited to extreme short-range missiles and guns. This meant they could not use the simulation of their highly advanced Krait short-range air-to-air missiles, which greatly out-performed even the very best of the current crop of standard AAMs. It was going to be a visual fight.

In effect, this would force them to rely upon their combined skills, and the agility and power of the Super Tornado, if they hoped to achieve success against the F-16s. They would have to work as a team in order to get the kind of result that would please their commander, and they knew it. Fortunately, they were allowed to use at least one vital item out of the ASV's formidable repertoire. They could use the Chameleon.

This pleased McCann enormously. The old McCann who hated losing in the air was back, and he was getting impatient.

"Major?"

"Cut me some slack here!" Morton retorted. "What do you think I'm doing? Holding my dick?"

"I wouldn't know," McCann said infuriatingly. "I'm in the backseat."

"Jesus!" There was a slight pause, then Morton went on sharply, "Er . . . okay, okay! I've got them!"

"Hallelujah!" Elmer Lee muttered.

"Say what?"

"Nothing, Major. Just watch those bozos. Okay? Let's rip 'em open!"

"I know all about you, McCann. I know what happened before you joined this outfit. Back in the States, you called a major an asshole during a turning fight. You got a thing against majors?"

"Who me? Little ol' me? Hell, I was only a lieutenant then and . . . *fight's on! Break right. Break right!* C'mon, Major! Let's have some action here!" McCann glanced upwards. Something streaked high above the canopy. "Forget the guy up top. The one below's the shooter. Go get him! Jeezus! Move it!"

● ● ●

Down in the hole, many of those listening in on the conversation had smiles on their faces.

Helle Hemelsen glanced at Jason, who was determined to keep a straight face. Next to him, *Freg-attenkapitän* Helm wore a similarly poker-faced expression, but a slight crinkling about the eyes betrayed him.

The hole, as the Operations Center was more colloquially known, was buried deep within the confines of the airfield, which had its own wooded areas, well away from the runways. Innocuous, low-lying buildings housed the entrance to the Center, as well as its filtration equipment and guard posts.

The Center was itself some distance from the buildings, beneath the effective screen of one of the wooded clusters. There was thus no evidence from the air of its location, and there were no heat emanations for infrared sensors to home on to; nor were there any returns for hopeful radar snoopers. Some of the powerful sensor and receiving units were sited at other parts of the airfield, while equally high-powered passive ones were located at well-camouflaged positions within the wood. For emergency evacuation there were emanation-free exits, also within the wood itself. The Center had its own catering, sleeping, and medical facilities for use by the duty shifts. It was manned twenty-four hours a day.

The personnel, like the air and other ground crew, were from various NATO and EU nations. They continued to wear their national uniforms, as no one had currently been politically brave enough to sanction a dedicated November design. Thus, for the time being, each country was identified by the national patch on one shoulder, while the other bore the NATO patch with the familiar two-tone blue, four-pointed star. There were plans to superimpose blue silhouettes of the EU's circle of stars upon the NATO emblem, but as yet no agreement to allow this had been reached.

Jason had taken the doctor to the heart of the Center, the operations room itself.

"I know you've been down here a few times," he began in a low voice to her, "when we've carried out the emergency evacuation exercises; but you've been so occupied with your own responsibilities during the triple E, you've never actually seen how this section functions."

He pointed to a huge screen that took up an entire wall of the large room, whose design was reminiscent of an auditorium. Banks of substation consoles with individual monitors were arranged in stepped semi-circles, where an audience would normally be seated.

"That's the tactical situation screen," Jason informed her, as they watched the computer-generated wire-frame drawings of the aircraft going through violent maneuvers, "usually called TACSIT. Many things can appear there: messages, relayed photo images from recce aircraft, AWACS, even from tactical strike air-craft or fighters on a mission, via their own sensor pods. We can also call up computer-generated images from the ACMI, during air combat training. What you're seeing on the screen at the moment is a version of that."

He went to the nearest console and spoke to the sergeant operator. The NCO handed a remote to him.

"I'll just point out some of the main features to you," he said to her as he returned. He held the remote towards the screen and a bright red arrow appeared. "As you can see," he continued, using the arrow to indicate as he spoke, "we're looking at Morton and McCann in the blue drawing of the ASV, doing battle with the orange F-16s. This is all happening in real time."

The wireframe images had wingtip trails that graphically displayed a "ribbon" wake as the aircraft went into their maneuvers, accurately marking their paths in a three-dimensional trace. The trail was bordered in red for the left wing and green for the right. If an aircraft executed a roll, the "ribbon" would corkscrew across the screen.

Jason pressed various switches on the remote, and the viewpoint on the screen changed several times. Among these were God's-eye view, edge-on from different points, or from the ground looking up. Individual speeds, heading, and altitude could be displayed onscreen, or be omitted, though all such information would continue to accumulate in the database. Terrain, where appropriate, could also be depicted. As the ACMI range was over the sea, there were no land formations onscreen.

"Normally," he said, "we place a line across the bottom of the screen to signify hard deck. We can set that at any level we choose. An aircraft going through that line is considered to have hit the ground—or as in this case the sea—and is therefore out of the fight. Today, hard deck is really hard deck: the sea itself. That should concentrate both their minds."

He then picked each aircraft in turn and "flew" along with it. He showed Doctor Hemelsen how the scale could be manipulated to cover a vast area or made so large that a cockpit would fill the entire screen. He hopped from cockpit to cockpit, to show a simplified head-up display, through which the computer image of a given targeted aircraft could be seen.

"You've just heard McCann and Morton, but we've also got another little trick up our sleeve. We can hear the F-16 pilots as well. In a real situation, it is possible for a backseater to attempt to eavesdrop on the opposing aircraft. This does not mean he would succeed, especially if the adversary has secure comms. However, for today's exercise, Morton and McCann are not allowed to try, simulating a hard transmission environment. The reverse is also true.

"The aircraft transmissions are coming to us via secure datalink, just as they would be on a hot mission, if the situation permitted it. Short of actually shooting at each other with real rounds, this fight will be conducted as if the enivironment in which they are currently operating is truly hostile. I expect them to fight hard, and to win this engagement." Jason raised his voice slightly. "Sarn't Thomas . . ."

The NCO who had given him the remote turned to look, shifting his headset slightly to hear better. "Sir?"

"Could you patch in the F-16s on voice, please?"

"Yes, sir."

The sergeant hit a key on his keyboard and the F-16's transmissions flooded through to join those of McCann and Morton.

". . . and those November boys think they're Sierra Hotel," one of the Falcon pilots came through in midsentence. "Let's ruin their day."

"Roger," the other F-16 pilot responded determinedly.

"I think *their* day is about to be ruined," Jason said, adding ominously, "It had better be." Then he cleared his throat softly. "You know of course that Sierra Hotel is the polite term . . ."

"I know what it means," Helle Hemelsen told him. Her eyes showed that she was enjoying his apparent uncertainty. "And don't worry. I wasn't about to ask you to translate."

"Of course in the real thing," he went on quickly, "an enemy would do his damnedest to ensure we could not listen to his tranmissions, while *we* would do our very best to make sure we could. Now let's see what kind of a show they're going to put on for us."

McCann was forcing his head round against the punishing G-forces as Morton hauled the ASV into a tight descending turn.

"Okay," he grunted. "You've spoiled the shooter's aim. Leave him for now." The G-forces eased. "They've switched the game. The top boy's the shooter now, and he's on his way down. Go up and make like a rocket. *No burners! Leave* the throttles alone for now. I'm going to random Chameleon for over water. Let's see how he likes that."

"Roger. Going up. No burners."

The descent had given the aircraft plenty of speed. Keeping the throttles at max dry, Morton hauled firmly on the stick and the ASV began to spread its wings automatically, maneuver slats and flaps deploying to generate more lift as it curved into the climb. As soon as the nose began to rise, the wings began to sweep and the maneuver devices to retract. The Super Tornado hurled itself skywards.

Morton reveled in the sheer power under his control. This was flying! He glanced over his left shoulder, at the fast-receding surface of the sea. He checked his right, then looked through the top of the canopy.

"See him?" he asked McCann.

"I've got him," came the assured voice from the backseat. "We've gone past. He's below and is gonna try to follow, but he can't see us properly. Go over the top and haul down on him."

"Roger."

Morton was somewhat astonished to discover how readily he was accepting McCann's directions without question. He pulled the ASV tightly onto its back at the top of the loop, kept the pressure on until the sleek nose again began to point seawards.

He kept pulling. The nose began to ease off the vertical, rising once more. The wings began to spread, biting at the air. Superheated streamers boiled searingly off the LERXes, tortured ribbons that stretched themselves over an airframe that had become indistinct.

"Do you see the goodie in the box?" McCann asked.

On the HUD, the diamond box of the infrared missile seeker head had neatly framed a distant dot. It was pulsing as the numerals of the range-to-target counted down.

"Got him!"

"Don't let him get away. That's our shooter out there. Play with the throttles all you want now."

"His buddy . . ."

"I'll worry about his buddy. Just get that bozo! Speed of light, man. Do it!"

Morton continued to sneak up on the F-16, which clearly had no idea where the ASV had got to.

In the hole, Helle Hemelsen had listened to McCann's barked instuctions to Morton and had watched, fascinated, as the computer image of the ASV had performed its tight maneuver. She watched as it drew inexorably closer to to unsuspecting orange drawing and found she instinctively wanted to shout a warning. *Behind you!* She smiled at herself.

Jason noted the reaction. "Something amuses you?"

"Only myself." She did not tell him why. "What has just happened?"

"McCann used the optical stealth system as they went into the maneuver. The combination of the Chameleon and the sudden change of direction, plus the ambient light values, have all helped to make the aircraft difficult to acquire visually, even though the F-16s are using their radars."

As he spoke, Jason used the remote-controlled cursor arrow to indicate each stage of the maneuver.

"McCann will also be jamming heavily," he continued, "cluttering their screens or simply disappearing off them altogether. As he's not using his own radar at the moment, he's not registering on their threat warners. See there? Orange Two should be backing up his leader; but he's lost sight of the threat. For very precious seconds, Orange One is naked.

"If Morton is quick about it, the ASV will soon get the first kill. This will then leave them with a one-on-one scenario. Breakfast for the ASV. That was good, fast thinking by McCann. There's no second-best in air combat. He who's first, wins."

In the ASV, Morton was curving towards the still-unaware F-16, watching as the range continued to decrease.

"Don't you lose that sucker out there," came McCann's voice on the headphones.

"Hey. I *know* how to fly this bird."

"Hey yourself, Major," came the unabashed rejoiner. "Think I'd be sitting back here if you didn't?"

In the Ops Center down in the hole, some of the operators at the substations were having great difficulty keeping straight faces. A few of them cast sneaky glances at the wing commander, taking note of his expression. While they could not detect any evidence of smiling, they thought they saw him twitch.

Helle Hemelsen gave him a quick glance. "It won't be bad for disclipline if you did crack your face slightly," she suggested in a soft whisper.

He favored her with a stern glance of his own, but made no comment.

Helm, seemingly deeply preoccupied with studying the maneuvers on the big screen, looked neither right nor left.

Morton saw the IN RNG cue appear on the head-up display. It pulsed once, then solidified. They were in range. All firing parameters had been satisfied. The tone sounded. He squeezed the missile release button on the stick.

"Fox Two!" he called, signifying a short-range missile shot.

The F-16 seemed to leap like a startled foal before rolling away to the left.

"There goes one pissed-off guy," McCann said gleefully, as he turned his head to observe the defeated Falcon's retreat. "Good kill, Major Morton, sir. Now it's back to business. His buddy's going to be even more pissed with us. Revenge is going to taste sweet to him, so let's make it sour. Here comes buddy boy. Three o'clock, and feeling mean."

Morton glanced over to his right. A speck was growing rapidly. A rapid scan of a three-inch-square display, tucked near the central warning panel on the right forward console, told him that McCann was still operating the Chameleon in random mode. The F-16 pilot would be wondering whether his eyes were deceiving him as he tried to visually acquire the ASV. It didn't help that his intended quarry was now into sun.

"I've got him," Morton said.

"Okaayyy," McCann said. "He's all yours. Keep him visual. Don't let him extend. Go for guns. I'll keep the Mark One eyeball on him, but the rest is up to you. No prompts from me. Think you can hack it?"

"I can hack it."

"Hey, Major . . . I'm not getting at you. I just thought you'd like to do your own thing, seeing he's close enough. If you want me to . . ."

"No! I can hack it, I said."

"Okay." There was a definite smile in the voice.

This served to infuriate Morton, who nonetheless decided it was far wiser to remain silent and to concentrate on ensnaring the nimble F-16.

In the Operations Center, they watched as the the ASV and the remaining F-16 battled each other for advantage. Their traces streaked and twisted across the screen, the ribbons of their trails entwining each other like a writhing mass of vipers.

"McCann seems to be as good as his word," Jason commented to Helm, who was continuing to study the big screen intently. "Not a peep from him."

"You sound suspicious," Helm said, not looking round.

"I'm always suspicious of that little imp."

Now Helm did turn to look at Jason. "He is doing right with Morton."

"Yes, damn it. That's the problem. He *is* good up there."

Helle Hemelsen had listened to the exchange with curiosity. "Your expression says you believe he has gone to the cookie jar," she said to Jason.

"He's up to something," Jason said.

"Oh, *men han er sød*," she murmured, switching briefly to Danish.

"What?" Jason looked at her. "Was that Danish?"

"Yes. I said, 'But he's sweet' . . . 'cute,' if you like."

The wing commander looked as if he wanted to turn his eyes heavenwards. "Not you as well."

"He's harmless."

"*Porcupines* are harmless. McCann . . . *no.*" Jason turned to the senior NCO he'd spoken to before. "Sarn't Thomas."

The man went through the headset-moving routine as he turned to look at the wing commander.

"Sir?"

"Check Captain McCann's frequencies, will you?"

"Check them, sir?"

Jason stared at him. "Do you have a problem with that?"

The sergeant had a slightly prominent Adam's apple. It moved nervously. "Er . . . no, sir."

By now both Helm and Helle Hemelsen were looking at Thomas, who became even more uncomfortable.

"Get on with it, Sergeant," Jason ordered in a dangerously quiet voice.

"Er . . . yes, sir," Thomas acknowledged quickly, "but he may be using one that's secured to the aircraft. Local transmission only . . ."

"Are you stalling, Sergeant?"

"No, sir!" Thomas began to tap swiftly at his keyboard.

On his monitor, a string of frequency channels scrolled upwards until one filled the monitor screen, to be framed by a yellow, pulsing box.

"Got the channel he's using, sir," Thomas, a twenty-four year old, said in a strained voice. He couldn't quite control the expression on his face, which hovered between enjoyment and concern. "He hasn't secured it."

Helm and the doctor glanced at Jason before—curiosity now well aroused—returning their attention to Thomas. The senior NCO was now looking as if he wished he were somewhere else at that moment. As far away as he could get, his expression telegraphed.

Jason reached for Thomas's headset. "Excuse me, Sarn't Thomas. I'd like to hear what's making you look so happy." He eased the set off the NCO's head and brought the phone to his right ear.

Bon Jovi's "Raise Your Hands" blasted at him.

"God God!" he exclaimed, snatching the headset away. "What the devil's that?"

He passed it back to Thomas, who took it as if expecting it to bite.

"Er . . ." Thomas began, "Bon Jovi, sir. Heavy metal."

"Heavy . . . !" Jason stared at Thomas, not quite trusting himself to speak.

"He's still on cockpit frequency, sir," the sergeant said urgently, hoping the wing commander wouldn't consider this an insubordinate interruption. "He'll not miss anything if Major Morton checks with him for . . ."

"What's this, Sergeant? You're suddenly Captain McCann's defense counsel?"

"Er, no, sir. What I mean, sir . . ."

"All right, Sergeant. Carry on."

"Sir!" Thomas said with relief and clamped his headset back on, looking as if he'd just escaped some unmentionably dire fate.

Jason looked at his two officers. "Heavy metal. Bon Jovi. I've heard of them. And as for you, Doc," he went on. "Cute. Harmless." He shook his head slowly. "I don't know. I just don't know."

They kept straight faces, though Helle Hemelsen lightly passed the tip of a forefinger along the corner of an eye, as if wiping something away.

Jason did not see, or pretended not to see, the surreptitious smiles on the faces of the other operators. They were quite used to McCann's impromptu rock broadcasts, when he chose not to secure the channel he happened to be using at the time.

Morton, unaware that McCann was following the fight to the accompaniment of blasting guitars and thumping, rolling bass, could not decide which was the more frustrating: trying to nail the hard-to-catch F-16 or the backseater's unnervingly continuing silence.

He felt as if he'd been hauling the ASV punishingly about the sky for hours. His entire head felt damp within the helmet. Several times, the F-16 had tried to extend the fight, in order to get into position for a good missile shot. Each time, Morton had used the phenomenal acceleration of the ASV to close the gap and reel in the darting aircraft, forcing the other pilot to remain within gun range. Unfortunately, the man in the F-16 would not oblige by staying within the shoot parameters long enough to be zapped.

Morton's perceived hours were little more than ninety seconds. He should have nailed the little electric jet by now, he felt. He once used to fly one of those dancing things, didn't he? He should at least know some of the other pilot's possible tricks.

So he should.

But whatever he thought he knew didn't seem to be working, just when he needed it.

McCann's silence didn't help either.

It was strange. Morton found himself realizing with some astonishment that he was actually beginning to miss the Kansas City boy's irreverent comments. He also had the uncomfortable feeling that the silent McCann was assessing his performance. He felt very much the subordinate, despite outranking the backseater. McCann had real missions under his belt. McCann was a wounded veteran. McCann had contempt for majors who were pilots. What the hell was he doing back there anyway?

Morton racked the ASV into yet another tight, diving turn and plunged after the elusive Falcon.

In the backseat, McCann continued to enjoy the rippling guitar sounds as the ASV streaked along at what seemed almost like sea level, before hauling into a steep climb in pursuit of the fleeing F-16.

The major still had a long way to go, McCann thought dispassionately, before he could begin to hack it *really* low like Selby or Hohendorf. This was still kids' stuff.

Morton would have been devastated by the appraisal, had he known of it.

Throughout, McCann had constantly kept a sharp lookout and, had the other aircraft succeeded in getting into a good position, he'd have warned Morton. But Morton seemed to be coping, even though the fight was becoming long-winded.

Then the Falcon twinkled away.

McCann decided it was time for some intervention. With regret, he stopped the Bon Jovi cassette and killed the channel he'd been using.

Morton had found that he was becoming more and more uncomfortable with McCann's silence and because he was distracted by this, lost concentration for the briefest of moments. It was enough.

"Jesus, Major!" came McCann's voice suddenly, "the guy's getting into our six!"

Morton cranked his head round. McCann was right. The Falcon was curving in from the left rear quarter. How the hell had he got there?

"*Don't* tighten the turn!" McCann was saying. "He's expecting that. Stay as you are. When I give the word, continue the roll through one-eighty, then haul tight-ass round, *immediately*. Don't give him warning. He'll try to follow, but he'll be too late if you're quick. *You'll* be too late if you're not. You should be getting on *his* six while he's still looking for us. You got that, Major?"

"I've got it." Morton sounded as if he was gritting his teeth. *I was right,* he thought with chagrin. *The little SOB's been assessing me.*

"Okay, Major. The Chameleon made it tough for him but now he's reckoning he's got us. He's good, but not *that* good."

"Look. Will you stop calling me 'Major' all the time?"

"You're a major . . ."

"I know, dammit! My name's Chuck . . ."

"Okay, Major Chuck . . ."

"Jesus . . ."

"Now!"

Morton rolled the ASV through one hundred eighty degrees as McCann had advised, abruptly changing to the opposite direction, and pulled hard into the turn, grunting and straining against the sudden slam of the G-forces. In his mask, the noises he made sounded as if he was having a hard time on the toilet.

Don't black out. Don't black out.

The words pounded in his mind as nearly eight times the force of gravity momentarily tried to flatten his body into his seat. Blacking out was a certain kill for your opponent in a real shooting fight. While you were having your enforced nap, all he'd have to do was stand off and take his potshot. Gun your brains out, in fact.

But McCann was again being proved right.

The F-16, caught out by the sudden maneuver, was looking very naked. The targeting box had found the aircraft and the gunsight pipper was drifting in, the ranging circle on its outer rim beginning to unwind in a counter-clockwise direction, as the range closed. The dotted "snake" came on, indicating precisely where the cannon shells would strike, had this been a real shoot.

But that won't last for long if I stop to admire the view, Morton thought.

He watched as he fed the hard-turning target aircraft into the open end of the test-tube shape on the guns HUD. When the target box, superimposed by both the pipper and the snake, was well inside the tube, it would be time for the kill.

The ASV tightened its turn and the Falcon slid inexorably down the tube.

The box stopped blinking and he got the tone.

Morton had already uncaged the gun trigger. He now squeezed it. In the headphones of both the ASV's crew and the F-16 pilot, the kill tone sounded.

The F-16 stopped turning and its pilot gave an unconventional waggle of his wings to show he accepted the outcome.

"Knock it off, knock it off," came their erstwhile adversary's voice on an open channel, indicating that the engagement was over. "Where did you guys disappear to?"

"Ah," McCann replied. "That would be telling."

An indefinable sound came back at them, then the Falcon pilot went into a flashy roll and dove out of sight, on his way back to base.

"And there goes another pissed-off guy," McCann said. "Good kill, Chuck," he added.

Morton, his entire head feeling as if it had been doused with water, experienced a sense of elation. "Thanks for the help. I appreciate it."

"Hey. That's what backseaters are for. Now what say we head on back home?"

"On our way, Mighty One," Morton acknowledged, euphoria briefly usurping common sense.

"Mighty One. Hey. I like that."

"Oh Major, Major," Jason murmured to himself. Like everyone else, he'd listened to the inter-cockpit conversation. "You'll live to regret those rashly spoken words."

Helle Hemelsen overheard the wing commander's comments. "Do you mean what he's just called Elmer Lee?" She seemed to find the idea amusing.

Jason nodded. "That's all we need," he said with the air of resigned experience. "McCann, the Mighty One."

Helm had also caught the remark.

Still sporting his hard, don't-mess-with-me expression, he said, "It is a good result, although the second engagement was beginning to look like a stalemate until McCann came back in. Morton is still a little behind the power curve with the aircraft, and is not yet quite sure of himself with it. But he is getting close. As for Captain McCann, in my opinion he is ready to go up with Hohendorf, and then back to his crewing with Selby. He has done well, even if he did misuse one of the cassette slots . . . again." The expression looked dangerously close to cracking into a smile.

Jason turned to Helle Hemelsen. "Doctor?"

"I could detect nothing in his voice to cause concern.

He sounded just like the old Elmer Lee, and on current evidence, you have no need for worry. I agree with the *Fregattenkapitän*. If you're asking me whether he's fit to return to combat duties . . . based upon what we've heard today and on my other observations over the months . . . I say yes. As for how he will react under actual combat conditions, he'll just be Elmer Lee. If you want to be absolutely sure, ground him. But then, you might as well ground everybody else too, including yourself, on that basis."

"Very well. All right, Doc. We'll go with that. Thanks for coming down."

"It was an experience."

"An experience . . . yes. And I haven't forgotten cute. Shame on you, Doc."

She gave him one of her brightest smiles.

"Come on," Jason said. "I'll take you back to your office. Coming with us?" he added to Helm.

"I'll stay here for a while," the deputy CO said. "I want to check out the replays. There are some aspects of the engagements I'll need to discuss with Major Morton, at debrief."

"Very well, Dieter. I'll leave it in your very capable hands." Jason looked round the room at the operators and controllers and raised his voice slightly. "Thank you, ladies and gentlemen."

A chorus of "sirs" responded as he and Helle Hemelsen left.

"Cute," Jason repeated as they walked out.

4

Jason's description of McCann as an imp was not far from the truth.

McCann had the sort of face that made you think he had just done something he shouldn't have, or was about to do so. It was a face that throughout his flying career so far had put every superior officer instantly on the alert, the moment they set eyes upon him for the very first time. It was a face that many a teacher from his days at school would retain searingly within their memory. Like a cat that in a room full of people will unerringly find the one person who hates cats, trouble made a point of hunting him out.

But there was no denying that in the backseat of a high-tech fighter, McCann was a wizard.

His childhood in Kansas City, *Missouri,* as he would stress bitingly to those who dared made the mistake of assuming Kansas, had been an exceedingly comfortable one. Being an only child had meant that his parents had lavished everything they could upon him. In truth, McCann should have been horribly spoiled. His idiosyncracies were tolerated because those who really liked him—though they wouldn't dare say so to his face—understood him, as Helle Hemelsen had said, to be a puppy that wanted to please.

Jason had once remarked that when he'd poached him from the U.S. Air Force, the entire vast organization had heaved a collective sigh of relief. That McCann would be in somebody else's hair was a mental refrain that could almost be heard aloud, and majors everywhere who were pilots might well have wept for joy.

McCann was not very tall, and had a round, chubby face topped by a close crop of hair that really was corn-colored. Whenever his hair grew beyond an inch, it became totally unruly. There was an inherent cockiness about him that tended to annoy some people, while others tolerated it with long-suffering good humor. The bright blue, wide-apart eyes and the button of a nose gave him the look of a slightly malicious imp, neatly fitting Jason's description of him.

He sat in the backseat of the ASV, humming to himself as Morton brought the Super Tornado low along the main runway, to pull up into a smartly executed fighter break. He closely monitored the systems as Morton began to set up for the landing and made a final check of the configuration. If anything went wrong at that moment, there was still time and enough fuel to call for an abort, and they'd have to go round again while attempting to resolve the problem.

It could all happen so easily. You've had a good flight. All systems functioning properly. You're positioned nicely for the runway and looking forward to the touchdown and getting out of the turkey suit. Then whammo. A birdstrike, or an in-flight fire, or one gear deciding not to lock down. Just about anything could happen to catch out the unwary. It was never over until you had climbed safely out of the aircraft.

But no problems manifested themselves.

"Wings to twenty-five," he announced. "Flaps to full. Gear down and locked. Three greens. Looking good."

He looked out and saw the runway slightly to the left and sliding neatly into line as Morton brought the ASV smoothly onto the centerline.

Morton put the aircraft down with practiced ease, and the thrust reversers came on, cutting the ground speed dramatically. Soon, they were taxiing off the runway.

"Not bad, Major," McCann said approvingly.

"Why thank you, Captain."

"Anytime."

They were sauntering back to the squadron crew room in their flight gear when McCann seemed to be staring at a burly figure approaching purposefully from that direction.

"What the hell is *he* doing here?" McCann exclaimed to himself.

Morton glanced towards the unknown person, who was still some distance away. "You know that guy?"

"Engineer officer," McCann replied tersely. "Well before your time. He was a flight lieutenant, then they promoted him to squadron leader . . ."

"Like . . . major, you mean . . ." Morton said, suddenly becoming interested.

"Yes, yes. Major, if you like. They posted him to the States on an avionics liaison detachment. He's supposed to be out there a while yet. God*damn*. Who in hell brought him back?"

Morton was giving McCann profoundly interested glances as they walked. "You look kind of sick, Captain.

What have you done to this guy? Stolen his woman?"
Morton paused. "Wait a minute. Wait a *minute*.
Revelation dawns. *This* is the guy Karen Lomax was
seeing?"

"What if it is?" McCann countered defensively.
"Yeah. That's Pearce. Geordie Pearce. His name's not
really Geordie. It's where he comes from. Like calling
some guy 'Yank,' or 'Reb.' He's a geordie from
Sunderland."

"Gawd . . ." Morton stared at the enormous form
coming towards them and could scarcely believe it.
"You really are crazy. Look at the *size* of the guy.
That's a tank on legs! No wonder he plays rugby. Do
they *call* him tank? You went after that guy's woman?"

"I didn't know they were an item when I saw her for
the first time. When I found out, it was too late. She's
one hell of a woman, though. You've seen her. Isn't she?"

"Are you going to be in one piece long enough to
appreciate that?" Morton demanded sympathetically.
"You like suffering, McCann. I'm outta here."

"Thanks, Major. I'll do the same for you one day."
McCann kept staring at the squadron leader, whose
approach was ominously determined.

"Hey. Who am I to meddle in a cosy triangle?"

Morton walked on, then stopped to look back as
Pearce came to a menacing halt in front of McCann. He
wondered whether Pearce would be mad enough to hit
the backseater. The engineer squadron leader would
be risking his career if he did that.

"Captain McCann," Pearce began.

"Sir?" McCann replied innocently.

"I've been looking for you in the crew room."

"I've been flying, sir, as you can see. Didn't they tell
you?"

"They told me."

"Glad to see you back, sir," McCann said politely.

Geordie Pearce was indeed a big man. His solid hands looked as if each could encircle McCann's throat with ease. His bushy black eyebrows met in the middle above eyes that were a strange, opaque black. They looked dead. Yet Pearce had a finely chiseled face and a powerful chin. There was little doubt that he was handsome in a cold, but brutal, way.

The added flavor of an undoubted hint of this latent brutality, which he so ruthlessly displayed upon a rugby pitch, carried with it an air of danger that some women found irresistible. This whiff of danger had clearly once enticed Karen Lomax.

The opaque eyes bored into McCann. "Are you?"

"I don't understand the question, sir," McCann now said ingenuously.

Pearce had planted his feet firmly across McCann's path. Fists on hips, he stared down at what he saw as little more than an umpudent tick.

"You don't fool me, McCann," Pearce snapped in a grating voice. "Don't believe you're immortal because you've apparently come back from the dead. Oh yes. I know all about your little escapade over Bosnia, and the tender attention you've been receiving while I've been away. Surprised?"

"No, sir. Just relieved I made it back."

"Don't get funny with me, Captain."

"Sir . . ."

"Shut it! You listen to me, Captain McCann. Keep well away from Flight Lieutenant Lomax. You're not a cat. You've still only got the one life."

"Going to beat me up, are you, sir?" McCann asked with suicidal bravery.

Pearce bared rampart-like, perfect teeth at him. "Forget it, McCann. You're not going to trap me into hitting a subordinate. There are other ways to do so, within regulations. I can challenge you to a boxing match. That's allowed. Can you box, McCann?"

"No."

"Good. Take heed, Captain." Pearce turned and stomped away without another word.

McCann took a deep breath, let it out, then walked on to where Morton was still waiting.

"Cheated death again," he said brightly to the pilot. "Don't know how I do it."

Morton was staring at him as if he'd just dropped out of the sky without a parachute and continued to walk around normally.

"What is *it* with you and people who are majors?" he asked. "You're going up the nose of yet another one."

"Talent," McCann replied, unabashed.

Momentarily lost for words, Morton carried on for a few steps, his dark hair, flattened by his helmet, contrasting sharply with McCann's corn-colored thatch.

Then in a slightly dazed voice, he asked, "You reckon he could have beaten the both of us?"

"If we were in a dark alley somewhere, out of uniform, and no one was watching? In a heartbeat."

"So you're going to back off?"

"Not a chance."

Morton shook his head despairingly. "Like I said. Crazy. Well, let's get out of these things, then head on to debriefing to hear what deputy boss Helm has to say about our hop."

"I think we did good up there."

"Let's hope he thinks so."

"A good result, gentlemen," was what Helm had to say. "You made good calls up there, Captain McCann.

Major, my personal opinion is that you're coming to grips with the new ship. Sometimes, you're a little behind the power curve; but not enough to worry me. You took on two Falcons and lived to tell the tale. In my book, that's a win. Keep this up and you'll be fully recommended for the super-superflick."

"Thank you, sir," Morton said, very pleased with himself.

"Don't thank me. I do the training, but you've got to have the application. Do bad, and I ground you. No argument. But you did good, and you had a good backseater to hold your hand."

Helm turned to one of three terminals in the briefing room. Each had a direct link to the Ops Center.

He switched one on.

As the screen came alive, a replay of the recent combat was being run.

"There are some weaknesses in the engagement," he went on, "although you did come out on top. Can you see what I am getting at, Major?"

Morton studied the replay of the cavorting aircraft, noting the moves the ASV was making.

Helm tapped a key, and the replay paused. "Can you see what's wrong with this?"

The pause was at the moment where Morton had lost sight of the second F-16.

Helm was looking at him. "What *were* you thinking of? Up to that moment, you were giving him no quarter. Doing fine. Then for some reason, he began to maneuver into your six. McCann gave the call, and a potential failure was converted into a win. Lose sight, lose the fight. You know that from your rookie days at flight school, Major. Am I right?"

"You're right, sir," Morton admitted.

"I'm not doing this to embarrass you. Here at

November, we go beyond what other units might find acceptable."

"I understand that, sir."

"Good. You're a very fine pilot. The boss always says he doesn't want dead crews because they are no use to him. My job, and the job of the other instructors, is to make sure you stay alive in combat. Okay?"

"Yessir."

Had Dieter Helm been around in the eleventh century, he would have been a crusader. His squared jawline, angular yet strong physique, blond Romanesque hair lying moss-like upon his skull, his piercing eyes, all gave the impression he would be equally at home attired in an eagle-plumed casque upon his head, chainmail and white surplice, with the black cross of the Teutonic hospitalers upon it. He could be imagined with broadsword at his hip and massive lance in armor-gloved hand, galloping in a thundering charge. His modern steed was a fearsome mount that would have sent those old crusaders fleeing in terror; but when he was in flying suit and helmet, he still looked the part.

"All right, Chuck," he now said, less formally. "There are going to be some changes with your crewing. Captain McCann will be moving to the next stage of his work-up, and you'll be paired with Major Carlizzi for now, until we have a permanent backseater for you. Do you remember Carlizzi?"

"I do, sir," Morton answered ruefully.

Carlizzi was an instructor backseater and had occupied the rear cockpit on one of the less powerful ASVs, when Morton had begun his initiation into the joys of the extreme flying practiced by the November unit. Carlizzi had also been the backseater when Morton had been introduced to his first air combat try-out against

Helm himself. Not surprisingly, he'd been comprehensively beaten.

Helm appeared to smile. "I can see you do." He turned to McCann. "Captain, you will now be paired with Hohendorf. Your hop will be at 1000 hours tomorrow; a one-on-one. Your adversaries will be Cottingham and Christiansen in the second ASV. This will be a series of three full engagements: long, medium, and gun range. If the long-range engagement continues all the way up to gun range before a kill is made, both aircraft will disengage after whoever has scored and move on to the next. Pilot helmet sights will be activated."

"Yes, sir."

"Major Morton, I want you to study the replay as often as possible over the next few days. Judge your own performance, and check out any mistakes you spot. I don't want a repeat next time you're up."

"Sir."

"All right, gentlemen. Thank you."

A mountain road in Bosnia.

The rusting carcass of the bus lay exactly where it had been forcibly stopped, just over eighteen months before. Its rear still pointed silently and gapingly to the sky, its nose dug into the soft, waterlogged ground at the side of the narrow, unpaved road. Every pane of glass had been shattered by the long-ago gunfire, and only jagged slivers, like sharks' teeth, protruded from the window and door surrounds.

It had long since lost its wheels and bullet-pocked seats, commandeered for the war effort by the very people who had fired upon it, killing all those they had previously captured and made their prisoners. They had promised the frightened people safety. Instead, the slopes beyond the bus were littered with the remains of their victims. The vehicle itself was a mass of holes, bearing grim testimony to the slaughter that had taken place. There were other buses, in other places, that bore witness to similar crimes.

Less than ten kilometers away was the village from which the buses had come. Once, it had boasted two hundred inhabitants: men, women, and children, belonging to all the Bosnian ethnic groups. They had lived peaceably together for generations. Their families were mixed.

They had wanted nothing to do with the war; but the war had come to them. Unlike in many other towns and villages in that tortured country, the inhabitants had stood together when the Black Lynxes descended upon them, and had refused to take sides. For that refusal to debase their honor and betray their friends and each other, they had paid the ultimate price.

The village did not make the news like places such as Srebrenica. There were other small pockets that never would, though they had suffered just as horrendously when the work of savages had been visited upon them. One man and his group of homicidal maniacs had been responsible for many of these atrocities.

Drago Serenic.

The hard-packed mountain road was little more than a wide track. The column of four armored personnel carriers came up it at a leisurely pace on dirt-smeared wheels, as if on routine patrol. All were Russian built. The three bringing up the rear were variations on the BTR-152 theme, long-wheelbased and six-wheeled. Their tops were open, and the six troopers in each were clearly visible.

The command car in the lead, though equally six-wheeled, had a shorter wheelbase and an armored roof. A sliding panel allowed the commander to stand head out, as if in the turret of a tank. Though the BTR-152 had its genesis in the fifties, these were not old machines. The command car itself had the very latest secure satellite communication system. A six-barreled rotary minigun, stolen from one of the NATO IFOR stores, was mounted proudly on the roof. Originally intended for an IFOR assault helicopter, it was now for the commander's use only.

The column's camouflage pattern was unusual. In addition to a normal version of the shades-of-green design favored by many ground forces throughout the world, there was also an overlaid speckle of black. The troopers and their commander wore combat outfits that were similarly camouflaged. There were no unit insignia, either on their vehicles or on their uniforms.

The commander himself had his own version of the Yugoslav Army hat upon his head. It was all black, with green piping, and clamped upon it was a headset and mike. His troopers wore black berets. The commander also called himself "general," but his followers were not regular troops.

He carried a 9mm automatic in a shoulder holster, the harness worn over his combat gear. The weapon was not of Russian manufacture, as would have been expected, but was a Beretta 92R, as carried by many Western forces. He had personally "liberated" it from its previous owner.

He was Drago Serenic, and they were the Black Lynxes.

Unlike the militia commander that MacAllister had encountered, Serenic had not been a petty criminal before the conflict. Serenic was not his real name.

Highly intelligent, he had been a lawyer and a partner in a very successful firm, with both national and international clients on their books. He had been exceedingly ruthless in his legal battles, with a high rate of success. This ruthlessness was matched only by his lack of humanity, which pleased his clients enormously, considering they were never on the receiving end.

Then had come the war.

Already a reserve officer, he had volunteered for unspecified special duties. The nature of those duties soon gave him a new area within which to give this innate ruthlessness, and inhumanity, new rein. Before long, his regular army commanders began to detect an uncomfortable smell about his activities, as the country went through its spectacular and savage disintegration. Then came the news that he had died in battle. The command, growing mindful of the aftermath of the war, and international reaction to it, heaved a sigh of relief.

Months later, a group known as the Black Lynxes began making an odious name for itself among the mountain villages and towns. While no one openly claimed support for this band of marauders, many tacitly approved of its activities, which included decimating whole communities in an orgy of killing. Soon, the Black Lynxes were called upon to carry out "unofficial little jobs" of cleansing. Their commander, Serenic, had never been seen in public without a balaclava beneath his black cap.

With the conflict supposedly over and IFOR troops patrolling in various parts of the country, it would have been expected that the Black Lynxes had been disbanded. Nothing was further from the truth. They still operated, and no one seemed able to stop them.

Whenever the alarm came that they had struck somewhere, the response was always too late, long after
they had vanished, leaving another village or hamlet
devastated and emptied of inhabitants. They struck
fear through the mountain communities, prompting
people to leave their homes before they too could
become a target for the Lynxes.

Which was the very intention.

Lip service was paid to calling them criminals and
murderers. Noises were made locally—with much public wringing of hands—about bringing them to justice.
In reality, many secretly approved of what was being
done.

Serenic now stood out of his BTR, a cigarette dan-
gling nonchalantly between lips bared by the slit in the
balaclava. His eyes and ears were similarly bared; but
the eyes were hidden by dark sunglasses, the ears by
the headphones.

As his BTR had neared the skeletal bus he had raised
a gloved hand briefly, to halt the column. He now made
an imperious gesture and the troops piled rapidly out of
the APCs to fan out on both sides of the road. These
were not all the troops under his command.

They waited.

Serenic stared for long moments at the bus, drawing
deeply on his cigarette. This had been one of the Black
Lynxes' jobs. He took another long drag on the
cigarette, removed it carefully, pinched it out between
gloved fingers, then flicked it over the side of the BTR.

He turned slowly, carefully scrutinizing the slopes
about him, picking out the strewn bones of his victims. If
his eyes could have been seen, there would have been no
reaction mirrored in them. It was even doubtful that, if
the young girl from the café had been placed before him
at that moment, he would have remembered her. He had

long ago learned to anesthetize himself by deliberately erasing his victims from memory. It was something he had perfected since the days of his legal practice.

He made a chopping motion.

Instantly, the troopers spread out into the woods on both sides of the road, clearly on a search mission of some kind. Serenic remained where he was, barely moving. Like some alien reptile, he appeared to be basking in the sun.

Half an hour later, the men began to filter back. It was a further fifteen minutes before the last one returned, to run up to Serenic's vehicle.

"No one's been here, Commandant," the man reported, speaking the language of the region. "The whole area is as we left it last year. Are we going to clear it?"

Serenic did not immediately reply. He looked once more about him, eyes surveying the slopes as his subordinate waited patiently.

"There is a stench of death here," he remarked at last. He sounded amused, as if he had made a joke. "No. We will not clear it up. Let the foreigners do it. They can do their excavating and their re-burying. It eases their consciences. This hasn't made the international news and it will take IFOR, or one of those do-gooding Scandinavian burial groups, a long time to find this place . . . which is as we want it. Let us go on to the village. See if anyone has been stupid enough to move in. Tell the men to board. We may find some action."

"At once, Commandant!" The man ran to comply.

Soon, the column was once again on the move. Serenic remained standing in his command car.

He lit a fresh cigarette.

● ● ●

The village looked as the bus had.

Gutted, empty shells stood just as gapingly, imploring the heavens like emaciated arms, travesties of the homes they once had been. Their walls seemed held together only by the latticework of holes that had been punched through them. Many were severely charred, the aftermath of the fires that had been deliberately started in them. Most had no roofs.

It was as if no life had ever existed there, so profound was the silence. Not even a dog skulked through the ruins.

The road neatly bisected the silent village, beyond which were the slopes of the mountain range. It ended there and was the only motorable road in or out. Radiating footpaths led from it, some going across the moutains.

There were unequivocal signs at each end of the village, warning of the consequences to anyone found moving back into a cleansed area. Once, the village had been a thriving community of neat, pretty houses, in a picture-postcard landscape. It was the sort of place wealthy tourists would have fled to—had they known of its existence—to enjoy its clean mountain air, and to escape the stressful rigors of city life for a precious couple of weeks. Now, its dead buildings stood in mute reproach as the column of APCs, manned by the very people who had desecrated it, rumbled in.

When the vehicles were halfway along, Serenic again raised a hand to call a halt.

The APCs stopped, engines running. He did not give the order to dismount. Instead, he once again looked slowly about him, as he'd done by the bus, masked head turning with a lifelessness that was reminiscent of a robot.

The head stopped.

The second cigarette was almost down to its filtered tip. Still looking in the direction of whatever had grabbed his attention, Serenic slowly removed it from his mouth and pinched it as he had done before. Then he flicked it over the side.

Unhurriedly, he reached for the minigun and swiveled it towards whatever he had seen; then he put a hand beneath the lip of the hatch to flick a switch. There was a hum as loudspeakers came on.

"You there!" he barked. "Come out! It will be better for you. If you do not, I will send my men to get you. They will not be gentle. You will come out immediately!"

The sound of his amplified voice seemed to startle the very mountains with its suddeness. There was no movement from within the ruins as the subdued humming of the speakers hung forebodingly upon the air.

The burping roar of the minigun was an even greater shock as Serenic poured a stream of 20mm tracer shells at the dead building he'd been looking at. A billow of pulverized cement and paint erupted from it in an expanding dust cloud, obscuring the already severely damaged house as the shells struck explosively.

Then a relative silence returned abruptly. Serenic had stopped firing. The only sound was that of the whirring of the minigun, its rotary barrels gradually spinning down to a stop in an unnerving, dying sibilance.

Movement.

Three people came hesitantly out from the cover of the wreckage of a house that was behind the one Serenic had pulverized with his cannon; a man in middle age, a much younger woman, and a child—a girl— of about eight.

A click indicated that Serenic had turned off the loudspeakers.

No one said anything, watching them with chilling detachment as they approached Serenic's command vehicle. They stopped, standing directly in front of it.

The man had prematurely aged. His clothes, which had once been of reasonable quality, now looked as if they belonged to a tramp. It seemed as if he'd been sleeping in them for some time. He had. His once rich and full head of black hair had degenerated into thin wisps of gray, most of which had fallen out. His cheeks were sunken as if he hadn't eaten for weeks, his body just this side of emaciation. His eyes were haunted. Incongruously, on his feet were dirty trainers, in unexpectedly good condition. Allowing for their recent use, they seemed almost new.

The young woman—in her mid- to late twenties—appeared perfectly healthy by comparison, with long black hair that looked well cared for. There was a ripe plumpness to her body that was beginning to generate a dangerous interest from Serenic's men. But her dark eyes remained unafraid.

She wore a simple print dress of red and white, with a thin sweater of plain blue pulled over the top. The sweater accentuated the fullness of her breasts. Many of the men had repositioned themselves in their vehicles, so as to get a better view of her.

Her legs, strong and sensually shaped, were bare and mud-streaked. She too wore trainers. In keeping with her general physical appearance, hers was a powerfully attractive face with equally strong contours; a woman whose genes had come from the mountains. But there were clear signs of fatigue upon that face, as if she had come a very long way.

The child held on to the woman's hand tightly and

stared blankly up at Serenic. There was neither fear, nor curiosity; just a terrible emptiness in the eyes. They were the eyes of a child who could no longer cry; who had already seen far too much in her barely commenced life. Perhaps that was the greatest crime of all the crimes already committed in that brutalized country: children who could no longer cry.

It made little difference to Serenic. He looked down upon the little girl in her crumpled denims and a sweater that was a smaller version of the woman's and saw only someone who should not be there. Like the other two, she was also wearing reasonably new trainers.

Serenic's dark glasses surveyed them coldly. "Who are you? And where have you come from?"

It was the man who answered, replying to the second question first. "We have come from Sarajevo . . ."

"Sarajevo!" There was a palpable contempt, as well as surprise, in Serenic's voice. "That place of mongrels! You are a very long way from home. It is nearly two hundred kilometers on foot, over these mountains. Did you walk all the way? With your child?"

Serenic was not really interested in the welfare of the little girl.

"We . . . we were fortunate . . ."

"Fortunate . . . !"

Serenic's men laughed at the thought that these people could think themselves fortunate. He did not join in, but neither did he stop them.

The man waited until the laughter had died down. "We . . . we . . ."

"We . . . we . . ." the men echoed, laughing again.

Serenic held up a hand. The laughing stopped immediately.

"What he is trying to say," the woman said coldly, "is that we were given a lift."

The glasses, like curved reflecting sockets, turned their focus upon her. "Your husband is so old you must talk for him?"

The dark eyes looked up at him with their own contempt. "He is my *father*. My mother is dead. People like you put them in a concentration camp . . ."

"They must have treated him well. *He* is still alive and walking."

The laughter from the men bellowed out again. This time, Serenic let them continue for a while, prolonging the humiliation.

The woman's contempt did not falter. Her eyes said it all.

"Who gave you the lift?" he demanded, when the laughter had at last died down.

"A British patrol . . ."

"The *British*." Serenic spat the words out. "Meddlers! Just like the Americans. But this land will be their grave, and the graveyard of all those other foreigners. British, Americans, French, Italians, Germans . . . and the rest. It does not matter who. First, we had the worthless UN bringing their African soldiers and other black tribes here to tell us what to do. *Africans! An insult!* Now we have the stupid IFOR." He paused suddenly, the lips in the mask briefly tightening before abruptly relaxing in what could have been a smile. "How far did the British take you? I would advise you not to lie to me. I do not take kindly to lying."

The woman knew there could be only one outcome to the encounter, but she gave no evidence of this. She maintained her stoicism and kept her face expressionless, though she was well aware of the leers from the grinning men.

"About eighty kilometers from here," she replied.

"Eighty! So you have walked the rest of the way?"

"Yes."

"How long did this take?"

"Seven days."

"About twelve kilometers a day."

"Yes. It was difficult for my father, and my daughter. We also had to be careful about mines."

"The British gave you these shoes?"

"Yes. And some food. They were pleasant young men."

"And what did you have to pay to these 'pleasant' young men?"

She stared at him. "Pay?"

"Don't pretend with me! You know what I mean. A woman like you would be attractive to men a long way from home."

She could sense the eyes behind the glasses undressing her.

"They would find you . . . enjoyable, I think."

"They did not touch me! They were civilized."

"Civilized," Serenic repeated coldly. "So you think my men are not civilized? You think *I* am not civilized?"

"I did not say that."

"No. You did not."

He paused again, continuing to stare at her. The father had begun to shake slightly.

"You!" he barked, causing the increasingly frightened, broken man to jump involuntarily. "Why are you shaking?"

"Please, Commandant," the man began, using the highest form of address he could think of in an effort to appease. "Can we go? We have done nothing . . ."

"Nothing? *Nothing? Did you not read the signs? This is a cleansed area!*" In another of his abrupt switches of attention, Serenic turned once more to the woman. "Where did the British get the shoes?"

She glanced briefly at her father before replying, "They were taking supplies to a small refugee camp."

"And you told them you were coming here."

"Yes. They had never heard of this place."

"I see." It sounded ominous. "And they will report this, of course."

"No."

"No?"

"They are dead."

This revelation surprised even Serenic. "How?"

"Just after they let us off, their truck hit a mine. It fell down a ravine and burst into flames. We tried to help, but there was nothing we could do."

"I see," Serenic repeated softly. This time, he sounded pleased. "I see."

Suddenly, a shot cracked into the silence that had followed. The piteous man was staggering back, frantically trying to stop the blood from pouring out of the wound in his chest with his bare, ineffective hands.

Releasing her daughter's hand, the woman rushed to him as he fell. The child remained where she was, staring at Serenic and the automatic he now held, still pointing it at her fallen grandfather. Her face was impassive, and she made no sound.

"Now he'll be happy," Serenic said to the woman. "He can join your Turkish mother, since he misses her so much."

The woman turned from her dying father to look up at Serenic with cold hatred.

She pointed to one of the gaping buildings. It was a small church with half a steeple. "Do you see that over there? Does that look like a mosque to you? That is where we worshiped when I was a child, and where my parents still worshiped after I had gone to

Sarajevo." She pointed to another of the ruins. "Over there is the mosque where our neighbors prayed."

"Then your family should have done something about it."

"We were *all* friends here!"

"Too bad."

"Damn you!" she yelled at him. "This was a beautiful country until you madmen started all this. *Damn all people like you!*"

"That is not a wise attitude," Serenic said, calmly responding to her condemnation. He removed his headphones and began to climb out of the APC.

She stood up slowly. Her father was now dead. Bright red splashes of his blood stained her dress, merging with the patterns on it. On her hands, other splashes glistened wetly.

Serenic went up to her, the gun still in his hand but pointing downwards. He went very close until he was practically touching her. She did not move back a single step.

It was unexpected and he paused in fleeting surprise, the hunter faced by a prey that had suddenly turned upon him.

The child watched him.

He reached forward with the gun and slowly raised the hem of her dress with it, pushing forwards and upwards now, until it stopped between her legs. She did not flinch.

"You have nice thighs," he murmured, rubbing the gun up and down them. "Did your brat's father go to a mosque?" he enquired softly. "You like screwing that kind, do you? Did he enjoy feeling those nice, soft thighs around his waist? *Did* he?" The final words came out in a hiss, as the gun kept moving slowly up and down her flesh.

She said nothing, nor did she back away from him.

"My mask does not frighten you, I see. Good. I like a strong woman with spirit. One of you look after the child," he ordered loudly to his men, "while I . . . talk to the mother."

For the first time, she allowed her real concern for the child to show. "No. Please! Don't hurt my baby. She's only a little child! I'll . . . I'll do anything you want but *please* . . . leave her alone!"

"We will not touch her. What do you think we are? Savages?"

For reply, she glanced pointedly at her father's body.

"Let us discuss this further," Serenic said tightly.

He grabbed her roughly by the arm and led her towards the nearest of the houses.

"Don't worry, darling!" she called to the child. "I'll be all right."

The child looked at the two of them but gave no reaction.

The men began to grin shamelessly. One of them had climbed out of his vehicle to come to stand by her, while Serenic and the woman disappeared inside the building.

Soon, there came the ripping sound of clothing being torn. Not long after that, a rhythmic grunting was heard. The men smirked as the rest of them clambered off their vehicles.

No sounds came from the woman. Her father lay where he had fallen, but no one took any further notice of him.

The child stared at the house silently, eyes expressionless, while her mother was brutally raped.

It was nearly half an hour before Serenic came out of the house, ostentatiously tidying himself and making a big show of doing up his trousers. There were streaks of blood on them.

"All right," he said to his men. "Your turn. She's got a great body to enjoy. Great tits too. Don't all rush at once," he added as they began to hurry towards the house, laughing and whooping in excited anticipation.

He looked at the child, who had not moved from where she stood. "I am always good to my men," he said to her conversationally.

Then he shot her. The little girl fell brokenly to the dried mud of the road, without uttering a single sound.

He stared at the dead child, the obscene mask giving an added callousness to the murderous act.

One of the men had come to look.

"When it's all over," Serenic told him, "get those damned shoes off them. Strip them of everything. There are others more worthy who could put those things to better use."

"Yes, Commandant."

Whatever the terrible experience the woman had been suffering at that moment, she'd heard the sound of the shot through it. For the first and only time, she screamed. It was a continuous keening wail, until it was abruptly cut off.

Then it began to rain.

It was as if the mountains themselves had begun to weep.

5

November base, the next day, 1000 hours.

"Goshawk Zero-One, Zero-Two," the tower said. "Clear to take off." It wasn't Karen Lomax's voice.

"Roger," Hohendorf acknowledged. "Zero-One."

"Zero-Two," Cottingham responded.

"Let's roll it!" came McCann's voice on the cockpit channel to Hohendorf. "The Double-C are in for a whupping on this fine day!"

Hohendorf was already firmly pushing the throttles forward through the gate and into burner. He had not held the aircraft on the brakes and it was rolling virtually as soon as the engines began to roar. By the time the afterburners cut in he was lifting it off the deck, bringing the gear up, and reefing the ASV Echo in a steep climb.

It was a classic Hohendorf takeoff.

McCann glanced over his right shoulder. The aircraft of Cottingham and Christiansen had been left slightly behind by Hohendorf's rapid rotation and climb, but it was rapidly pulling into formation, matching the near-vertical ascent.

"Gawd," McCann said. "I love this every time. I'm a jet junky!" he warbled.

"Don't sing!" Hohendorf pleaded before adding, half-guiltily, "Are you okay back there?"

As this was the first time they'd flown together since Bosnia, he wondered whether McCann felt any unease with the pairing.

"Sure," came the cheerful response. "I'm fine. Quit worrying, will you, Axel? I'm okay. Really. Like coming home."

"Well, I will try to get you back down in once piece this time," Hohendorf said, making a weak joke of it.

"Look, Axel," McCann said, knowing only too well how Hohendorf felt, "like I've been telling you for a while now . . . it was not your fault. Hey, man, I got hit. It happens. Look at it this way . . . if *you'd* been hit instead, I might really have bought it. I know you jocks think you're God's own but hey, sometimes we need pilots to drive us around."

Hohendorf felt his face crease slightly in his oxygen mask in a fleeting smile. Staying down was not in Elmer Lee's vocabulary.

"Goshawk, we have traffic inbound two-two-zero, one-zero miles. Maintain climb to high altitude transit. Repeat two-two-zero, ten miles."

This time, the controller's voice was Karen Lomax's.

"This is Goshawk," McCann said, making the acknowledgement. He also kept to procedures. "That's a roger. Traffic two-two-zero inbound, ten miles. You guys copy that?" he added to Goshawk Zero-Two.

"We copy," Christiansen confirmed.

Had the message not come, they would have leveled out at twenty thousand feet and headed out to the air combat range. High altitude transit for the day meant going up to forty thousand. The direct climb was no problem for the ASV. He wondered what prompted the change.

"Have a good flight, and a good fight, Zero-One," came the warm tones of Karen Lomax.

McCann forced himself to behave and did not make the reply he wanted to. "Thank you, November. Will do. Zero-One out."

"Very restrained of you, Elmer Lee," Hohendorf suggested.

"Yeah," McCann said, after making certain they were on cockpit frequency only. "The boss had a little talk with me yesterday. He heard my goodbyes."

"Tough luck."

"Yeah. He's always where you never want him to be. How about that?"

"That's what being a boss is all about. You've got to be everywhere."

"Well, I'll never be one."

"You? Elmer Lee, you're the kind of person who makes it to general."

"Yeah. And sharks don't have teeth."

"Some don't."

"You know what I mean."

"Yes, Elmer Lee. I do know what you mean."

While they'd been talking, McCann had been closely monitoring his systems. His genius in the backseat was such that he was always in complete control, no matter what else he may be engaged in. McCann and his systems were one.

On the ground, Jason and Helm were again in the air

traffic control tower, again standing on the balcony. One of the small but heavily armed MD500 Defender gunships of the airfield perimeter defense squadron thrummed away in the distance. There was at least one of those on patrol, twenty-four hours a day.

"It's always a pleasure watching Hohendorf take off," Jason was saying. "The man flies the aircraft as if he's glued to it. Selby's virtually the same, but there are perceptible differences."

"Selby and Hohendorf," Helm remarked thoughtfully.

"Our two dominant males, and constantly in rivalry."

"You do not mind?"

"As long as they do not endanger themselves and their crews, their aircraft, or the interests of this unit, they can keep their rivalry. But should they slip up because of it, they are not immune to being grounded."

"I think they are aware of that."

"I should sincerely hope so," Jason said firmly.

"They're due for promotion," Helm went on. It was almost a question, left hanging.

Jason nodded. "I've read the recommendations from Mario da Vinci and yourself. Selby to squadron leader, and Hohendorf to *Korvettenkapitän*, which makes them equivalent to a major. I don't have a problem with that. In truth, they're well overdue. We'll give Hohendorf charge of Zero-One squadron and Selby, Zero-Two. Their rivalry will now be transferred to their respective squadrons, but that will be to the good. A spell of command should sort them out. Is Selby still up in London?"

"Yes. He's due back in two days."

"Seeing that young woman, no doubt. Miss Mannon, isn't it? The one with the financier father?"

"That is the one. And Hohendorf is still very tight with Selby's sister."

"Ah yes. The sister. The real source of the rivalry."

"Perhaps Selby doesn't want a German . . ."

"Steady on, Dieter. You can't seriously believe that. I've once had Selby carpeted, if you remember, for nearly allowing this thing to put his aircraft into the drink. We could have lost not only an expensive aircraft, but also two members of an extremely valuable crew. McCann was in the backseat. He could have died that day too."

"I remember."

"Selby does not have an antipathy towards Germans. Morven Selby's his only sibling, and a younger sister to boot. With both parents dying when they were relatively young, he is, not unnaturally, sometimes over-protective of her.

"But you do know what those two gentlemen are like in combat. Formidable. Quite terrifying for an enemy, in fact. They work together in the air like smoothly interlocking machinery. Deadly stuff. The crews of Hohendorf and Flacht, and Selby and McCann have no equals. Only Bagni and Stockmann, and now Cottingham and Christiansen, come near. Those four crews are our top men."

Helm said nothing for a while, then he began speaking, as if to himself. "Recently, the whole business with the football made me think that we Germans will never be seen to do anything right, no matter how hard we try . . ."

"Dieter . . ."

"Please, boss, let me finish."

"All right, old man," Jason said quietly.

"We Germans," Helm continued, "at least the majority of us and especially all the German personnel here on the base, have a permanent nightmare of Europe returning to what it used to be. We have so much to lose, you see. That is why I want to make sure that what we do here succeeds. It must."

"And it will, Dieter," Jason assured him, vividly recalling Helle Hemelsen's expression of remarkably similar views the day before. "It will. I consider myself most fortunate with the team I have assembled. I need people like you, and Mario, with me. I need *all* of you who have come here to this station to maintain your support. You senior officers have the responsibility of passing this on to your subordinates. Though we must currently hang on to our low profile, we are the genesis of what will one day become the norm. I shall fight for that, as long as I can draw breath."

"You have us," Helm told him solemnly, "for as long as it takes."

"Thank you, Dieter. I value that vote of confidence." Jason looked out over the airfield. "And I'm going to need as much of it as I can get. We're about to have another test of our resolve." He pointed to a distant aircraft on approach. "Assorted Eurocrats descending on us out of the blue, so to speak. Probably yet another check to see we're not wasting their precious money. Whose idea was it, I wonder, to spring this unexpected visit? We could do with the air vice-marshal at a time like this."

Just then a sharp roar made them look up. The distantly small shape of a standard Tornado F.3 passed high above, on its way to enter the circuit behind the executive aircraft that was making its way to the airfield. Air Vice-Marshal Robert Thurson, about to arrive.

"I think he heard you," Helm said drily.

Jason looked much happier. "And *I* think I may have an idea of just how this came about. Let's go and greet our uninvited guests. We'll take them down the hole and give them a show; but I do hope whoever set up this little jaunt have done their jobs efficiently and sorted out the proper clearances. No clearances, no peep at anything remotely sensitive. And I don't care who they are." He paused. "Oh my God. McCann's up there. With my luck, it would be today of all days."

"They've decided to visit us without warning," Helm began uncompromisingly, "let them see us . . ."

"Warts and all?"

"Yes."

"When McCann's upstairs, he's the kind of wart that worries me in a situation like this," was Jason's heart-felt comment.

"It's the minister, isn't it, sir?" Helm said. "*He* thought up this lunatic scheme in order to wrongfoot us. After all we've accomplished, one would have thought he'd have given up by now."

"My dear Christopher," the air vice-marshal began soothingly, "*per ardua ad astra*. The Royal Air Force motto. As its members, we should be used to it. 'Through hardship to the stars' . . . and all that. It doesn't end as the years pass. You're facing some hard-ships of your own, as I fully understand. But from a certain point of view, you're nearly more fortunate than the poor old Royal Air Force itself.

"One would also have thought," Thurson went on, "that *you* would have realized by now that no level is too low to stoop, for a politician who wants to hang on to power and look good in the eyes of his peers and supporters, however infantile. These are the people who once said that, as missiles would be the weapons of the future, there would be no further need for fight-ers; then they had a good go at killing off our fighters, and virtually succeeded."

"So this impromptu visit *is* the minister's idea."

Thurson nodded. "I'm afraid so, dear boy. So terribly sorry. He was hoping to catch you off-guard, of course, and with me absent from the proceedings, exposed to the chill wind of the *fait accompli*. Fortunately for both of us, a little bird warned me just in time. I thought the most practical thing would be to grab the kite and get up here as fast as I could. Went high and out to sea to break the sound barrier, then made a rapid descent. Rather amusing, arriving on their tail like that."

Not only did Jason have the AVM as a shield against those inimical to the November idea, the wing commander was also Thurson's protégé. Once Jason's flying instructor, Thurson had since taken a continuing interest in the younger man's career. He'd steadfastly supported Jason throughout the extremely difficult period of setting up the first of what was hoped would be a series of November bases. But though Jason had succeeded in bringing nearly two full squadrons to operational status, the pressures to close him down were as great as ever.

Thurson, a slim, tall man with the classical features of an aesthete, was well aware of this. He thus kept an efficient information network which served as an early warning system, whenever something was being planned to catch Jason out. This network was remarkably successful. The November program had allies as varied as its enemies. It did not mean, however, that Jason could get his own way with everything.

As soon as he had arrived, the air vice-marshal had rushed to the wing commander's office to brief him on the situation. There were three European representatives: one each from Germany, France, and the UK, plus a James Applegate, their general minder, who just happened to be employed by the minister's office.

Jason had left them to be seen to by Helm, while

they were being put through security checks by the RAF Regiment squadron leader who was boss of the unit's ground security forces. This officer, David Mearns, was notoriously stringent. The very worst thing a privileged visitor could do was try to pull rank. In such circumstances, Mearns would prove to be even more rigorous. He was fully backed by Jason and, in turn, by the air vice-marshal himself.

Mearns's deputy, Nathaniel Pike, a helicopter pilot seconded from the Parachute Regiment, was a captain who was no less rigorous. Those on the receiving end of their security attentions tended to say there was nothing to choose between them. It was Pike who was currently flying the perimeter patrol in the MD500.

"What's their excuse this time for being here, sir?" Jason now asked. "Another fault-finding exercise? Yet another budget snoop in the hope of justifying a chop in the funding?"

Thurson had entered the office still in his flight gear and carrying his helmet. He had put that down and was now in the process of removing his survival gear— immersion suit included—and G-suit.

"Don't mind if I get rid of these in here, do you?"

"Er . . . no, sir."

"Shan't be a minute." Soon, Thurson was wearing just his flight overalls and boots. "Ah! That's better."

"Would you like me to have a tea or coffee brought in, sir?"

"I'll have a tea, but I'll wait till we're down the hole."

"The real reason?" he repeated.

"I'll answer that obliquely, if you don't mind. The Eurobods are quite harmless. I think they're genuinely interested in the project itself. Of course, they're very mindful of budgetary constraints. But they're also wise enough to realize that the wild hopes of the 'New

World Order,' with *perestroika, glasnost*, and the fall of the Berlin Wall that had enveloped so many in a euphoric bout of wishful thinking, are as dead as the proverbial dodo. Dead at the starting post, as those of us a little more open-eyed about human nature realized from the very beginning; though it was politically incorrect to say so at the time.

"Those of us who hoisted warning flags were roundly condemned as wanting to continue playing with our high-tech toys. Reality—in the guise of the Gulf War, to Chechnya, to Yugoslavia, to a currently rumbling Middle East, and all those other little disagreements around the globe—soon intervened and began to drag a few people away from eating the lotus. Still too few, but it's a beginning. I believe our Euroguests are some of that few.

"The one you've really got to worry about is the creep named Applegate. Direct from the minister's office, and here to snoop. The way to spoil his little game is to impress the Eurobods. If they like what they see they'll be on-side, and Applegate will be isolated. We want them leaving here singing your praises, while Applegate skulks back to his master with egg on his face.

"Remember, Christopher, there are two things the minister hates more than being forced to steal your successes as his own . . . the fact that you know it, and that you're still in business. That knowledge chokes him."

"It doesn't seem to prevent him from appropriating them."

"Of course not. The man's a political animal. Anything that enhances his stature is to be grabbed with both hands. Shame does not come into it. So . . . anything planned today that might excite our guests?"

"Two of the Echo ASVs are currently up," Jason began warily. "They'll be carrying out a series of engagements against each other, from long range to gun range. They're using the ACMI, so everything will be onscreen down the hole."

"Excellent! That should definitely excite them. Will there be voice transmissions?"

"Yes, sir," Jason replied cautiously.

"Good. Even better. Who've you got upstairs?"

"Cottingham and Christiansen . . ."

"An American and a Dane," the AVM said appprovingly. "A good way to show the multi-national flavor of the unit. Who else?"

"Hohendorf . . ."

"That should please our German guest . . ."

"And McCann . . ."

"Oh dear Lord . . ."

"Yes, sir. Exactly. Today of all days."

"Indeed," the air vice-marshal said, looking stricken. "McCann on voice transmission. I can barely wait."

In the hole, Thurson began making the introductions. They were in the VIP reception area, prior to entering the Ops Center itself.

"Gentlemen, I have the pleasure to present Wing Commander Christopher Jason, who is in overall command of the November project. Wing Commander . . . Doctor Otto Eschenbeck . . . Monsieur Maurice DuClos . . . Mr. Jack Makepeace . . . and, of course, Mr. James Applegate of the minister's office."

Jason shook hands with each in turn.

Applegate was a small, round man who tended to look at everyone with a sideways-tilted head, as if sighting along his left cheekbone. This odd posture meant that he frequently had to brush away locks of dark, lank hair. The way he did it gave the impression that he thought it looked elegant. His handshake was much as Jason expected: slightly damp to the touch and weak, as if the mere effort tired him.

"Your security officer was most uncooperative, Wing Commander," he protested. "We've all got perfectly good clearance."

"I'm certain you have, sir," Jason said with nicely measured respect, "but my officers cannot be too careful. We are responsible for a highly sensitive project. It would not do if we were to be lax with the national interests of the NATO and EU nations, or with the taxpayers' hard-earned money."

The air vice-marshal remained commendably expressionless as Jason fired the first broadside at Applegate. The Eurocrats looked sufficiently approving. Clearly, they could almost be heard thinking, the wing commander took his job very seriously indeed.

"Yes," Applegate said with apparent calm, though he was furious. "Quite." But he wasn't ready to give up just yet. "Shouldn't Group Captain Inglis, the station commander, be in overall command? He is your superior officer . . ."

"If you'll excuse the interruption, Mr. Applegate," Thurson joined in smoothly, "Group Captain Inglis is in overall charge of the administration of the base. But command and organization of the November project itself rests with Wing Commander Jason, who happens to be, let us not forget, the founder of the entire program. It was felt that this command structure enabled the operational status of the unit to be achieved more quickly and efficiently. Efficiency has to be the word in an important project such as this. Don't you think?"

"Er . . . yes. Yes, of course." Applegate had a glazed look about him after these opening broadsides. "Perhaps we should now see the Operations Center."

"Certainly."

As they made their way to the Ops Center with Jason in the lead, the three Euro representatives glanced at each other, then with contempt at the back of Applegate's head.

Thurson spotted this, and allowed himself the most ghostly of smiles.

"Fight's on!" Hohendorf called and immediately broke hard left to go into a one hundred eighty degree turn. He then off-loaded the wings by easing off the stick pressure and lit the burners.

The ASV leapt away like a scalded cat, rapidly putting distance between them and the Double-C's Tornado.

McCann in the backseat wrenched his head round to look. Cottingham had gone into a sharp break to the right and was already accelerating so rapidly in the climb, the other aircraft virtually vanished even as he looked. From McCann's vantage point, it had seemed to disappear. He knew that Christiansen, in the backseat, was already working the Chameleon for all he was worth.

"But you're not as good as ol' Elmer Lee," McCann murmured as he turned round again.

Christiansen, he knew, was still coming to grips with the system. Cottingham's backseater was well versed in its use; but he had not yet got to the stage where he could manipulate as instinctively as either McCann, Flacht, or Stockmann. Of those three, McCann naturally considered himself the best.

"All right, Baron," McCann now said to Hohendorf, who really was a baron, "let's kick some ass. I don't want to lose to these guys."

"Neither do I," said Baron Maximillian Axel von Wietze-Hohendorf mildly. "And enough with the 'Baron.'"

"But you are . . ."

"I know, Elmer Lee. But you also know I never use the title."

"Okay," McCann agreed cheerfully. "So let's get down to business. They're going to play a little hide-and-seek with us at long range."

"We'll be playing some hide-and-seek too."

"Okay by me. So why don't we do a quick turn-round, just long enough to let me give them a quick flash of the radar before they pick *their* turnaround position?"

Hohendorf knew what McCann was getting at. It was sneaky, but then, air combat was all about cunning as well as ability. The ASV Echo's radar had a long reach of at least one hundred fifty nautical miles, although both Flacht and McCann were known to get much better performance than that under certain conditions. They regularly hit a range of one hundred seventy nautical miles and were certain they could do even better. Coupled with the performance of the dedicated advanced long-, medium-, and short-range missiles that were the aircraft's normal fit, this made the ASV a formidable combat adversary from extreme long range and all the way down to the devastating firepower of the internal, 20mm six-barreled rotary cannon. The gun, especially when slaved to the helmet sighting system, was fiendishly accurate; a fact that pleased all the crews enormously.

The ASV Echo also had a new self-repairing program incorporated into its control system. If serious damage were suffered—battle or otherwise—the program would seek out the best possible means by which to give the pilot some control authority, to help him bring the aircraft back. This was in addition to the quadruple, self-repairing channels of the fly-by-wire control system. If part of a wing was missing or so severely damaged as to seriously affect flight integrity, the new program would gauge the extent of the damage and, in effect, attempt to rewrite the aerodynamic laws and *make* the battered aircraft airworthy long enough to get it home. No one had as yet been put in a position to find out just how effective this new program really was. No one wanted to.

"Like teaching a goddamned brick to fly," McCann was heard to comment when he'd heard of it.

The ASV's air-to-air missile capability far exceeded that of the normal weapon load of other NATO aircraft. It was capable of multiple target engagements at all ranges. These ranges merged so that there were no gaps within the kill zone, from the time the target came within the long reach of the first group of missiles.

The Skyray Beta, Skyray Alpha, and the Krait were the long-, medium-, and short-range weapons respectively. All were lighter, faster, and more agile than those used by other aircraft. They were also more accurate and far harder to evade. The Skyray B could reach out to one hundred thirty miles.

What McCann was therefore suggesting was that a quick flash of the radar would catch Cottingham and Christiansen still extending, in preparation to coming round for the first engagement. They would thus still be vulnerable to surprise. The radar would then store the position, while no longer broadcasting its presence. Using the speed, altitude, and heading information it had gained of the target aircraft, it would then proceed to quarter the area with the most likely position update and wait to adjust this when another sweep was commanded. Definitely a sneaky thing to do.

"Elmer Lee," Hohendorf now began, "I *like* the way you think. That was mean, and sneaky."

"Mean and sneaky. That's little ol' me."

"They'll know as soon as we hit them."

"Yep. But it will be too late by then."

"Okay. Do this quick."

"I'll be real quick."

"Okay. Here we go."

Hohendorf racked the ASV round suddenly, pointing the aircraft very briefly in the direction the Double-C had gone before plunging seawards.

"Did you get them?"

"Oh I got them, all right," McCann said gleefully. "He glanced out of the cockpit. "Going deep-sea diving are we?"

"Something like that."

"As long as I know."

Bip.

In the other Tornado, Cottingham heard the brief warning tone of the radar flash.

"Shit!" he cried, immediately hauling the aircraft into a rapid change of both altitude and direction. "God-*dammit,* Lars! They just gave us a radar hit while we were still extending."

"Yes," Christiansen acknowledged calmly. "That was a little . . . ungentlemanly."

"Ungentlemanly, my ass. We should have done it to them first. God*dammit!* I hate that!"

"Sorry."

"Not your fault. It's that McCann. Real mean, low thinking little zit. Coming back from the dead sure hasn't reformed him."

Cottingham could remember the very first time he'd ever set eyes on McCann; although the Kansas City Dude's reputation had traveled so widely, Cottingham had already known of him. It had also been Cottingham's first day at November One. McCann, on seeing the black USAF captain, had greeted him in the officers' mess with palm up, and a "Yo, bro!"

McCann's well-meaning—but embarrassingly clumsy —attempt at the time to make him feel at ease had failed spectacularly. And in front of all those Brit officers too.

"That McCann," Cottingham repeated. "Sometimes, it's pretty hard to tell where that guy's coming from. He may be a pain in the butt on the ground but up here, he's a nightmare in a fight. We're going to have to be real mean today, Lars."

"I can be mean."

"So let's do it. Hey . . . are we broadcasting to the hole yet?"

"Every word."

"Sheeit! I hate that!"

Down in the hole, the Euro VIPs were staring at the big screen in wonder and listening to the transmissions in amazement. Jason had a neutral expression pasted on his face while the AVM shot him penetrating glances from time to time, in between answering questions from the guests.

Dieter Helm had decided to stay away, pleading the need to check out the instructors on Zero-Two squadron. Jason knew Helm couldn't stomach the stage-managed charade of the visit, but he accepted the lame excuse. He would have ducked the whole affair himself, had he been able to; but as the man in command, he did not have that option open to him.

"What's happening now?" Jack Makepeace asked, watching the image of Hohendorf's and McCann's ASV begin to lose definition as the craft continued to plunge seawards. "That airplane is not going to pieces as it's falling, is it?"

Jason restrained a smile. "No, sir," he replied. "What you're seeing is the operation of a system on the aircraft which makes it indistinct to an adversary. The ACMI's computer-generated images mimic everything that's happening. That way, we can easily tell how a crew performs, under any circumstances."

Makepeace grinned. "So they can't do lousy up there, then come back to you and fake it?"

Jason shook his head. "They certainly can't. I want all my crews to be the very best. I have no time for passengers."

Makepeace looked about him. "Very impressive, Wing Commander. And you push your men. I like that." He turned once more to the large screen. "What happens when they make mistakes?"

Jason sensed Thurson looking at him. He knew the AVM was waiting to see how he would answer that. He also knew Applegate was eagerly hoping he'd make a mess of it.

"Mistakes do occur," Jason replied calmly. "In an organization such as this, where young people take tons of potent machinery into the air and use the machinery as a weapon, frequently at limits that the average citizen cannot even begin to imagine, one would expect a rash of accidents. Happily, I can tell you that our selection process is so stringent, those who are fortunate enough to make it this far are not the types to drive themselves into the coffin box. The coffin box is . . ."

"I've never heard that term before, Wing Commander," Makepeace interrupted with a tight smile, "but I have a pretty good idea what you mean. Very graphically put. You play a hard game."

"Never a game, Mr. Makepeace."

Makepeace stared at the wing commander's expression. "No," he remarked, a tinge of respect in his voice. "I expect not."

Jason glanced fleetingly at Thurson. The AVM looked pleased with the way the potentially awkward question had been handled.

"Wing Commander." It was DuClos.

"Sir?"

"I am assuming that some French personnel managed to get through your tests?"

"I am very pleased to tell you that we do indeed have two members of the *Armée de L'Air* with us. Both former Mirage pilots. They are currently undergoing instruction with Zero-Two squadron."

"And they are performing well?" DuClos raised both eyebrows, waiting for the reply.

"Very well indeed, sir. I chose excellently."

"Good, good!" The eyebrows went down. DuClos looked pleased. National pride had been satisfied. "I would not expect you to be soft with them, of course. I am confident they can take the pace."

"I can promise you, sir, we will most certainly not be soft with them. And they know it."

DuClos was not sure how to take that, and a brief look of uncertainty came into his eyes. Then he brightened. "Good, good. It is obvious you will not accept any but the best."

"There is much at stake. We need the best."

DuClos nodded and turned to the screen. At that moment, Goshawk Zero-One seemed to be skimming the sea.

"Mon dieu!" he exclaimed. "He is in the sea!"

"Not quite, sir," Jason said, thinking Hohendorf must be aquaplaning. "But he is low. He's employing a tactic to confuse his opponent."

"And what will the opponent do?"

"I expect him to counter, or the pilot in that aircraft, *Kapitänleutnant* Hohendorf will nail him. Hohendorf is one of my very top pilots. He never gives an opponent the slightest chance. When you're up against him, you're in serious trouble."

"Marineflieger." This came from Otto Eschenbeck. "Do you have others like him?" Eschenbeck had a satisfied expression on his face. He had clearly found Jason's comments about Hohendorf to his liking.

"Yes, sir. There's Flight Lieutenant Mark Selby, Royal Air Force. Sometimes, very little appears to be the choice between them, but there are very perceptible differences. Then we've got *Capitano* Nico Bagni of the AMI; an exceptionally graceful flyer. At this moment, Hohendorf is pitted against Captain Cottingham of the USAF. Cottingham, a former F-15 pilot, is a good man. Their backseaters are all top notch. I hold these four crews up as models for the rest of my crews. If they can achieve standards approximating these four, I shall be well pleased. They do not have to be as good, because these are exceptional men. The fact that the others have made it here at all means they're already well above average."

Eschenbeck was nodding approvingly. "I too am very impressed, Wing Commander. By the time we are finished here, I believe we shall have good things to report."

"Thank you, sir," Jason said with the right amount of gratitude.

Another glance at Thurson showed the air vice-marshal keeping a very straight face as he maintained his attention firmly on the screen.

Applegate looked sick.

6

McCann glanced behind him. Twin trails of steam boiled in their wake, searing off the water in the heat of the engines.

Hell, he thought. *This is* low, *low flying. Morton should see this!*

He took a quick scan of the repeated HUD symbology he'd called up on one of the three multi-function displays in the rear cockpit. The altitude numerals were at one-five.

Fifteen feet between the flat belly and the surface! Jeez!

He took another glance over his shoulder. The twin superheated plumes of water, continuously streaming, followed like gigantic tails that seemed to stretch for miles, as if attached to some hyperfast speedboat. If they actually hit the water, it would be like colliding with a mountain.

He'd put on "Raise Your Hands" at background

volume, but, for once, he was not really listening to the music.

"Uh," he began to Hohendorf. "This is seriously low, man."

"Don't worry, Elmer Lee," Hohendorf's assured voice came back at him. "We're not going to hit." The pilot had accurately judged what was on his backseater's mind. "When I was with the *Marineflieger*, some of us would practice this approach to a target ship."

"Uh, yeah?" McCann said, glancing out at the racing sea. He had the bizarre impression they were hurtling along a trough, with high water definitely above them. "But wouldn't that mark out your position? I mean those tails can be seen from way off."

"Ah, but you see, there is a trick to it. Watch."

Hohendorf suddenly hauled the ASV into a punishing climb to twenty-five hundred feet, rolled one hundred thirty degrees, pulled into a slanting dive, rolled level, and descended once more, this time to one hundred feet, going away from the trail of plumes which still hung like strange, tubed clouds, apparently on the surface of the water.

"To anyone visually sighting from a ship—their radar would have lost us—the steam trail would make them continue to look in that direction. But of course, we are no longer there. Our attack is now from a direction they do not expect." Hohendorf chuckled. "If the Double-C are combining radar with infrared and optical while they search us out, they may be having two nice trails on their display. But where are we?"

"I like it!" McCann said, already forgetting how close the water had been. He swiftly called up the attack plan on the radar display. "According to our picture and allowing for our own acrobatics, they should be at eight-zero miles, heading three-three-one. Altitude ten thousand, five hundred. Way too high, even if they are trying for a look-down shoot. Speed six hundred knots. They're burning some wind."

"Let them. They don't know where we are. Get ready for another flash to update."

"You got it."

McCann again glanced out of the cockpit, this time to his right.

In the clear distance, the twin plumes could still be seen as Hohendorf banked hard into a right turn, bringing the aircraft round on an intercept heading to where the systems had predicted the second ASV should be.

"They'll be spoofing," Hohendorf said. "It might take you a little time to get a return."

"I can burn through," McCann told him confidently. "Lars is pretty good with his kit; but he's up against *me*, not some fighter jock in another kind of ship, working his own radar, which isn't as good as this beauty." He patted the MFD. "I'll get 'em."

"I can hear something," Hohendorf said. "Kind of faint . . . you've got *music* on?"

"Just background stuff," McCann replied nonchalantly. "Da-da-daaa . . ." he went on, accompanying the guitars, ". . . boo-boo-di boo-boo-di boo-boo-di boo-boo-di . . . daa-daa-daaa . . ."

"Elmer Lee . . . !"

"Radar looking up. . . . got 'em! Right where they ought to be. And locked. It's on the HUD. Hit the helmet sight and let 'em have a Skyray BVR shoot for breakfast."

Hohendorf immediately put McCann's music out of his mind as the target box appeared on the head-up display. The tracking arrow on the helmet sight was pointing unerringly to its own locked diamond, within which Cottingham and Christiansen's distant, and beyond-visual-range, ASV was lurking. Their aircraft was pinned like a trophy butterfly on the invisible board of the sky.

Having already selected the missile for the long-range shot, Hohendorf reacted swiftly, easing the aircraft round to bring the targeting box into the missile steering circle as the shoot cue came on. He squeezed the missile release. The computers worked out the parameters of the launch of the inert missile and compared that with targeting and distance values, as Hohendorf turned sharply away. In a real engagement, he would have done the same, rapidly changing position to deny an enemy a possible acquisition in response.

No point launching at him, if you're going to give him the chance to launch at you in return. While you're both ballet dancing around trying to evade each other's missiles, you are both defensive, unable to continue the attack, giving a possible opportunity to an alert wingman. But sometimes, even under threat from an incoming round, a good pilot could still get off a double-shot within the launch time, if he had somehow managed to acquire and lock. Making life that easy for him was not an option.

"We got 'em!" McCann announced with certainty, although the computers, calculating the time of missile flight, had not yet given the results.

Bip. Bip.
  B i p - b i p - b i p - b i p - b i p - b i p - b i p - b i p .
Beeeeeeeeeeeeeeeeeeeeeee!
  Then the characteristic rising hoot of the attention getter, following hard on the sound of the unbreakable lock-on, told the dreaded story.

"God*dammit!*" Cottingham swore furiously as he pressed one of the small red flashing oblong buttons, positioned on either side of the base of the head-up display.

The hooting stopped.

"Where the hell did that come from?"

"From two hundred feet at seven-five miles, at one-six-eight," Christiansen replied precisely, reading the information off his MFD.

"The bastards are *behind* us? I thought you'd got an enhanced infrared image of something on a heading of three-four-one."

"I did. It was them. But Hohendorf pulled a trick. That double trail was a decoy. I should have remembered."

"*Remembered?* Remembered what?"

"When I was back home," Christiansen began, speaking quickly as he rapidly worked the search radar to hunt out Hohendorf and McCann for the next engagement, "we used to have exercises in the Baltic with the *Marineflieger*. As you know, I was a recce pilot on RF-35 Draken; but you do not know I wanted F-16s. In a great misfortune for me, there were more pilots than seats in those sweet little airplanes. So . . . I considered leaving." He paused to mutter something in Danish at the radar.

"Then the chance came to go to the States on secondment," he went on, continuing to speak rapidly as he worked, "but only if I converted to the backseat, on F-4G Wild Weasel Phantoms. I took it. That secondment was a good fortune. Now I am with the November squadrons."

"What's this leading to, Lars?"

"The *Marineflieger* Tornados were the attack aircraft, and we had to defend. I heard a story about a pilot spotting trails low down and he went to investigate, thinking he had found an easy target. But there was nothing. Next thing he knew, this Tornado was in his six, zapping him with a Nine Lima simulated shot. He was really pissed off."

"This a true story?" Cottingham sounded sceptical.

"It is what I heard. You have seen the trails for yourself."

"You telling me it was *Hohendorf* that time back then?"

"I wasn't there . . . but it could have been."

"Sheeit."

Then Christiansen grunted in annoyance.

"What, what! Let's hear it, Lars."

"I can't burn through the jamming. This kit is supposed to burn through anything."

"Yeah, but MCann's got some moves all his own. Be nice to him one day, and get him to tell you what he does with that box of tricks. Meanwhile, find those suckers."

Cottingham searched the sky while Christiansen fought McCann's jamming.

"I have got source-location on auto," the baskseater said. "It is tracing the direction of the jamming. We'll soon find them . . . ah . . ."

"That sounds ominous," Cottingham said. "What've we got?"

"I . . . think he expected me to do this. The jamming has stopped; but we have not got a return."

"So they could be anywhere."

"Yes."

"This is not good, Lars."

"No."

"God*dammit!*"

● ● ●

Down in the Ops Center, Applegate had a sly look on his face.

"Do your aircrew make a habit of listening to music when airborne, Wing Commander," he began, "and making strange noises in accompaniment?" The sly look had become smug, as if he'd somehow scored a major point.

"Personally," Makepeace joined in, before Jason could make a suitable reply, "I don't care if they listen to 'Colonel Bogey' if they feel like it, as long as they get the job done. From what we've just seen, they do that with astonishing efficiency. If they can be like this against fellow crews—who are as highly skilled—*in a similar aircraft*, imagine their performance against an enemy."

Makepeace was a member of Her Majesty's Opposition, and had little time for Applegate.

He received support from both Eschenbeck and DuClos.

"I agree," Eschenbeck said. "There on that screen, we have witnessed remarkable flying. We ask these young men to do very dangerous work on our behalf . . ." he stared at Applegate, ". . . which *we* cannot perform for ourselves. I too do not care if they listen to music, if they do not put their airplane, themselves, or our citizens on the ground in danger because of it. It is also quite simple to realize they are very dedicated people. The spirit I find here symbolizes what we are trying to build in Europe."

DuClos said nothing, but was nodding vigorously in agreement.

"Thank you, gentlemen," Jason said respectfully, studiously avoiding a glance in Applegate's direction. "Now let's see and hear what further developments of the fight await us. You will note that Hohendorf and McCann—

that's the blue image with the figures zero and one attached to it as identification—have once again gone low. Zero-Two, Cottingham and Christiansen—the orange aircraft—are still trying to find them.

"Those dashes you see—arranged in semi-circular groups—following each other from one aircraft to the next, are representations of search radar pulses. Pulses from the originating aircraft spread outwards from the source. You'll also note that neither aircraft keeps that up for long because . . . *there* . . . that bright line that just flashed in the opposite direction is a jamming signal. The search pulse has vanished. A successful jam.

"But of course, nothing is for free. That red, dashed line that came almost simultaneously from the searching aircraft, riding the jammer, was a locator beam attempting to find the source of the jamming. But now it's wavering. Zero-One suspected what would happen—as you've just heard Christiansen remark—and jammed only long enough to achieve its purpose. Now both aircraft are sniffing each other out as they draw closer, but keeping their radars on standby for the moment. They will engage passive systems, while trying to out-maneuver each other. It's a bit like dancing in the dark, not knowing where your partner may happen to be at a given moment. This is where the skill of the individual backseater really begins to count."

"Thank you for that very informative appraisal, Wing Commander." Applegate spoke so gracelessly, everyone looked at him.

The silence that greeted his remark was eloquent.

"I reckon Lars is one unhappy guy right now," McCann said, sounding very pleased with himself. "They've got to try and even the score. But we're not going to let them, are we?"

"Not if I have anything to do about it."

"And me. And me."

"And you, Elmer Lee. How could I forget?"

"Just checking."

"Are you still listening to that music?"

"Umm . . . background stuff. Now hold the chat for a second. I'm kind of busy back here. Got me a brainfart that should help us keep ruining their day."

"Yes, sir," Hohendorf said drily.

McCann had recalled the stored radar display on one of the MFDs, checking out the historical location of Zero-Two's last updated position. Each display screen was bordered by several square, soft-key buttons. He repeatedly pressed one at the edge of the screen that was currently the focus of his attention. The system gave him a series of probability readouts, of where the opposing ASV might now have re-positioned.

He released the button. The readouts stabilized to one that kept changing, continuously making updates, quartering the screen and suggesting a choice of options. The screen also superimposed a bi-color track display of the last thirty seconds of Zero-Two's most recently recorded maneuvers. Heading, altitude, and speed were also onscreen. A series of small, pulsing orange diamonds were displayed, marked alphabetically to denote priority. This too constantly changed. The letters on each diamond kept swapping priority, as the system continually made predictions.

Then McCann saw a position he felt was most likely. He pressed another key, and the display held. All the other diamonds had vanished. The single target now began to move about the screen as the computers offered up possible solutions. The new, accompanying readouts of altitude, course, and speed were also displayed and constantly changing. The previous information had moved to the lower left corner of the screen, enabling rapid comparisons. From the single diamond, six bright tracks radiated. At the end of each moving line were the triple numbers denoting the current heading. They too were frequently changing as the systems went through their multiple calculations.

One particular set of numbers attracted him.

"'Kayyyy . . ." he said. "Brainfart solution coming up. Go right, one-five-five."

"One-five-five," Hohendorf acknowledged without hesitation, turning onto the new heading.

"Now take us to five thousand feet. Easy! A gentle little stroll upstairs. Get ready to break real hard . . . *left* . . . when I say . . . then do all your fancy bits. I'll drop them a couple of decoys to play with."

"Roger."

"Okay . . . here goes. I'm going to give them a flash. When I do, they're going to be on to us like a rattlesnake with a sore butt, or what passes for a snake's butt. Those guys are good and hungry, and mad as hell. Okay?"

"The O is kay."

"Okay . . . okay . . ." McCann murmured, watching the display. *"Go! Aaah shit!"* he groaned as Hohendorf, doing his "fancy bits," suddenly hauled the ASV tightly into a hard, G-intensive, climbing turn to the left. His speed jeans squeezed at his lower body. His pressure-breathing, anti-G vest briefly forced air into his lungs, to prevent them from collapsing under the punishing assault of the high-G forces that pummeled him. In a 9G-plus aircraft, it was the soft machine in his protective cockpit that was likely to break first.

The pressure eased slightly as Hohendorf relaxed the turn.

"Sometimes," McCann said with reproach, "I *really* hate pilots. You know that?"

"You called it," Hohendorf grunted unrepentantly, flinging the Tornado onto its back to pull it into a steep dive, once more plunging headlong towards the water. "I'm carrying it out. Going down."

"Just give a guy some warning, is all."

"Warning? What's that?"

"You pilots kill me."

"We try very hard not to, Elmer Lee."

"Oh yeah."

McCann watched calmly as the ASV Echo seemed hellbent on becoming a submarine. He had complete faith in Hohendorf's flying abilities; but the water, shimmering in the brightness of the sun, was coming up a little too rapidly for his peace of mind.

But Hohendorf was already initiating the pull-up, even as the aircraft continued to plummet. Then the sleek nose was moving from the vertical, hauling itself away from that greedy-looking water.

"Going hydroplaning again, are we?"

"Worrying about getting your feet wet?" was Hohendorf's super-calm response.

"Nah."

McCann took a studiously cool glance behind. They were not as low as he'd thought. The spectacular, but tell-tale plumes were not streaming like great swirling banners in their wake.

Above them and well away from their last position, the decoys—two small cylinders that in succession gave off rich returns to a questing radar and a long-burning sunburst flare—went into their spoofing routines for the benefit of Cottingham and Christiansen.

"Did you get them?" Hohendorf now asked.

"I surely did," McCann replied in triumph. "Picked me a location and guess what? They were there, naked as virgins."

"Virgins," Hohendorf repeated, as if tasting the word. "Is your mind on someone in particular?"

"Who? Me?" McCann was innocence personified. "Okay," he went on quickly, before Hohendorf could make a response. "I've got these aces locked up . . ." he watched as the radar display marked out the possible tracks of Cottingham and Christiansen's aircraft since the recent sweep, ". . . and they'll be evading like their lives depend on it—which they would, of course, if we were shooting at them for real. But if *we're* quick, they won't get out of the missile envelope in time. They're going through ten thousand feet at four-three miles, and coming down. Should do nicely for a Skyray Alpha."

"Skyray Alpha selected."

"Okay. On the helmet sight, and on the HUD. Go . . . two-six-one . . . *now!*"

"Roger. Going two-six-one."

Hohendorf banked hard onto the new course and looked up. The helmet sight immediately picked up the other aircraft. The Skyray began to give its oscillating tone. It was ready. The targeting boxes on both the HUD and the helmet sight had fixed, glowing diamonds within them. Target well and truly locked.

He squeezed the release.

The entire series of maneuvers, from the moment that McCann had directed them onto the course of one hundred fifty-five degrees, had taken just twenty-five fleeting seconds.

● ● ●

The moment Cottingham heard the short, telephone-like, pulsating burst of the radar warning receiver, he went immediately into a series of violent evasive maneuvers in an attempt to break the lock. The sound had died almost instantly.

Christiansen was not convinced they'd escaped. "He has given us a quick tap on the shoulder, long enough to mark our position. Now he is working out location probabilities. We should get out of this sector. Fast."

"I'm on it."

But it was already too late.

Bip.

Bip, bip, bip, bip, bip, bip, bip, bip . . .

"*Damn!*" Cottingham swore. "Those guys are quick."

B i p - b i p - b i p - b i p - b i p - b i p - b i p - b i p .
Beeeeeeeeeeeeeeeeeeeee!

Cottingham grunted and strained as he used high-G avoidance maneuvers, in a ferocious attempt to evade the simulated missile shoot.

To no avail.

The loud, rising hoot of the attention getters brutally told him he'd not made it.

"Shit!" he said in frustration. "Shit, shit, *shit!*"

It was to his great credit that he did not seek to blame Christiansen. He knew Christiansen was an excellent backseater. They'd been in real combat before and had scored. It was just that they were now up against two of the top men on the entire November unit.

It still didn't make him feel any better.

"All right," he said roughly. "Let's see how they do in the next two engagements."

The Double-C lost the short-range missile contest as well; comprehensively. Then it was down to the final guns engagement.

This turned out to be more protracted. Cottingham, the ex–F-15 pilot, was very good at close-in maneuvering. He used all the skills he'd learned while flying that highly agile big fighter to prevent Hohendorf from achieving a gun solution.

Trouble was, he could get nowhere near Hohendorf's six, no matter how hard he tried. He could feel the dampness on his entire body like a second skin, as the fierce combat went on.

In the Operations Center, people were on their feet as they watched the screen. Every so often, a collective cheer or groan would fill the room as a good, or bad, move was made. It was difficult to tell which of the two pilots—Hohendorf or Cottingham—they supported.

Eschenbeck was torn between admiration for his fellow citizen Hohendorf and for Cottingham. He nibbled at a fingernail while staring, transfixed, at the screen.

DuClos had his hands in his pockets and kept rising on the balls of his feet every time one of the aircraft came close to the water.

Makepeace simply looked on astonished while Applegate, despite himself, could not hide his wide-eyed stare at the screen.

Jason glanced at each of his visitors, a surreptitious twitch of a smile touching his lips briefly. Then he saw the AVM glance at him. Thurson gave a barely perceptible nod. Opposition defeated. Applegate would not have the support of the Euro representatives when he attempted to make a case against the project to the minister.

The wing commander was—as Thurson once described him to a fellow instructor during Jason's student pilot days—a rare bird. First impressions were that he was unremarkable; a clear indication of how seriously misleading first impressions could be. A man of medium height, his regular features were spotlessly clean-shaven. His dark eyes contrasted sharply with his slightly receding sandy hair. He tended to joke about the retreating hairline, calling it his bone dome tidemark; a reference to the fact that it was the price many aircrew paid for wearing the vitally necessary protective helmet in the high-G environment in which they worked. He had a habit of removing his cap and wiping his forehead with the back of the same hand, before putting the cap back on again.

When the situation called for it—which was often—the intensity of Jason's gaze tended to rivet those upon whom it fell; his presence in any room could never be ignored. At times, this quality could sometimes be dominating, irrespective of the rank or status of those present.

Jason was well aware of the nature of the power within him and was quite capable of manipulating it to his own advantage. Given the scale of his responsibilities, this was not surprising. Yet none of his personnel—even of the most junior rank—found him intimidating. However, none would dream of crossing him, unless they had taken complete leave of their senses.

The wing commander looked at the cavorting images on the screen, and felt justifiably proud of his aircrew.

"You going to keep . . . playing with these guys?" McCann asked, straining against the crush of yet another punishing turn to the left. "Or . . . are we going to . . . zap them and go on home?"

Hohendorf snap-rolled the ASV into a descending right turn, spiraling down behind Zero-Two.

"You may have noticed," he replied, "that . . . they're not standing still."

"You can take 'em."

"Thank you, Elmer Lee."

"Anytime."

Then the Double-C aircraft was sweeping its wings as it rocketed skywards once more.

Hohendorf followed, as if tied to it. But Cottingham was still managing to keep out of the gun's reach. Every so often Hohendorf would get the tone, which would last for just the most fleeting fraction of a second. However, no matter how hard Cottingham tried, he was given no opportunity to turn the tables and put Hohendorf in front.

"We're getting close to bingo fuel, man," McCann warned. "Nail these guys and let's head back. I don't like the idea of swimming home. Besides, the boss would have our balls if we let his airplane run out of the juice."

The two aircraft were once again very close to the water, with Hohendorf still in unshakable pursuit. He was even lower than Cottingham, who was not as confident in a hard turning fight at such ultra-low altitudes. If there was going to be a mistake made by the other pilot, this was where it would happen.

And it did.

For the barest of moments, Cottingham's nerve must have deserted him when he saw how close to the water he really was. He hesitated briefly, and Hohendorf got the perfect gun solution.

"You've got him!" McCann crowed. "Oh shit! You've lost him, man. He escaped!"

"We're nearly at bingo, as you've said," Hohendorf remarked. "No time for another try." Then he called to Zero-Two, "Knock it off, knock it off!"

"Roger. Knock it off."

"I call that an honorable draw."

"Yeah," came the other pilot's voice drily. "But you made me work for it."

"I couldn't take the chance of letting you get near my six. I'd never get you off!"

A chuckle came back at him.

"Let's go home, Zero-Two."

"Amen to that," Cottingham said, repositioning on Hohendorf's wing.

In tight formation, the two ASVs climbed to thirty-five thousand feet and headed back to base.

Jason understood quite clearly what had happened.

Cottingham had not escaped. Hohendorf had let him go and it had been done so subtly, not even Cottingham himself or McCann, for that matter, had been aware of it.

But Jason approved. After having won all the previous engagements, Hohendorf had decided to be magnanimous in his triumph and had deliberately chosen not to further add to Cottingham's discomfiture.

Hohendorf had displayed the sort of team spirit Jason expected of his crews. Cottingham and Christiansen were among the very best, and humiliating them would have proved nothing. A lesser person, Jason decided, would have gone for a clean sweep of victories.

"Wing Commander." Eschenbeck's voice intruded upon Jason's thoughts. "This was most, *most* impressive. I am very happy to have been invited to see for myself."

Jason kept a neutral expression on his face. It would have been graceless to admit that the invitation had in fact, not come from him at all.

"I am very pleased that we were able to show you something of what we do here, sir."

"My colleagues and I will have many good things to say about your program when we return."

"Thank you. We need all the help we can get."

Eschenbeck's shrewd eyes looked at him. "I know it is not easy for you, and I understand what you are doing. Those who try to stop you will not have an easy time." Eschenbeck did not look at Applegate when he said that, but the message was unmistakable.

Applegate showed no reaction.

"And now, Wing Commander Jason," Eschenbeck went on, "if it is all right with you, my colleagues and I would like to see more of your base. Yes?"

"Everything is waiting, sir. We have also arranged lunch for you in the Mess."

"Thank you, Wing Commander."

Jason inclined his head. "Sir."

He stood aside for them to file out. Thurson brought up the rear.

"We'll make a politician of you yet, Christopher," the air vice-marshal whispered as he came up.

"In my nightmares . . . sir."

Thurson smiled to himself.

McCann was uncharacteristically silent for most of the return flight. All that came from him were the usual navigator's pronouncements relating to the efficient operation of the aircraft. But even those were kept to a minimum. Most telling of all, he played no music; positive evidence that something was nagging away at him.

This continued all the way to recovery to base, taxiing to the aircraft shelter, and eventual shut-down. It wasn't until they were walking away from the Tornado that he at last chose to speak about what was really on his mind.

"C'mon, Axel," he began. "You let him go, didn't you?"

Cottingham and Christiansen were some distance ahead, well out of earshot.

"I did?"

"Sure you did. I had the HUD repeater on one of my displays. You had the guy nailed. It was a perfect straddle. The snake had him from nose to tail, and box was right on the cockpit. You'd never miss out on a gun solution like that. There was plenty of time to take the shot. So what happened?"

"He was too quick . . ."

"Bullshit!"

Hohendorf stopped.

McCann did likewise, looking at him.

In Hohendorf's confidential file, his height was given as 1.8288 meters; exactly six feet. Even more than Helm, he looked like Hollywood's imagined version of a Roman, his own crop of fine blond hair lending greatly to that impression. Had he really been a Roman citizen, the palest of blue eyes—almost like Helle Hemelsen's —would have placed him north of the Po.

His slim body looked tough, his unlined face seemingly that of a teenager. A look into those eyes, however, would soon dispel that notion. The awareness in them spoke of a knowledge of life's travails. The teenaged face had the eyes of a man who had grown up a very long time ago, and quickly. At Tecklenburg, on the edge of the Teutoberger Wald in Germany, the walls of the Schloss Hohendorf were adorned with the portraits of similar countenances.

His old squadron commander in the *Marineflieger* had once said that there were many good pilots on the squadron, but that Hohendorf was the genius; that Hohendorf possessed the instincts of the old pioneer flyers, combined with a total empathy with the current, high-tech machines. It was a rare gift that Jason himself had zeroed in on when he'd poached the pilot away from his former unit.

McCann had no knowledge of what Hohendorf's old squadron commander had thought, or of Jason's reasons for making the choice; but he knew what his own instincts and expertise were telling him. There was no way Cottingham could have escaped that gunshot, unless Hohendorf had deliberately chosen to miss the chance.

"You could have taken that shot with your eyes closed, Axel," he now said. "It just doesn't get any better than that. Hell, even *Morton* could have gotten a few rounds in, assuming he could have made the opportunity in the first place."

Hohendorf pursed his lips briefly. "You don't believe our newest colleague could have made the opportunity by himself?"

McCann shook his head slowly. "No. He's getting there, but he's not yet good enough to pull something like that. Which, from where I'm standing, tells me you had the Double-C colder than dead mutton . . . and you let them go."

"Hey!" someone shouted. "You guys coming to debriefing, or what?"

They looked round. Cottingham and Christiansen were waiting for them.

"Well?" McCann whispered fiercely as they resumed walking. "Did you? Look. If you gave them a break because we zapped them three times in a row, I can understand that. It's a cool thing to do. I don't think they've realized it."

"*You* did," Hohendorf said after a pause.

"Yeah. But they couldn't see what I could."

"The computers will have recorded it."

"Sure . . . but it will still look as if you screwed up, and missed the chance. You even fooled the computers. I *know* you didn't screw up."

Hohendorf decided to give in. "All right, Elmer Lee. But no one else is to know this."

"The boss will. He's razorblade sharp. But he's not going to tell anyone and for sure not the Double-C."

"And you?"

"My mouth is sealed."

"Even to Mark?"

"I can't tell him something I don't know about, can I?" McCann said.

Hohendorf glanced at him with some warmth, and patted him briefly on a shoulder. "Thanks, Elmer Lee."

"You're welcome."

Later in the Mess, they found a pleasant surprise waiting.

"Yo, pretty-pretty!" McCann greeted. "When did you get in?"

"About half an hour ago," Caroline Hamilton-Jones replied, smiling as McCann gave her a kiss on the cheek.

The others stood round with silly grins on their faces.

"Well?" she challenged. "Is Elmer Lee the only one who's going to give me a welcome?"

They each kissed her cheek, rather more hesitantly than McCann, as if unsure whether they should. Hohendorf gave her a gentle hug.

"Did you fly in?" he asked.

She shook her head. "Drove up in my little Fiesta."

"What we're all dying to know," McCann said, "and these guys are too cool to ask, is this: are you here to join us? As a pilot, I mean."

"That's what the orders say," she replied, eyes bright with anticipation. "I'm going to Zero-Two squadron."

"*Yes!*" McCann cried, punching the air with a fist. "You made it! Good stuff. Good stuff!"

Remarkably, while part of him still envied the men in the front seat, he had no such feelings when it came to Caroline. Helle Hemelsen would probably have had an analysis to explain this supposed aberration; but only Elmer Lee could possibly understand the real reason, if at all.

They all shook her hand, congratulating her for having successfully made it through Jason's rigorous selection process.

"I haven't seen the boss yet. He's busy with some VIP guests."

"We need VIPs like holes in the head," McCann said uncompromisingly. "I suppose they're going to have lunch here. Well, Caroline," he went on brightly, "your coming back to us calls for a monster celebration. But first, I'd like a talk with you. Alone."

"Now wait a minute . . ." Cottingham began.

"Hey, hey, hey!" McCann interrupted. "Later." He took Caroline by the arm. "I really need to talk with you. Believe me."

Intrigued, she looked at the others helplessly and shrugged. "I'll see you guys in a minute."

"You'll be sorreee!" they chorused.

"Quite likely," she agreed.

"A wise man ignores the clatter of empty vessels," McCann said loftily.

"Oh no," Cottingham groaned. "Weak Chinese philosophy. Come on guys, buy me a coffee to help me get over this."

"With friends like these . . ." McCann said, watching them leave. "Um . . ." he went on to Caroline, ". . . you didn't mind me calling you pretty-pretty, did you? I mean . . . you probably think it's not politically correct and . . ."

"Elmer Lee, you'll never be PC if you live to be a thousand. But don't change. It would be too much hard work."

"Anyway, whenever I think of PC, I think of *Breakfast of Champions*. That's a book I found in my dad's library when I was a . . . um . . . kid. It was about bringing people down. You know, if someone was a good dancer, there was a law that forced them to wear heavy weights so they couldn't dance so well anymore, so they wouldn't make those who couldn't dance at all feel inadequate. In your case, it would mean *you* couldn't become a good pilot, in case you upset people who couldn't fly."

"Sounds ghastly. I couldn't bear the thought of that. Nobody comes between me and my airplane."

"So you didn't mind my saying pretty-pretty?"

"I didn't mind. Really. It's nice to be thought pretty."

"Oh good," said the unabashed McCann.

"And besides," Caroline said, "I have rather more important things to worry about . . . like am I going to hack it with the ASV."

"Sure you will. We're all rooting for you. We'll even try to persuade the boss to get you into our squadron."

"You've got the ASV Echo. I don't think he'll dare turn me loose in one of those for a while."

"Hey . . . what's this? Defeatism from the woman who left here a fighter controller working down in the hole, and returns as a *pilot*, on *fighters?*"

"I stand corrected. I hope I'll be good enough to get the Echo."

"That's more like it. You will."

"Thanks for the vote of confidence. Now, what was the big secret you wanted to talk to me about?"

"Uh ... yeah. Um ... look Caroline, you're a woman ..."

"I should bloody well hope so!"

"Er, what I mean. Ah hell. I'm not doing this right."

She gave him a sideways look, seeing the embarrassment spreading across his features and accurately working out why.

"It's Karen Lomax, isn't it?"

"Well ..."

"Elmer Lee. This is a marathon pursuit! Haven't you told the girl yet? She was at your bedside almost every day. When I came up to see you a couple of times, you were asleep on both occasions ..."

"I know. Sorry. But I saw all the cards, and the sweets. Thank you for sending them."

"Got to keep our turbulent navigator in good spirits," Caroline said. "I'd even fly with you in the backseat."

McCann stared at her. "You would?"

"Of course I would. I'd consider it a privilege."

"Well, I'll be ..." McCann said, quite taken aback, but feeling good about it too.

"When I came up on my visits," she said into his confusion, and continuing where she'd left off, "I had long talks with your Karen and ..."

"Not my Karen," McCann said gloomily. "We've been out a few times, sure ... but I don't think I've got a hope in hell."

"You wouldn't say that if you could have seen how she looked when you were in that hospital bed."

"You obviously don't know."

"Don't know what?"

"*He's* back. That guy haunts me. First, he breaks his leg playing rugby. Long convalescence, they say. I think I've got a good run, but hey . . . what happens? The guy's so damned fit, he gets better quickly. Then they send him to the States. A year's detachment, at least. Good news. I've got another chance. But guess what? Yup. He's back *early, and* he's a squadron leader now, outranking me. Worst of all, he warns me off. Threatened to challenge me to a boxing match, the big ox. I think he wants to beat me to a pulp."

She was staring at him. "I think you're right. But Elmer Lee, what about the person in the middle of all this? It's up to Karen. You can't fight over her like a couple of stags. If she wants to be with you, it's nothing to do with Geordie Pearce, squadron leader or not. Anyway, I believe Geordie was always much more keen on her than she was on him. She wouldn't have been seeing you at all otherwise. She's not like that."

"You think so?" McCann asked uncertainly.

"I know so. Elmer Lee, you're the man who came back from the dead. You can do anything. Go get her, boy!"

He grinned at her. "Thanks, Caroline. I will! You're great! Now let's go join those rats who call themselves my friends."

"Yep," she said drily, seeing the crazy, eager look on his face. "I'm definitely back. By the way," she added, "where's Mark Selby?"

"London, with Kim Mannon."

7

He felt himself go deep into the furnace of her body. She gave a sudden vibration, like a taut string about to snap, as she levered herself up slightly on her heels to draw him in even deeper. Her hands, gripping at the uprights of the brass bed, whitened at the knuckles. Ripples of tension briefly ran along her arms, like strange creatures playing hide-and-seek under the skin. The dampness of her stomach and her breasts sucked at him as she shuddered and strained beneath him. His arms were wrapped about her upper back, gripping her tightly as he drove deeper and deeper, until it seemed as if he was trying to put his entire body into her.

"Oh God!" she cried in a high, small voice. "You're going right through me!"

He immediately began to ease off.

"For God's sake, don't stop!" she wailed, locking her legs about him to ensure he wouldn't. "Not now! Not now!" Then she was surging wildly at him. "Oh now! *Now, now, now!*" she gave a high-pitched squeal that changed into a long, rising scream.

He strained at her, the muscles cording in his neck. He held on to her as he felt his very soul flowing out of him and into her. They remained like that for long moments, her screaming wail mingling with his own strangulated roar. Then slowly, their bodies relaxed, collapsing damply against each other.

He eased himself sideways, intending to shift his weight off her.

But she gripped him tightly. "Don't you dare pull out! Don't you dare! Mmm!" she added softly, when he didn't. "I like that. Oh yes . . . I do!"

He lay against the body he loved so much, pulsing gently into her. Every so often, she would move a thigh slowly in such a way that the action generated a languorous arousal within him. The pulses increased each time she did that.

"You're milking me," he said.

"Mmm-hmm," she said. "I like."

She moved her thigh again.

November base.

The VIPs had at last gone back, and Jason was in his office with the air vice-marshal. The roar of a pair of Tornados taking off made the windows hum. Jason waited until the sounds had faded before speaking.

"I think that went off tolerably well, sir. Don't you?"

"*I* think," the AVM said, "it went better than tolerably. They were most impressed. Not only were they totally awed by the performance of your two crews, and fairly amazed by the way you've developed this unit, but you also charmed them, my boy. Applegate had a most hangdog expression upon his unfortunate visage. Not much cheer for his master, the minister."

"Thank you for being here, sir."

"I've got to protect my investment," Thurson remarked, only half-jokingly. "But let us not rest upon our laurels. Our enemies will never give up. Neither must we."

"No chance of that, sir."

"Glad to hear it. Now I must be on my way. Got to prize my backseater away from the coffee-maker, or his nerve ends will be jangling." Thurson held out his hand. "Aways onward, Christopher."

"Sir," Jason acknowledged as he shook the AVM's hand.

"Give Antonia your love, shall I?" Thurson had a wicked gleam in his eye.

"Er . . . yes, sir!"

"Good. She will be pleased. Now I must really be off . . ."

A knock interrupted him.

Jason quickly glanced at his watch. "She's right on time. I'll ask her to wait, sir . . ."

"Who is it?"

"Flight Lieutenant Hamilton-Jones . . ."

"Ah! Young Caroline! Do let her in. It will be good to see her."

"Yes, sir. Come in!" Jason called.

Caroline entered, saw the air vice-marshal, drew to attention, and gave a snappy salute.

"Stand easy, Caroline," the AVM said, then surprised her by taking her hand and shaking it. "Congratulations on making it this far. I must say that when the wing commander first told me he'd recommended you for flying duties, I was not totally in agreement. You have proved me wrong. I wish you every success with the November squadrons."

She was both astonished and pleased. "Thank you, sir! I'll do my best."

"I'm sure you will. I was on my way out, so I'll leave you in the wing commander's capable hands."

"Yes, sir."

"If you wouldn't mind waiting a few moments," the AVM added, before turning to Jason. "Walk with me a little way, Christopher."

"Make yourself comfortable, Caroline," Jason said to her, not sure of the AVM's motives. "I'll soon be back."

"Yes, sir."

Jason followed his superior into the corridor.

When they were some distance from the office, Thurson said, "Remarkable work, Christopher. You got her up here."

"Do I detect a note of disapproval, sir?"

"Disapproval's too strong a word."

"Then what was that all about in there? You congratulated her."

"And I meant every word. She has done well."

"But?"

"She could be your Achilles' heel."

"I don't understand, sir."

"Christopher, Christopher. Your intentions are quite admirable. And I do know—before you say it—that you do not care whether she's a woman, as long as her piloting skills are of the high standards you require. Very commendable. But don't forget that there's still a very strong antipathy towards women combat pilots. Let's face it, even female transport and utility pilots are still frowned upon in some quarters.

"You're playing with a hot potato. Not only is she being groomed to be a combat pilot, which—to some—is bad enough, but in *this* of all units. One might say you're not only tempting fate, but tweaking its nose rather painfully. The slightest error she makes will be seized upon by those who desperately want to close you down. I know, and appreciate, that her quite outstanding airmanship saved your life when the Hawk went down. However, you also know as well as I do, that those who wish to do so will see only what they wish to: that she had a crash. The circumstances will be conveniently ignored. Just watch your step, dear boy, and your back."

"Yes, sir."

"Anyway, as I know you'll be as scrupulously rigorous with her as you are with all your candidates, she might not make it."

"She will."

"Yes," the air vice-marshal said. "That, unfortunately, is what I'm afraid of."

Caroline Hamilton-Jones was about average height. Her hair, a rich dark blond that had more than a hint of red in it, was crisply cut and a little shorter than she used to wear it. In her days as a fighter controller, her ears were hidden. Now they were bared, but the cut had been softly done, so as to remove all hint of severity.

Her body was full and rounded, without being overly voluptuous. She had a firm stomach and a small waist, the overall impression being one of subtle sensuality. Her eyes were a pale brown, her face smooth and rounded but with a determined chin. It was an attractive and warm face, and, on close inspection, a very fine layer of blond hairs, rather like a baby's, could be seen on her cheeks near her ears. At certain angles in sunlight, that layer seemed to glow, giving her an ethereal look. Her slightly loose-fitting flying overalls tended to accentuate her curves.

One of the first November casualties—Neil Ferris—

had been a navigator with whom she'd been in love. His aircraft had crashed into a mountain. From time to time, the pain of the loss showed in her eyes; but it had not prevented her from fulfilling her desire to be a fighter pilot. It was almost as if she felt that to succeed was in some way to pay tribute to him.

Currently in her 2B shirtsleeve, summer dress uniform, she stood up as Jason returned and was about to put on her cap, which she had removed.

"Please sit down, Caroline," he said. "And leave your cap off." He went round to his desk and sat down. "I've studied your file," he said to her. "Most impressive. You're an excellent pilot, and I'm very glad you were able to come to us. Are you ready for the ASV?"

"Yes, sir! I am."

"That's the spirit. I'll not promise you it will be easy. It won't. I've been forced to reject many a good pilot and nav who have come here, hoping for a place. Many of them were the best people on their respective units. I'm not trying to dissuade you, either. You would not be sitting here before me, if that had been the case.

"You are here because, so far, you have proved to be good enough. But the hard work is only just beginning. You will be taught to be a warrior who can beat other warriors who are far better than even the kind of pilot you would consider exceptional on other units. You will receive no favors. Judgement will be severe. I want only those who can go out there and be a serious danger to the adversary, but not to either yourself or your squadron. There will be no shortcuts. Are you still prepared to stay with it?" Jason's eyes bored into hers.

She did not drop her gaze. "I am, sir," she replied firmly.

He stood up. "Good!" He came from behind the desk, hand outstretched. "Welcome back, Caroline."

She shook the hand. "Thank you, sir. It's good to be back."

"Settling in all right?"

"Yes, thank you. I ran into some of the guys in the Mess earlier. Elmer Lee wants to plan some sort of celebration."

"Ah yes. Captain McCann." Jason said, speaking with the voice of long-suffering experience. "I well remember his little surprise at our inauguration ball."

She smiled at the memory. "There's only one like him."

"Thank God!"

"He's a bit like a mascot though, isn't he, sir?"

"Mascot from hell, more like."

"But we'd miss him if he wasn't here."

Jason looked sharply at her. "Not you as well."

"I . . . don't understand, sir."

"Since his near-death experience, everyone appears to be treating Captain McCann like some rare creature. Where is it all going to lead, one wonders? On reflection, I don't think I want to know the answer to that."

"Will you come to the party, sir? Whenever it is?"

"Must I?"

"Imperative, sir."

"Orders for the boss?"

"Would I do that?"

"You probably all would, given half the chance. All right, Caroline. Whenever it is, I'll put in an appearance."

"Thank you, sir."

He nodded at her, indicating that the meeting was over.

She put on her cap, saluted, and went out.

Jason went to a window to look out at the main runway. Three Tornados taxied past, in trail.

"Mascot," he said. "Hm!"

They had not spoken of the crash in the Hawk.

London, the same day.

Kimberly Mannon gave a regretful sigh as she shifted her body and Mark Selby came out of her.

"Oh," she said drowsily. "Put him back."

"Are you going to leave me with any strength for flying?"

She punched at his chest playfully, then snuggled closer. "I'll feed you with lots of high-protein stuff before you go."

"Will I even make it to the table?"

"Shut up," she said, rolling on top of him and kissing him fully on the mouth. She stopped long enough to say, "Mmm! You're not that exhausted, I see!"

She straddled him to quickly impale herself upon him, giving a shuddering squeal as she descended.

"Oh . . . *God! Oh, oh, oh, oh, oh* . . ."

She punctuated each utterance with a rise and fall of her body, in a rhythmic plunging that soon had him grabbing tightly at her.

He rolled her over and a great urgency seized him as he moved once more within her.

"Oh my God, Mark!" she gasped. "Mark. Mmmmmmark. *Mark!*" The high-pitched squeal again reverberated round the large penthouse flat, with its panoramic view of the Thames. The squealing went on and on until gradually, it faded into a whimper as their bodies once again fell into pleasant exhaustion.

He felt a wetness against his chest and was astonished to discover tears in her eyes.

"Kim! Oh God, I've . . . I've hurt you!"

A slow smile came to her lips. "No you haven't," she told him softly. "I was so . . . it was so . . . I just couldn't help it. I'm not crying because I'm sad. I think . . . I think I was just . . . it just happened. I wasn't even aware. See? You've done that to me. And I like it."

"Should I be worried?"

Her tongue reached out slowly and licked at a corner of her mouth. "Oh yes," she said. "But in the best possible way." She started moving against him.

"Kim! What's got into you?"

"You have."

She gave a throaty, sensuous chuckle and started kissing him again.

Kimberly Mannon was a complete contrast to Morven, Selby's sister. In normal circumstances, a Mannon and a Selby would never have met. But who could say what was normal? Selby had been dragged—under great protest—to a ball to which his sister had been invited. The invitation had not come from Kim, but from a friend of Morven's. She had dragooned her brother to play it safe, not really wanting an escort who would expect a payment in kind at the end of the evening.

A bored Selby, watching the antics of what he'd considered to be the idle offspring of the rich and privileged, had been accosted by one of those very offspring. Kim Mannon was the only child of Sir Julius Mannon, financial tycoon.

He had looked at the woman with the small, neat body and had decided she was trouble on two legs. He wanted nothing to do with her, but he'd reckoned without the woman herself. Kim Mannon had decided she very much wanted Mark Selby and had single-mindedly set about achieving that goal.

Her perfectly shaped head was covered with gleaming black hair that she wore short. Thick eyebrows were set above dark eyes that were wide apart, deep pools of hidden mischief. A generous mouth contrasted with the unexpectedly small, sharp nose. Her walk was something else. It was a flowing, feline gait that signaled danger with every step.

Enter ye here at your peril, Selby had found himself thinking, the first time they'd made love.

He was still entering, and peril was deliciously sweet.

But theirs was a protracted and sometimes fraught affair. At first not wanting to, Selby had eventually surprised himself by asking her to marry him. A close shave in combat had brought home to him the fact that he'd found the woman with whom he wanted to spend the rest of his life. He'd also discovered that since meeting Kim, a recurring nightmare he'd suffered had stopped. It was about an old friend, Sammy Newton, who'd died in a ball of flame against a mountainside. The incident had occurred long before he'd been chosen for the November program; yet the nightmare had followed him there too. Then he'd met Kim, and now he flew with a pair of her red knickers in his flying suit.

But Sir Julius had other ideas, and had made it quite plain he did not want his daughter married off to a lowly RAF flight lieutenant. In fact, no suitor except the one he had already chosen would be satisfactory.

Sir Julius's choice was a sleek financial barracuda named Reginald Barham-Deane. Sir Julius's problem was that Kim hated the man.

Barham-Deane had an even greater problem. He refused to believe that Kim could not see the great advantages that being married to him would bring. Selby could not understand the kind of man who could hang around waiting for his supposedly intended bride to make up her mind, while she slept with someone else.

The convoluted frictions had caused a split and she had gone round the world on a trip generously financed by a father, who'd thought he had won. He hadn't. Kim had discovered she didn't want to be away from Selby. For the time being, they no longer spoke of marriage and Sir Julius left them alone, certain that in the end, she would come to her senses.

Unfortunately for Sir Julius, his daughter was very much like him in some ways: stubborn and single-minded when she wanted to be. It was a contest of wills that each was determined to win.

"Do you really have to leave tomorrow?" she now asked in tones of languid satisfaction.

"Do you want this fancy apartment of your father's . . ."

"It's mine. He may have paid for it, but it's still mine."

"All right. Do you want this fancy apartment of yours crawling with security coppers? I don't turn up, they come here. The boss knows where I can be found."

"Would he really do that? Send the police after you?"

"Not really. I was exaggerating."

"I remember when were just getting to know each other, our talking about that. You were joking then too."

He was pleasantly surprised. "You remember that far back?"

She smacked him playfully. "It's not that far back. Bored with me, are you?"

"Never!" he said. "But I'm not joking about the boss. He really would not be pleased; when the boss is not pleased, it's far better to be hauled in by the military cops. An unhappy boss can mean a very short flying career."

"I wouldn't want that."

"Paid killer, you once called me."

"When we first met. Don't remind me. God. That was so trite. I thought I was being so clever. I wanted to hit back at you because you had a look of such lofty disdain on your face. I wanted to take you down a peg or two. You were watching people I called my friends make fools of themselves at the ball. Not all of them were close, but they still passed muster as friends. I thought you despised us."

"Barham-Deane making a sick joke about going into mountains didn't help, especially after what had happened to Sammy Newton."

"Yes. I remember. Reggie was particularly obnoxious that night, even for him."

"I just didn't want to be there."

She stroked his inner thigh. "And now?"

"And now . . . I want to be . . . here . . ."

"Oh yes!" she said, her voice a high, stifled gasp as she moved sinuously to accommodate him.

The soft friction of her body began to work on him, rapidly sending a new frisson of arousal that shot through him like an electrical charge. It caused an involuntarily shudder that traveled down his body, and deep into her.

"*Ooh!*" she squealed in that high, plaintive voice. "In here? *Oh!* In . . . in here . . . is . . . nnniice . . . very . . . very . . . nice. Mmm."

A deep sigh of pleasure came out of her.

The Pentagon, two weeks later, 0800 hours.

General Bowmaker strode into his office, hung his cap on the coatstand, then began to remove his jacket before he sat down at his desk. He was patting at the jacket, as was his custom, to check he'd got everything out of it before hanging it up, when he felt something unfamiliar in one of the side pockets. He'd certainly not put anything in there. He was sure of it.

He reached in and found a postcard. He took it out and stared at it, feeling suddenly tense.

The card was of a Norwegian fjord.

He turned it over carefully, as if expecting something hidden within it to explode. There was no stamp, and no postmark to indicate when, or where, it had been posted. There was no address, and no sender. Just two letters, written in heavy capitals, were on it.

O K

That was all.

He could not even begin to understand how that card had found its way into his pocket; but it could only have come from one source: Mac.

She certainly had a network in the damnedest of places, he thought. He could not identify a single moment that would have allowed someone to place the card. Yet, it had found its way to him. The simple message meant just the one thing: she had agreed to do things as he'd suggested. It still didn't mean she was happy with every aspect, but it was a start.

She was going in, and was probably already there.

There was no telling how long the card had taken to reach him. Time to get moving, just in case she'd already been days in the field.

He shredded the card with his desk shredder, then put his jacket back on. He grabbed his cap and went into the outer office to speak to his staff officer, who was also his deputy.

"Arrange the earliest flight to Europe for me, will you please, Colonel?" he said to her. "Lakenheath, England. I'll take anything that's going."

She had risen to her feet when he'd entered. Now she

looked at him severely, almost like a head teacher looking at a boy who had dared ask to leave school early.

"*Europe, sir?*"

"You make it sound like I said Mars."

"You were only there . . ."

"Yes, yes. I know. Perhaps I'm getting to like the
place."

Her expression clearly showed she did not appreciate the joke. "Will I be having to deputize for you at
any of those embassy dinners like the last time, sir?"

"You still holding that against me, Marlene?"

"Sir, those people just *hated* women in positions of
authority." Her nose wrinkled in outrage at the thought
of it.

"And as I said at the time, they're in the U.S. of A. As
I also said last time, they want our F-16s or anything
else from us, the least they can do is treat our women
officers with the respect due to them. We observe their
customs when we go to their country. We require the
same of them when they're here."

"I don't know which would have been worse, sir. The
forced politeness I got, or the real way they might have
behaved."

"But you did a good job. They got their airplanes,
and we've got some clients who owe us favors."

"Yes, sir." She did not sound enthusiastic.

"Well, Marlene? Will you see to that flight for me?"

"Yes, sir. But promise me one thing."

"Shoot."

"Try to get back before another of those functions
comes up. Please?"

"I'll do my best, Colonel. I'll do my best."

"Sir."

● ● ●

Moscow, the next day, 0900 hours.

General Feliks Alexandrovitch Kurinin, formerly KGB but still effectively doing the same job, pressed a button on the intercom unit on his desk.

"Gregor!"

"Yes, Comrade General . . ."

"Gregor, Gregor . . . How many times do I have to tell you about this 'Comrade' business? We are all democrats now."

"Of course, General." There was a definite hint of laughter in the voice.

"I know, I know," Kurinin said. "It's a crazy zoo out there, and the election only makes it more so. It will get crazier still. Bombs on the metro are only the beginning."

"Inevitable, General."

"As night follows day. Now tell me . . . anything of interest from those burial teams going into Bosnia?"

"Not what we're looking for."

"Keep monitoring the situation. I want an update by 1500 hours. Bring it in person."

"Yes, General."

Kurinin cut transmission, then leaned back in his richly upholstered swivel chair of gleaming brown leather.

"A zoo," he said. "They should be charging admittance."

Lakenheath, 1000 hours, British Summer Time.

The large RAF station was the USAF in Europe's nesting place for F-15E Eagles. Bowmaker's Sabreliner taxied to its alloted parking space on the ramp and shut down. Carrying an overnight bag, Bowmaker got out of the aircraft and saw a black Jaguar saloon waiting close by. Standing next to it was a familiar, immaculately dressed figure.

"I'll be damned," he said to himself softly.

He acknowledged the salute of a lieutenant waiting by the aircraft steps and walked up to the Jaguar. He held out his hand.

"I'm not even going to bother to ask how in hell you knew I was going to be here, at this precise moment."

"A wise decision," Charles Buntline said with a tight smile as they shook hands. "You wouldn't have got a reply." He opened a rear door. "After you, General."

Bowmaker slung the bag into the car and got in. Buntline followed. The car was moving almost before the door had shut with expensive solidity.

The general looked about him. They were separated from the driver by a wall of soundproof, tinted glass.

"Some car," he remarked.

"Armored, with bullet-proof glass. The partition slides open if one desires it. This was ordered for a head of state who needed protection from his own people. Unfortunately, they got to him before the car. We sort of . . . inherited it."

"I don't suppose this luxury APC was . . . sort of delayed, by any chance? You know, trouble with export licenses . . ."

"Why, General. One would think you were suggesting we had anything to do with the poor man's demise."

"As if," Bowmaker said.

"Sometimes in life, things simply do not synchronize," Buntline said mysteriously.

"Synchronize. Sure. Let's talk about synchronicity. Did you arrange for me to get the card?"

They had come to the gates and Buntline delayed his reply. The armed guards peered at them, saluted smartly, and waved them on their way.

"I know nothing about any card," Buntline said as the Jaguar powered off, on its way to London. "I was simply informed that you would be arriving, when, and where."

Bowmaker stared at him. "You people, whoever you really are, have got a whole damned underground network that seems to . . ."

"What you really mean, General, if you'll excuse the interruption, is that we're a shadow organization, supra-national and supra-international. You would only be partially correct. We owe our allegiance to our countries, not to this . . . organization that may, or may not, exist; whatever your impressions might otherwise lead you to believe."

"A dangerous weapon."

"We are quite aware of that and keep a very tight control."

"And who controls the controllers?"

"Ah. The eternal question."

"Which no one's ever been able to answer to my satisfaction."

"Or mine," Buntline said unexpectedly. But he still didn't give an answer. "So," he went on. "To business. The person in whom we're both interested is already in the field."

"How?"

"With one of the burial parties. We . . . er . . . have reason to believe that others may already be looking for her."

"You mean they *know* she's out there? So soon? I told her to be careful."

"She will be. She's quite capable of looking after herself. Of course, if she's to bring the package out—which, if you remember, is *your* idea—it will complicate matters for her. She'll need cover."

"You're saying if she'd gone in to do what she wanted to in the first place, there'd have been no risk?"

"There's always an element of risk. But she had considered them in the original plan. In. Take him out. Out. She'd have had just herself to worry about, and could have made her exit through any number of routes. Your way, she has to tow along someone who's not going to come willingly, and who will have his own psychos hunting her down. The risks are now considerably greater."

"You're saying I've put her in extreme danger."

"Bluntly?"

"Please be blunt," Bowmaker said, with a slight edge to his voice.

"Yes. However ... even the most ostensibly hazardous situation can be neutralized; or at least, some degree of neutralization can be brought to bear. So let us concentrate on that. Who knows? Bringing this wretched man out may yield substantial benefits."

"You have a plan."

"I have indeed."

"Worked out before."

"One must have contingencies."

"Contingencies. You Brits have a way with words. Why do I get this feeling I'm getting a ride here?"

Buntline gave a sharp laugh. "Now *that's* very American."

Bowaker's look was steady. "Sometimes, I wonder which side you're on."

"Ours."

"Ours?"

"Yours, mine, this country's, the Alliance ... ours. But

do let us concentrate on our friend out there, who will need our help. Even with the supposed cease-fire, the situation is as volatile as it ever was; perhaps even more so. There's a lot of boiling hate, and the need for revenge grows exponentially, every time a new mass grave is found. It will not take much to set off the powder keg.

"IFOR's presence will only be of minimal effect if the thing is allowed to blow. I would hazard that they'd roll over the IFOR troops, unless we went in hard at the very beginning. You and I both know that political wrangling will make that virtually impossible, exactly as occurred before. The result will be even worse, because there is fresh cause for revenge. We have done a scenario model and I can tell you, General, that the omens are not good. It is not inconceiveable that if we are not very careful, we shall have a conflagration that spreads beyond the the borders of the present combatants."

"Is that code for a European war?"

"Western Europe and its allies versus the rest. Yes."

Bowmaker said nothing.

"Therefore," Buntline went on, "we should endeavor to haul out those two—our friend and her package—with as little fuss as possible. Now, that may not be how the situation eventuallly resolves itself. We must thus be prepared to put out any fire that may come alight, and do so swiftly and tidily.

"We will not be using the same pattern of rescue as the last time. No helicopter, no people on the ground. They'll be expecting that. Instead, we have an airstrip identified. No interest has been shown towards it, so as to avoid unwanted attention. The aircraft, a C130 Hercules, will make the one and only landing. It won't come to a halt. They'll have to board on the run. If she's not there, the aircraft will leave. The Hercules must of course have protection. An escort . . ."

"I can fill in the rest," Bowmaker said. "The November boys."

Buntline nodded. "Right up their street. For obvious reasons, we cannot and will not use the IFOR aircraft."

"There's more, isn't there?"

"There's more. A flight of six Su-27K Flankers are in the area, on a goodwill visit."

"Goodwill . . . !"

"They've been giving airshows. But we have definite evidence that they're fully combat-ready. Further, they do not belong to any *officially* declared fighter unit."

"Unit insignia?"

"None."

"Are they 'gifts' perhaps? Sweeteners for an eventual purchase?"

"Possibly," Buntline said. "But we have no truly hard evidence to go on."

"A rogue group?"

"That's the most likely probability."

"More of the same people after our friend?"

"For what it's worth, that what *I* think."

"So we may assume they're allowing for some kind of air cover to get her back out."

"In their place, I certainly would."

"Then I guess we'd better talk to the November boys."

"They're expecting you."

"As I said," Bowmaker began drily, "I am on a ride. Why didn't we just leave from Lakenheath?"

"The minister wants to see you."

"That bozo? Why, for Pete's sake? Haven't I got enough troubles?"

"Air Vice-Marshal Thurson's going to be there. Damage limitation."

"The minister *knows* about this?"

"Someone's told him . . ."

"Jeezus!"

"Not me. Now we've got to sit on him and try and persuade him it will be to his enhancement."

"Jeezus!" Bowmaker repeated in exasperation.

"So who told him?"

For the first time, Buntline looked embarrassed. "I don't know."

Bowmaker just stared at him.

8

Moscow, 1500 hours.

Lieutenant-Colonel Gregor Levchuk entered Kurinin's office bang on time. He was a tall man with iron-gray, cropped hair, attired in a uniform that no one had ever seen to be anything less than totally smart. It was clear by his demeanor that he enjoyed a relatively informal relationship with his superior officer. He carried a thin file beneath one arm.

Kurinin looked up from his large desk. "Ah, Gregor. Sit down. So what do we have?"

Levchuk pulled a straight-backed chair close to the desk and sat down. He placed the file on the desk before Kurinin.

"Nothing much as yet, General," he began, as Kurinin opened the file and began to study its contents. "But my instincts tell me something will pop soon."

"Your instincts?" Kurinin remarked, not looking up from the file. "Or your spider's web?"

Levchuk's smile was fleeting. "There are vibrations on the 'web.' But nothing worth a report for the time being."

Kurinin shut the file. "So you have logged two of these burial parties, split into five groups each."

"Yes, General. Each of the groups has a particular area in which to initiate digging, collate the number of bodies found, then arrange for their re-burial."

Kurinin shook his head slowly. "The madness of that country. There are times, Gregor, when I do believe we inhabit a planet of lunatics. If we're not very careful, that bunch could drag us into a war we do not want, or before we're ready. This nation needs strength and stability before it can begin to engage in any major conflict. At this time, although we can manage the brushfires, we cannot deal with a conflagration. In time, yes . . . when we have obtained full control; but not now. Anyone who tells you otherwise is an idiot."

"We've had our madnesses too," Levchuk commented, a bold statement that, under normal circumstances, a subordinate officer would never have dared make to a general. But these were not normal circumstances. "And still do. What is going on is proof of it."

Kurinin nodded. "With our history . . . You are quite right, of course. But things are going our way, despite a few setbacks with that special NATO unit, and one of our number getting greedy and moving too quickly. But people are being slotted into place. The election gave just the result we wanted. A sick man in charge. We'll continue to remain in the background; behind the scenes. But our time is coming, Gregor, much sooner than most people expect, particularly those in the West. In the meantime, they must be prevented from expanding NATO eastwards. This process must begin now; with priority on the destruction, or shut-down, of the special unit. It is the one aspect we cannot leave for later."

He jabbed at the file with an index finger. "But . . . we must also find this woman. She is actually a *Russian* operative, and clearly one of the very best. I may even have met her; but as we know, she is able to change her appearance quite effectively.

"We need to learn about the people she works for, both here in Russia, and in the West. We must know who they are. They have such access to our computers, there's a whole area to which *we* ourselves have no access. An intolerable situation that must be rectified as quickly as possible. I once believed we controlled everything. So *who are* these people? And what do they want?"

Levchuk made no reply.

Whitehall, London.

While Kurinin and Levchuk were trying to discover MacAllister's whereabouts, the Jaguar pulled into the secure carpark.

"Leave your bag," Buntline advised as he climbed out. "It will be quite safe."

"Nothing in there anyone could make use of, anyway," Bowmaker said as he too got out of the car.

They entered the solid Whitehall building.

The minister's young secretary—deliberately handpicked for attractiveness—greeted them in the outer office. She smiled brightly at Buntline.

"Hullo, Mr. Buntline. Nice to see you."

"Always nice to see *you*, Louise."

Her smile, widening in pleasure, was turned upon Bowmaker. "Nice to see you again, General."

"It warms an old man's heart to know you recognize him."

"You're not old, General," she said, giving him a look that was at once coy and brazen. "I think you're flirting with me."

"Of course I am."

She grinned. "The minister and the air vice-marshal are waiting. Please go right in, gentlemen."

"Thank you," the said together.

"'Old man,'" Buntline whispered at him as they made for the door to the minister's office. "Shameless, General."

"What else is a general to be?"

Buntline pushed open the tall double doors. He never knocked. He stood back for Bowmaker to precede him into what could easily be the large office of a well-heeled gentlemen's club. A deep red carpet dominated the room. Three comfortable chairs were arranged in a wide semi-circle, facing the big inlaid desk. A low table was positioned next to each.

"Ah, gentlemen!" the minister opened the gambit brightly, as if really pleased to see them. "Do come in, Charles. A pleasure to see you again, General. And you do know each other, of course, Air Vice-Marshal."

"Indeed, Minister."

"Glad to be here, sir," Bowmaker said to the minister as they shook hands.

The correct way to address an air vice-marshal, if using his rank, was simply "Air Marshal." But the minister was sufficiently petty-minded and insecure to have the need to use any little put-downs he could find.

Thurson, elegant in civilian clothes, was standing to

one side, and couldn't have cared less; and the minister knew it. It annoyed him.

Thurson now went over to Bowmaker to shake hands. "Good to see you, Abe."

"You too, Robert. We keep meeting under these circumstances. Perhaps one day we should try having dinner when the outside world does not require our attention."

"That could take some time, if we had to wait for such an opportunity."

"You could be right. Let's just do it, anyway."

"My feelings exactly."

The minister, feeling out of the loop, cleared his throat loudly. "Please be seated, gentlemen, and let's see if we can find our way out of this delicate situation." He remained standing, leaning against his desk.

Bowmaker, Thurson, and Buntline glanced at each other expressionlessly in reponse to the minister's view of the matter, before taking their seats.

"Some tea and biscuits are being brought," the minister went on, "but coffee for you, General, as I'm sure you prefer. You Americans do so like your coffee, do you not?"

"Some of us quite enjoy tea," Bowmaker responded mildly.

"Oh! I'm sorry. Would you like me to change that?"

"Not at all, sir," Bowmaker replied. "I'm happy with the coffee."

"Er, quite. Very good."

Thurson and Buntline maintained neutral expressions, but they understood what Bowmaker had done, and why.

The minister cleared his throat again and turned to Buntline. "Now, Charles. How did this thing get so out of hand in the first place? There could be the devil to pay."

"It's not out of hand, Minister," Buntline answered firmly. "It never was."

The minister stared at him, perplexed. "But my information . . . "

"Was flawed, Minister," Buntline said.

Buntline's manner showed very clearly that while the minister would miss no opportunity to maintain the pecking order over members of the services, Buntline was a much tougher nut to crack. He also knew the minister understood this perfectly, never being quite certain whether Buntline was an ally or a foe.

"I don't quite follow, Charles. Ah! Here's the tea. And the coffee, of course. I'm quite happy to have tea brought, General," he added to Bowmaker. He clearly found it disconcerting that he had not totally controlled the preparations for the meeting.

"I'm happy with the coffee," Bowmaker said. "Thank you."

"Oh. Very well. We'll leave it as it is. Thank you, Mrs. Morrison," he said to the woman who had entered with a tray.

She was followed by a young woman with another tray.

They all waited as the tea and biscuits were placed on each small table, with the exception of Bowmaker, who got his coffee. Tea and biscuits were also placed on the minister's desk.

"Thank you, Mrs. Morrison," the minister repeated.

"Minister," she said, and went out, followed by her assistant.

"Gold dust, that woman," the minister said. "Please tuck in, everyone. No ceremony here."

Following his own advice, the minister began to

dunk one of his biscuits. Buntline hated the habit and covered his distaste by taking a swallow of his tea.

"Excellent tea, as always," he said.

"Yes," the minister agreed, popping the soggy biscuit into his mouth. He munched and swallowed then added, "Mrs. Morrison's quite a treasure. You were saying, Charles. Flawed information?"

Buntline put his cup down. "Flawed," he repeated. "Imagine someone, somewhere, wanting to seriously embarrass us out there. I can think of many candidates. They make certain a tale like this reaches your ears. What reaction can they hope for? Exactly the one they're receiving.

"You want to know what's going on. You call in those people you believe may know something about it. What's the likely result? There's either an operation running, or there isn't. If there is, the interested party hopes to find out more, which in turn can be manipulated to cause us maximum embarrassment. If one isn't running, denials will still leave a lingering doubt. Could it be possible that we're carrying out our own secret snatches? Do you see what I'm getting at, Minister?"

"Yes. Yes, I do, Charles." The minister looked vague, but all three men could read the expressions chasing across his features. The minister didn't want to be embarrassed and was clearly thinking of ways to get out from under. "But *is* there such an operation?"

"How did you get the information?" Buntline countered.

"A journalist came right up to me outside the house and asked if it were true that we were running a snatch operation in Bosnia. I denied it vehemently, of course."

"Who told *him?*"

"He said another journalist told him there was one, and he wanted to be sure. So he asked me."

"The old whispering trick," Buntline said, recognizing a ploy he had himself used in the past. "Someone tells someone who tells someone else and so on, while the originator of the story is conveniently lost in the mists. It always works, Minister."

"So there isn't an operation, after all?" He sounded hopeful.

His visitors looked at each other.

"There is," Buntline said.

The minister paled. "But you just told me . . ."

"I just told you your information was flawed, Minister. And so it most certainly is. It's a highly sensitive mission. We're going to bring out one of the worst criminals . . ."

"My God, man! You can't, Charles!"

"One of the worst criminals," Buntline repeated, "and get him to reveal more information than the UN, IFOR, or any of the other international agencies are likely to get hold of. Stuff that never made the news. There are plenty of those around. Think of it, Minister. You could hold the key to the prosecution of many, many more who would otherwise escape. Real details. Hard facts. Enormous feather in your cap. People would say you were smart enough to see the potential."

Buntline stopped, watching with interest the new thought processes being telegraphed across the minister's face. The desire for kudos was being challenged by the need to ensure nothing unpleasant stuck to him.

Vanity won.

"It would be quite a coup," he agreed tentatively.

"That will only happen if you continue to deny you know anything about any operation. I suspect this is a fishing expedition. They're after our operative. They've been after him for some time."

Buntline had deliberately given the minister the wrong gender identification. One never knew what might be said at official, or non-official functions. The tiniest comment in one location could at times develop into dangerous consequences for an agent in the field somewhere else. On occasion, these could prove fatal.

He was aware that the others had glanced at him, but he chose to ignore their looks for the time being.

"General?" the minister began to Bowmaker. "Do you agree with this scenario?"

"Completely, sir. That man out there will also need air cover for his exit with the . . . er, package. We're sending in a C130 to do the recovery. It will need an escort."

The minister turned to Thurson. "Air Vice-Marshal? I take it the escorting aircraft will come from that . . . unit of yours up in Scotland?"

"The 'unit,' Minister, belongs to several nations. Not to me." Thurson knew that the minister was still annoyed that his stooge, Applegate, had not been able to return with anything to discredit the November project.

"Yes, yes! You know what I mean."

"They are the obvious choice," Thurson said.

"Yes. I suppose you're right; though I do wish that insurbordinate wing commander could be given a different post elsewhere."

"Without Wing Commander Jason, Minister, there is no November program."

"The thought had crossed my mind," the minister said ominously. "But yes. I agree with you. The escorting aircraft will have to come from there. Of course, I know nothing of this."

"We understand, Minister," Thurson said.

● ● ●

The Jaguar purred away from Whitehall. All three men were in the back.

"Remind me not to play poker with you," Bowmaker said to Buntline. "You're dangerous."

"I've never played."

"You could have fooled me."

"You went along when I said our operative was a he."

"You dealt the cards," Bowmaker remarked drily. "I just played the hand."

"There's that poker analogy again."

Bowmaker grinned tightly. "Sure you play. Different stakes, different cards; but you play." He peered out of a tinted window. "Where to now?"

"Where else?" Thurson said. "We're catching a flight to November."

"And I've got all the information we need," Buntline added.

A small mountain town, Bosnia.

The van carrying the international investigating and burial team was escorted by two IFOR vehicles; one ahead, the other covering the rear. MacAllister was sitting directly behind the driver. Bowmaker would not have recognized her.

Her hair was now jet black, her eyebrows thicker. Skillfully inserted cheek and chin pads had so altered the contours of her face, she was unrecognizable. Subtle padding in the clothing she wore—suitable for mountain walking—had given her body the appearance of frumpishness, her determinedly unstylish glasses adding to that impression. Solid walking boots covered her feet. She looked the perfect stereotype of the sort of person cynics would usually judge to be a do-gooder. There was nothing else in her life, they would say with resigned pity. The power-dressed bombshell whom Bowmaker had met in Norway had effectively vanished.

She had deliberately chosen to be in this particular group. The information that had been passed to her had suggested that the town where they were going was frequently visited by Serenic. He did not do so as leader of the Black Lynxes. Under another name, he brazenly came into the town, in civilian clothes. His bodyguards came too, but they never seemed to be with him, and tended to take up positions within sight of him while appearing to be quite unconnected with his presence.

Serenic's visits owed as much to hubris as to the need to escape now and then from the restrictive confines of his mask and secretive mountain existence. It was his way of flaunting himself before those who sought him out. He had grown a designer beard and moustache and, with his inevitable dark glasses, bore little resemblance to the volunteer lawyer who had supposedly died in battle. But, as in so many cases, it was the little things that had betrayed him.

The person who had supplied the information to MacAllister had observed Serenic over a long period, after he had formed the Black Lynxes. Though never having seen his face before, he had paid close attention to one of Serenic's particular habits. This had subsequently proved to have been the clincher: it was Serenic's habit of pinching out his cigarette before carelessly flicking it away.

There was also an undeniable arrogance about the "civilian" Serenic that the man himself obviously found difficult to keep under control, even when he was playing his game of "bearding the foreigners." His vanity would thus be his undoing.

The little town was perched on rising ground that looked out upon a steep valley. It was a beautiful location, but like the village that Serenic and his men had destroyed, the immediate area hid monstrous secrets. The purpose of the burial party was to search the steep slopes for evidence of bodies in mass graves.

The convoy entered the town and made for the small central square, where it stopped. MacAllister looked out at the people who had gathered to stare at the strangers in their midst. They were unnervingly silent. One of the vehicle commanders was talking, through the interpreter who had accompanied the party, to a man who appeared to be someone of local stature. The man did not look pleased. His expression was clearly saying he wished these strangers would go away. The soldier was firm, demanding a place to stay for the investigating team.

After much discussion a small, indifferent-looking hotel on one side of the square was placed at their disposal. This was done with undisguised bad grace from the local man. There were some bullet pockmarks on the hotel walls but, generally, the war appeared to have passed it by. Contrary to expectations, what could so far be seen of the town also appeared to be reasonably intact.

The soldier, an American captain with IFOR, came up to the van.

"You've got somewhere to stay," he began laconically, "but don't expect flags of welcome. These people are hostile, uncooperative, and downright rude, all in one. I'm not even sure this used to be their town; at least, not all of it. Who knows with these folks. Your place is that little hotel with the outside café."

"What about you and your men?" the driver asked.

"We're staying with our humvees. We'll park right

outside the hotel when you're here, just in case. They won't try anything, knowing we can call in some choppers pretty damn quick. But you never know. Sane people wouldn't; but this damn country's out to lunch. Some nut tells them to start killing and they do, even their friends. They've been killing each other for hundreds of years and will do so again, once we've gone back home. Just like most of the goddamned planet, in fact.

"Uh . . . one more thing. I don't reckon there's anyone here who's keen to have you do any digging, so there'll be no volunteers. Best thing is to do some preliminary on your own—we'll help—then if we find anything, call up reinforcements." The captain gave an expressive shiver. "This place looks beautiful, but it gives me the creeps . . . like in some spooky movie. You know . . . bunch of people find this pretty town in the middle of nowhere, only to discover it's inhabited by werewolves."

"You've been watching too many movies, Captain," the driver, a Dutchman, said with a grin.

The captain glanced about him. "You reckon? These folks look like goddamned werewolves to me. They've got nasty secrets. It's in their goddamned faces." He looked at if he wanted to spit.

"Put like that, perhaps you are right." The driver, who was also the leader of the group, looked round at his passengers. Including MacAllister, there were two women and three men. "You have all heard. Let us see what the hotel is like, have a small something to eat, then go outside the town to see what we can find."

"How long will we be here?" MacAllister asked. They knew her as Jeanne Beauleon, a French citizen. She had decided that coming in as a Finn might have been too close to her own real background.

"It depends on what we find, Jeanne. You look worried. You're not letting the captain's talk of werewolves get to you, are you?"

"No!" she answered, nervously quick. "Of course not."

"All right, everyone. Out we go."

November base, 1500 hours.

The station basked in bright sunshine and a temperature of twenty-five degrees Celsius. A light, cooling breeze came off the Moray Firth. McCann was tinkering with his Corvette in the Mess carpark when the twin-engined HS 125CC3, from the RAF's executive jet squadron, passed overhead.

He glanced up, watching as it went out of sight beyond the building.

"Here comes trouble," he murmured, before returning to what he'd been doing to the gleaming engine.

The aircraft, based upon the civil version, curved sedately round to set itself up for the landing. It alighted, with small puffs of smoke from its tires, before whistling down to taxiing pace. By comparison to the roar of a Tornado, it was virtually silent.

Selby came out of the Mess and strode up to McCann. Now that they were once more paired as a crew, they had amassed several flight hours together since McCann's ACMI flight with Hohendorf. There had been no compatibility problems. They worked as a team as smoothly as they'd done before.

"Why don't you leave that thing alone, Elmer Lee?" Selby remarked as he stopped by the car. "It can't possibly work better than it does. It can't shine more than it looks, and you can eat off it, it's so clean."

"Hey. Anything is possible," McCann retorted without

looking up. "Things can go wrong. The flyer's mantra."

"*Mantra?*" Selby sounded as if he wanted to laugh. "What next?" He crossed his eyes. "Ommmmmm . . ."

McCann ignored the remark and the pantomime. "Anyway, I'm taking Karen out. Got to make sure everything's okay."

"So you've finally decided to brave Geordie Pearce's worst, now that he's back? That's really clever."

"What's he going to do? Kill me?

"He well might," Selby pointed out.

Knowing it was a wind-up, McCann remained unperturbed. "We'll see. Caroline says it's up to Karen."

"That's as may be. But Pearce is a big obstacle to climb over. A man like that is not going to take rejection lightly."

"We'll see," McCann repeated, still probing about the engine. "By the way, I think we've got trouble."

"That's not news. You're always in trouble."

"We. I said *we*. Us. The squadron."

Selby was at once interested. "What pounded that idea into your hot little brain?"

"A CC3 just entered the circuit. Probably landed by now."

"More VIPs?"

McCann continued to fiddle in the Corvette's engine bay. "Dunno. My hair's itching."

"Wash it."

"Have your fun. I think it's trouble," McCann insisted. "As long as I can take Karen out tonight, I don't care."

Unfortunately for McCann, he was right about the trouble. Even more unfortunate was that he would not get to take Karen Lomax out that evening.

● ● ●

Along with four other ASV Echo crews, McCann and Selby were waiting attentively in Briefing Room Alpha. The others were Hohendorf and Flacht, Bagni and Stockmann, the Double-C, and Morton with one of the backseat instructors with whom he'd flown air combat training missions, standing in as his navigator. Carlizzi was a major in the Italian Air Force, who spoke English like a New Yorker.

"Wash your hair more often!" Selby hissed at McCann. "Then this wouldn't happen."

"Hey!" McCann hissed back. "My hair didn't make this happen. *It* made my hair itch."

Stockmann was sitting behind McCann. He tapped the top on McCann's head with a knuckle. "You two sound like an old married couple, whispering to each other. I hear you're going into the ring with Squadron Leader Pearce. Think you're a boxer now, do you, Kansas boy? Hah!"

"The boss would never allow it," McCann countered. "Anyway, that's a nasty rumor."

"Hah!" Stockmann said again. "You know, I'm glad you're back from the dead, McCann. Think of the fun we wouldn't be having."

Whatever McCann had intended as a retort was cut short as the door to the briefing room swung open and four people came in. Jason was followed by Bowmaker, Thurson, and Buntline.

"Please remain seated, gentlemen," the air vice-marshal said as they began to get smartly to their feet. "This is a preliminary brief. A more detailed one will follow in a day or so. Mr. Buntline and General Bowmaker, whom you all know, have got a little task for us. Mr. Buntline?"

"Thank you, Air Marshal."

Buntline did not climb the dais to speak at the

lectern. Instead, he moved across the room to stand before the fighter crews.

"Gentlemen," he began, "I'll come straight to the point. We require an escort for an extremely sensitive mission over Bosnia." He paused, to allow his words to sink in.

Every one of the aircrew glanced involuntarily at McCann. Buntline knew why.

"Captain McCann," he said.

The child-like, misleadingly innocent eyes looked up at him. "Sir?"

"I am well aware of what happened after your last flight over Bosnia. I have already spoken to the wing commander. If you feel you would prefer not to go on this mission, there is not a single person here who would hold it against you."

McCann took his time while Buntline, and the entire room, waited for him to speak.

"Can I be frank, sir?" he said at last.

"Be as frank as you like. No one's going to pull rank."

Standing in a far corner of the room, nearer the door, Jason looked as if he thought Buntline was fanning a flame while putting his hand into it at the same time.

"So who's going to try and stop me?" McCann asked seriously.

Jason raised his eyes heavenwards.

Slightly taken aback, Buntline gave an uncertain smile. "I take it that means yes."

"You bet your . . ." McCann paused when he noticed Jason staring fixedly at him, ". . . er . . . that's a yes . . . er, sir."

"Thank you, Captain."

"You're welcome."

"Ye-ess." Buntline shot McCann a speculative glance

before going on. "To continue . . . a Hercules aircraft will be doing a rough field landing and takeoff, without coming to a full stop. It will require escort to and from its destination. I cannot stress too highly the importance of that airplane. It *must not* be shot down. Ingress and egress will not be over hostile territory, although the landing field will be close to a *potentially* hostile area."

"Question, sir," someone said.

"Yes, Mr. . . . Hohendorf, is it?"

"Yes, sir," Hohendorf acknowledged. "If the route in and out is not over hostile territory, where is the threat likely to come from?"

"Ah. Now we do come to the crux of the matter. It would appear—by one of those sometimes inconvenient twists of fate—that a flight of six Su-27K Flankers are on a goodwill visit . . ."

"Hah!" Stockmann whispered to Bagni. "Inconvenient! Goodwill!"

Jason saw him. "You'll get your chance to speak, Marine!" he snapped sternly.

"Sir! Yessir!"

"I share your scepticism, Captain Stockmann," Buntline said calmly. "This so-called goodwill visit, transparently, has other motives. In a general sense, this has implications for the Western Alliance in both the short and long term. In the immediate future, however, this will be of particular concern to our mission. As I've said, it is most inconvenient that they have chosen this particular moment to 'visit.' Given our information, we have strong reasons to believe that the Flankers will react with hostility, once your flight has entered the area.

"All may, of course, go smoothly. They may choose to remain on their side of the fence. But, equally possible, it may enter the heads of those who sent those aircraft there in the first place to give a demonstration of their capability. What better test than real combat? The last time you crossed swords with 'visiting' aircraft, they came off worse. They may well be looking for a re-match, with these more advanced examples."

Buntline looked at each in turn. "It would be nice to say to you that the mission will proceed smoothly; that the Hercules will get in and out, with no hindrance. It would be nice; but that would be to ignore reality. Anything can happen. Isn't that what you flyers say?"

"And it frequently does, sir," McCann said. He gave Selby a glance that was loaded with smugness.

Selby ignored him.

"Thank you, Captain McCann," Buntline said, raising an eyebrow slightly. "That was a rhetorical question. But to conclude . . ." he went on, ". . . questions, gentlemen? And this one's not rhetorical." His smile was almost invisible.

"May we know the purpose of the C130's mission?" Selby asked.

Buntline shook his head. "I'm sorry, but that has to be on a need-to-know basis. I do appreciate the reasons behind the question. However, I can but insist that you do everything in your power, should that aircraft come under attack, to ensure its survival. This is of paramount importance."

"Easy," McCann said.

Everyone stared at him.

"We can either do it," he told them, wide-eyed. "Or we can't. And I hate losing. Easy."

"Are you on the same planet as the rest of us?" Stockmann growled a whisper at him.

McCann tapped his foot once. "Sure feels like it."

"I think," Buntline said, eyeing McCann warily, "I

understand what Captain McCann, in his own inimitable way, is getting at. You simply do not, must not, contemplate the possibility of failure."

"We never do," Bagni said quietly.

Buntline glanced over his shoulder at Jason. "I do not doubt it. Wing Commander, anything to add at this moment?"

Jason came forward. "Yes, thank you, Mr. Buntline." As Buntline moved away, Jason's eyes zeroed in on his crews and continued, "No need to remind you that you will communicate, to no one, any information about this operation. You may not, however, be entirely happy with what comes next. You are all confined to the unit until this is over, as you will be required to deploy to Italy at very short notice, within the next forty-eight hours. It could easily be tonight."

He looked at McCann. "Captain, there's a constipated look upon your face."

"I'm all right now, sir," McCann said quickly.

"Glad to hear it. Would anyone else like to know whether they can go out with the object of their desires tonight? No? I thought not. Those of you with people off the station may telephone, provided you remember to keep it on a strictly personal level. I will accept no excuses to the contrary.

"The escort will consist of Hohendorf/Flacht, Selby/McCann, Bagni/Stockmann, and Cottingham/Christiansen. Hohendorf leads. Majors Morton and Carlizzi will remain on standby at the forward base in Italy. Don't even think of it, Major," Jason went on firmly as Morton tried to raise an objection. "You will get into combat soon enough. Don't be in a hurry. You are on standby. Any further questions?"

"No, sir."

"Good. You will all be informed of the time of the

pre-mission briefing," the wing commander continued, his eyes raking them. "In the meantime check your aircraft, prepare yourselves. A full load of air-to-air weapons will be carried." He turned to the AVM and to Bowmaker. "Anything you'd like to say, sir? General?"

Thurson shook his head.

"You seem to have covered it all for now, Wing Commander," Bowmaker said.

"Sir. That's all, gentlemen," Jason added to his crews.

"I just *knew* it," McCann said as the senior officers left. "As soon as I saw that CC3, I just knew trouble was a-coming. And to think I've been cleaning the car all day, all for this evening."

"You ought to know, McCann," Selby began, "in this country, when we clean our cars, it rains. Always. Or seems like it."

"It's not raining."

"Good observation. On the other hand, something has happened to stop you using it tonight. Same thing."

"You're making this up as you go along."

"Whatever you say, Elmer Lee."

"What do I tell Karen? You heard the boss. One wrong word and . . ." McCann drew an expressive finger across his throat.

"She's in the service. More to the point, she's a *November* officer. She knows things can change from one moment to the next. She won't need an explanation. Besides, if she really does need to know, SATCO will see that she's given whatever information is relevant to her duties."

The senior air traffic control officer, a squadron leader, was Karen Lomax's immediate boss.

McCann looked like someone who'd been presented

with an unexpected gift, only to have it snatched away before he could get his hands on it. "I *really* was looking forward to this evening, dammnit. Really, *really*."

"Hah!" the crop-haired Stockmann said, grinning—reminiscent of Geordie Pearce—powerful teeth at him. "The longer the wait, the sweeter the bait."

"C'mon guys. Help me out. Let's have some ideas here."

Stockmann gave an expressive sigh. "Use your brains, Kansas boy," he said, as if to a slow child. "This base is as big as a small town. There must be a hundred places where you can be private. Hell, the enlisted personnel don't seem to have a problem . . . "

"And you think the boss is going to smile at two of his officers . . . "

Stockmann did the knuckle trick on McCann's head while the others looked on, amused.

"She lives in quarters on the base," he said. "Right?"

"Yeah. With her parents, in case you'd forgotten."

"Would that be Wing Commander and Mrs. Lomax? The same wing commander who's Engineering boss?"

"Yeah."

"The same Wing Commander Lomax who went *off the base today*, with his wife, for a family visit somewhere in the south of England, leaving their lovely daughter *all alone?*"

"*What?* She never told me . . . "

"Tell him, guys," Stockmann said wearily.

"She wanted to make it a surprise," Bagni said.

McCann stared at them. They were all grinning at him. Even Selby.

"You guys *knew?* She *told* you?"

"No, Elmer Lee," Selby answered patiently. "She told Caroline. Caroline told us. We were sworn to silence. This business with the mission, coming out of the blue, has changed all that now. But you were never meant to go off the station, anyway."

"She is cooking a dinner for you," Hohendorf told him. "Tonight is your night, Elmer Lee. Enjoy. When you see Caroline, ask her yourself, if you do not believe us."

For once bereft of words, McCann stood there, mouth hanging slightly open.

"Catch a fly in that," Selby told him.

"Wow!" was all McCann could manage, eventually.

9

McCann, dressed in a featherlight, dark cream linen suit, was standing by the Corvette. He had asked Caroline Hamilton-Jones about the dinner and she had confirmed what he'd been told by the others. With the exception of Flacht—who lived in married quarters— and Caroline, they had trailed him to the carpark.

Stockmann whistled. "Will you guys look at that?"

They stood in a loose semi-circle near the Corvette. McCann hovered by the car uncertainly, looking self-conscious. In his right hand was something about the size of a beeper for an answering machine. He played his fingers over it absently.

"Seems like designer stuff to me," Selby commented, going up to McCann and inspecting him. "Never seen that one before, Elmer Lee. What's your rich dad been buying you? Armani?"

"My own money bought this," McCann said defensively. "It came from my salary. I stopped off in London on my way back from convalescence in the States, to do some shopping."

"You little devil, McCann. You're being civilized by Miss Lomax! Been doing Harrods in secret?"

"It wasn't Harrods, and it's not an Armani."

"Let's have a look-see," Stockmann said, and quickly moved forward to have a look at the label inside the jacket. "Baldessarini," he read. "This looks like serious stuff."

"It is."

"You are a surprise every day, Elmer Lee," Hohendorf joined in. "I know that label. It is supposed to be for the discerning."

"Oh God," Selby groaned. "Did you have to tell him that? We'll never hear the last of it. Off you go, McCann. You've got the flowers, and the wine. Don't let the side down."

"What's that gizmo you're playing with?" Stockmann enquired. "Some new kind of car security?"

McCann stopped playing with the object and stared at it as if wondering how it had got there. "This?"

"No," Stockmann replied sarcastically. "The golf club in my hand."

McCann grinned at him, ignoring the sarcasm. "One of my brainfarts. I call it my mobile-phone scrambler. I had a talk with one of the guys who works on the ASV Echo's defensive electronics, and he came up with this. It bugs me when I go to a restaurant and some person right next to my left ear starts shouting into a mobile, as if I'm really interested in what they're saying while I'm trying to eat. I reckon this will do some serious jamming."

"I'm sure it's illegal," said Caroline, who had just turned up. "Will it work on trains?" she added hopefully. "Can I borrow it?"

"Haven't tried it out yet, but it will work. You can all borrow it if . . . you're nice to me."

"That'll be the day," Stockmann said. He went on to the others, "C'mon. Let the guy go on his date. Get outta here, McCann."

"Don't forget, Elmer Lee," Caroline warned, "you know nothing about the dinner. It's a surprise. So don't greet her with a 'Yo, Karen. What's cooking?' It will be your last date with her if you do."

"Hey. I know how to behave."

"Of course you do," she soothed.

They stood back as he got into the car and started the powerful engine. He blipped the throttle and the Corvette gave a deep bark. He waggled his fingers at them, then drove off in a manner that was very restrained, for him.

"It's like watching your little brother go off on his first date," Caroline said. "Sweet."

Selby stared at her. "Do you mean someone we know?"

"Be nice, Mark."

"I'm always nice."

"Let's follow him," Stockmann suggested. "I want to see what he does when she comes to the door."

"Don't be a peeping Tom," Caroline admonished.

"It's just some fun. We're not going to stand outside the house and watch them all evening. Who's with me?"

They stood there looking at each other for a while. Then they all said, "Me!"

Including Caroline.

McCann held the flowers in one hand before him like a shield, as he stood at the door. The bottle of expensive wine was in the other. He poked a finger out to press the doorbell.

Karen Lomax opened the door instantly, it seemed. It was almost as if she'd been standing just inside, eagerly waiting. Given the time of year, it was broad daylight, and as he looked at her, McCann thought she was the most beautiful person he'd ever seen. The thinnest dress he'd ever clapped his eyes on was a pulse-racing bonus.

"Flowers!" she greeted warmly, taking them from him. The scent of her made him feel faint. "Thank you, Elmer Lee." She gave him a light kiss on the lips. "You've brought wine too. And why are you staring at me like that? We have been out before."

"Yes," he said, swallowing, "but . . . you look really . . . even more beautiful . . . tonight."

She blushed in the way he liked so much. "And you look very handsome and smart."

"Um . . . thanks. Um . . . we can't go off the base. That's why I brought the wine. I thought that perhaps . . ." He stopped, playing the part to the hilt.

"We're staying in. Can't you smell the cooking? We're having dinner here, so it was a good idea to bring wine. My parents are away and we'll be all alone." She widened her eyes at him. "Don't stand there like a statue, Elmer Lee. Come in!"

"Um, yes. Okay."

He was so intoxicated by her, he hadn't even registered the mouth-watering aroma coming out of the kitchen. He entered the house as she stood back to let him in, holding on to the bottle of wine as if for protection.

Now that he had arrived at the moment in time that he'd dreamed and fantasized about for so long, the Kansas City Dude was astounded to discover he was actually feeling out of his depth.

A short distance away, two carloads of McCann's colleagues, remaining out of sight of the lovebirds, had watched the little drama.

Stockmann placed a hand on his heart. "Get's you right there."

Caroline smacked him on the shoulder. "That's enough. Let's leave them to it. Come on. Back to the Mess."

"Hang on," Selby said. He was looking down the road from the Lomax house.

They looked at him.

"What?" Stockmann asked, then followed the direction of gaze. "Hey. Isn't that . . . ?"

"Geordie Pearce's car!" Caroline finished softly in alarm. "What's he doing here?"

"I say we wait," Stockmann said in a hard voice. "McCann's our little runt. *We* give him a hard time. *Nobody* else, except maybe the boss."

"I agree," Hohendorf said.

They watched as Pearce's car drew up next to the Corvette. Pearce, in civilian dress, got out, slammed his door, then stared at the gunmetal gray car. He looked as if he wanted to kick it over the house.

"Trouble," Hohendorf murmured.

"He wouldn't dare!" Caroline said.

"Who knows what a guy will do in a situation like this?" Stockmann remarked thoughtfully. "He's looking at the 'vette like it's that football he boots around on the field."

Pearce walked away from the car with seeming reluctance and went up to the door. He banged on it imperiously, twice.

"I think he's losing his marbles," Stockmann said in amazement. "What's he think he's doing? He's the deputy boss of Engineering, for crying out loud, not some enlisted man in a bar. We'd better . . ."

"No," Selby interrupted. *"I'll* go. Elmer Lee's *my* backseater."

"I'll come with you," Hohendorf said. "I have a stake in this. He was mine too, for a short while."

Selby shook his head. "This is for me. If Pearce beats me into a pulp, then you can all join in." He began walking towards the house.

"I do not believe the squadron leader could be so crazy," Bagni said.

"Who knows what love can do to a man?" Cottingham said philosophically.

"Lust, more like," Caroline remarked coldly. "Primitive man itching to fight over a mate."

"Hey," Stockmann said. "Enough of the primitive already, if you're lumping us with him. And don't say we're all the same."

"I won't."

"That sounds like a back-handed compliment."

She smiled sweetly at him. "Is it?"

But the door to the house had once again opened, and their attention had re-focused upon it. Karen Lomax was again in the doorway. Pearce's stance looked menacing, and Karen Lomax seemed fragile before him.

"What's *he* doing here?" Pearce demanded tightly. A massive hand jabbed in the direction of McCann's Corvette.

"I believe I have the right to invite a guest into my home, sir," she replied. She displayed no fear of him.

"'Sir?' What's this 'sir' business, Karen?"

"Karen? Are you okay?" McCann, jacket off and looking at ease, came out of a room and approached the door. "Oh," he said, startled, when he saw Pearce.

"'Oh' is right, Captain!" Pearce said through gritted teeth. "What the devil do you think you're up to? Wasn't one warning enough for you?"

"Please, Geordie," Karen implored. "Don't make a scene . . ."

"Scene! You have no idea what a scene can be . . ."

"Excuse me, sir."

Pearce's head snapped round. "*Who the hell are* . . .you. Oh, I see. Flight Lieutenant Selby." Pearce looked about him. "Are all the superstars here?" he went on, with biting sarcasm.

"I think you'd better leave, sir," Selby told him quietly, "before this whole thing becomes even more embarrassing and people begin to gather."

Pearce glared at him with eyes that seemed to blaze. "You *what?* You tell me nothing, Selby. Your lot seem to think the sun shines out of your backsides . . ."

"Sir, we don't . . ."

"Don't bloody interrupt *me, Flight Lieutenant!*"

"Sir." Selby waited.

Pearce stared angrily at him for some moments before abruptly turning away, to walk back to his car. The squadron leader wrenched the door open, got in, and slammed it shut. He started the engine in such a way, it sounded as if he wanted to rip the entire motor out of the vehicle. He crunched it into gear, reversed perilously close to the Corvette, before turning the car round to race off the way he had come.

"Oh boy," McCann said into the silence that had descended.

Karen Lomax had a film of tears in her eyes. "He's ruined the evening," she said.

"No he hasn't," Elmer Lee told her gently. He turned to Selby. "Are the guys here too?"

Selby nodded.

"I won't ask what you were doing here in the first

place, but thanks for coming. I think if you hadn't been there . . ."

Selby clapped him on the shoulder. "Take the lady inside Elmer Lee. Enjoy your evening."

"Sure."

Selby turned away as McCann took Karen back inside, and walked back to where the others were waiting.

They drove back to the Mess in silence, astonished by Pearce's behavior.

When they had returned to the carpark and had climbed out, Stockmann looked at each in turn.

"Guys, that dipstick *services* our airplanes. I don't know about the rest of you, but *I* hate the idea of a guy who loses his cool being responsible for the integrity of the machine I fly into the wide blue yonder. Think about it."

No one said anything to that.

The small mountain town, Bosnia.

MacAllister lay on her bed in the small, basic room, listening to the noises coming from the café below. The tables were occupied mainly by the investigating party and some of the soldiers. One or two locals were also there, but the majority of those townspeople who frequented the cafés and bars around the square had given it a wide berth.

The day's search had as yet yielded no evidence of mass graves; but everyone felt certain there were some. It was simply a matter of time. The local people were far too furtive for there not to be. As the IFOR captain had said, there were ugly secrets out there beyond the town. They would not have had time to dig up any evidence, in order to hide it elsewhere. In any case, freshly dug earth would have been suspicious in itself.

MacAllister was far more interested in the whereabouts of Serenic, and wondered how long she would have to remain in the town before he put in an appearance. That had been the real purpose behind her question to the leader of the group. The longer it took to find buried victims, the better it would suit her. On the other hand, the longer she stayed in the country itself, the greater her risks became.

She had just three days to find him.

The C130 would come to the landing site on the fifth day. Three days to capture him, and two days to make it to the site. Five days in all for the snatch mission.

"Five days for my Task," she murmured.

If she failed to make the rendezvous the aircraft would leave, with or without her.

The information she'd received had suggested, she reminded herself, that Serenic was due to make a visit about now. Perhaps he was already in the town. The news of the presence of the investigating team would have spread through the area like wildfire, and would have been irresistible to him. Perhaps he would turn up in the morning.

Perhaps.

She reached into the backpack she'd brought with her. It was generally similar to the ones used by her supposed colleagues; but there were differences that would have astonished her investigative "colleagues." In a padded section, effectively hiding its contours, was her automatic pistol and its silencer. In another compartment was a mean-looking combat knife. She checked that both weapons were in place.

Keeping the pack close, she rolled over to go to sleep.

In the morning, it would be day two.

November base, day two of the Task, 0900 hours.

Jason was in his office, but not at his desk. He was standing, cap firmly fixed upon his head. His eyes seemed ready to drill into something.

A knock sounded on the door.

"Come!" he barked.

Geordie Pearce entered and saluted smartly. "You sent for me, sir?" He looked puzzled.

"You seem surprised," Jason said coldly.

Taken aback by the wing commander's tone, Pearce's eyes widened slightly, then his brow furrowed.

"Is something wrong, sir?"

"You tell me."

"Has there been some bad servicing . . ."

"This has nothing to do with the servicing of aircraft, Squadron Leader Pearce; though you must have an inkling, I'd have thought."

Pearce was now very surprised. "Would you care to let me in on what the problem is, sir?"

Jason's eyes pinned his subordinate to an invisible wall. "Captain McCann. How's that for starters?"

"Ah. So he came running to you . . ."

"*Squadron Leader Pearce!* I did not ask for your opinions concerning another officer. I asked for an explanation of your behavior last night. And to get the record absolutely straight . . . it wasn't McCann—of whom you've just so contemptuously spoken—who 'came running' to me, as you have so rudely put it. I am not prepared to condone that attitude.

"It was Flight Lieutenant Lomax, in some distress, who gave a reply to SATCO when he asked her if she was all right. At first she was most reluctant to explain, and it was eventually wormed out of her, until SATCO understood what was going on. He then decided I should be informed. I would like to hear your own version of the incident. If I were you, I'd think very carefully before speaking. Well?"

"This is a very difficult one, sir," Pearce answered, looking straight ahead, face impassive.

Jason stared hard at his subordinate for long moments in total silence, his mouth a tight line. He then removed his cap and placed it on the desk.

"Take off your hat, Geordie. I'm going to make this informal. It will remain that way, unless you force me to revert to a more formal stance."

Jason waited until Pearce had slowly removed his own cap.

"You are one of the very best Engineer officers I have ever come across," he continued. "That was why I moved heaven and earth to get you. You have been with this unit almost from the very beginning so you know, even more than most people on this station, the importance of what we're doing here, and of our vulnerabilty to our enemies within the system.

"There are superbly dedicated crews out there. Some of their number have already made the ultimate sacrifice, while others have, more than once, laid their lives on the line in combat. They deserve to have officers on the ground who are capable of ensuring that the aircraft they fly are totally reliable; even allowing for the fact that fully serviceable aircraft can still go wrong. I want nothing that can possibly affect this fine balance to exist on my unit.

"Good God, man! What were you thinking of? Threatening a member of my aircrew like some brawler from a pub, and challenging him to a *boxing match?* Have you any idea what I would have done to you if you had seriously injured McCann, which you clearly intended to do? Hiding behind the dubious legality of such a match would not have saved you from my wrath. *You, a Rugby Blue,* versus McCann? Have you completely taken leave of your senses? You are the *deputy boss* of the Engineering wing, man! I recommended you for promotion to squadron leader. Is this how you repay my trust? What kind of example do you call this? We are supposed to be better than those we command."

Jason paused for breath and stalked the room for some moments. He stopped, turning to face Pearce once more. The squadron leader still continued to stand rigidly to attention, cap beneath an arm.

"Karen Lomax," Jason continued, "is a grown woman, free to make her own choice of men. Whether you agree with that choice is neither here nor there. Almost every man alive has covered that route. What does she see in him, we've all said to ourselves at one time or another, when she could have me? Like good intentions, the road to hell is also paved with that eternal question. I dare say you'll find as many women who say the same about us.

"But your personal problems are *yours* to solve. Do so any way you like . . . as long as they do *not* encroach upon the integrity of the unit and its ultimate purpose. I have said—and I do mean it—that I will ground any member of the aircrew who allows personal problems to put at risk the aircraft, the mission, other members

of the aircrew, and himself or herself, as the case may
be. I am giving you the same warning. Much as I think
very highly of you as both an officer and an engineer,
one more incident like this and you're out of here so
fast you'll think you're rocket propelled. If you resent
the way I have just spoken to you, I am quite happy to
put my cap back on and we shall conduct this formally."

Jason's eyes seemed to hold Pearce's in twin beams
of fearsome power.

"Which is it to be, Geordie? Do I put my hat on? Or
do you wish to look upon this as a roasting from someone who is your commander, but who also looks upon
you as an exceptional brother officer, and as a friend."

Pearce swallowed a couple of times. "Without the
hat, sir."

Jason gave an audible sigh of relief. "Good. Good.
You've made the right choice. I should have hated losing you." He held out a hand. "Let's hear no more of it."

Pearce gave a tight smile and shook the hand. "We
were sort of unofficially engaged. Well ... to be fair,
perhaps I overcooked it. I assumed, where I should not
have."

"Geordie, engagements—like marriages—break all
the time, leaving one of the parties hurt, and mystified.
Life has many sweet cruelties. I've been there. Not a
marriage, but a love affair I expected to last. There.
The wingco has admitted he's human, after all."

"It is a surprise."

"My being human?"

"No, sir," Pearce replied, looking more relaxed now.
"The affair."

"Ah. Lesson number one, or one hundred, Mr.
Pearce. Never assume."

"I think I got that one, sir."

"All right, Geordie," Jason said quietly. "That's the end of my lecturing. Now to more pressing business. I want the five ASV Echoes that are scheduled for the deployment to be fully tooled up, and every square inch of those aircraft gone over with microscopic thoroughness. I expect a max effort from your team."

Pearce put on his cap. Jason did likewise.

"You can count on it, sir," Pearce assured him.

"I know I can."

"Sir!" Pearce saluted.

Jason returned the salute. "Carry on."

Pearce went out, and Jason turned to look out of a window. "For my sins," he said to himself drily, removing the cap again and wiping his forehead with the back of his hand, "I'm now an agony uncle. The joys of command."

Bosnia, 1100 hours local.

Three kilometers west of the small mountain town and on one of the steep slopes above the valley, MacAllister felt the tool she was using strike something about a half a meter down. She began to dig around the probing hole she had made. She told no one, just in case all she had struck was nothing more than a piece of buried wood or perhaps metal of some kind.

Soon, the excavation was large enough for her to clearly see her find. She was hoping it would not turn out to be bones; at least, not yet.

She wanted to find Serenic first, and planned to take him out under the cover of the flurry of excitement and agitation that would follow the initial discovery.

She heaved a quiet sigh of relief. It was a lump of wood. She moved to another spot and began to dig afresh.

Some kilometers away and deep into the mountains, Serenic was putting the finishing touches to his civilian persona.

"What are you going to say to those people, Commandant?" asked one of the four bodyguards due to accompany him. The man was also in civilian clothes.

"First," Serenic retorted coldly, "remember *not* to call me "Commandant" in the town. I am Milan Pavlic."

"Yes, Comm . . . Milan Pavlic."

Serenic stopped what he was doing to turn chilling eyes upon the bodyguard. "If you make a mistake like that again, I will shoot you. *Understand?*"

"Yes!" the man said hastily. "Yes, Milan!"

His calm suddenly returning, Serenic continued his preparations. "As to your question about those meddling, grave-digging people . . . I shall just watch them." He laughed abruptly. It was a laugh that did not sound quite sane. "I might even offer to help. Who knows? They may have one of those pretty but stupid women who believe they can change the world by doing things like this. Perhaps she will like the company of Milan Pavlic." Serenic turned to the bodyguard and grinned. "And how do I look? Like a rich black-marketeer?"

He was dressed in a cool-looking pale suit. His black hair was slicked back, his dark eyes hooded beneath thick eyebrows. On his face was thick designer stubble. During his law-practicing days, he had always been scrupulously clean-shaven. His open-necked, buttoned-down, pale blue shirt showed the glint of a gold chain beneath.

"A playboy," the man replied.

Serenic nodded, pleased. "As I said. A rich black-marketeer. Well, come on!" he urged the bodyguard. "Get the others and let's pay our foreign, meddling friends a visit."

"Yes, Milan."

Moscow, 1200 hours local.

Kurinin looked through the file that Levchuk had brought in. When he'd finished, he looked up.

"You're certain of this, Gregor?"

"Absolutely. There are five teams in that particular group. She's got to be with one of them."

"The question is, of course . . . will she be found in time? According to what's in here, the teams are spread all over the place, all escorted by IFOR troops, who just happen to be American. Whereas the other nations sometimes hesitate to shoot when threatened, the Americans don't pause to worry about it. They *shoot.* Personally, I would do the same."

"So we must do this the subtle way," Levchuk said. "We've got the appropriate people out there."

Kurinin nodded. "All right, Gregor. Unleash the hounds. And warn the commander of the . . . 'goodwill' fighter detachment to be on standby for imminent action. If we don't get her, they'd better."

The smile of the inevitably smartly turned-out Levchuk was enigmatic. "I'll get on it right away."

"You know," Kurinin said, causing Levchuk to pause by the door. "These are stirring times for our country, and the world. There's a storm coming. It may be on the horizon, or it may be well back; but it's coming. And when it's passed, people like us will be in charge; as long as we are careful about how we play our own game. Bear that in mind, Gregor."

"I always do."

November base, 1200 hours local.

The standard ASV Tornado was at the threshold of the main runway, on final hold before takeoff. It was a two-stick trainer version with a full set of controls in the back cockpit, for the instructor pilot. Most instructors tended to hope they would never be in a situation where they would have to make use of them.

Dieter Helm had no such worries. Despite the reservations he'd expressed to Jason about women fighter pilots, he had elected to take the first ASV familiarization flight with Caroline Hamilton-Jones. He expected her takeoff to be well executed.

Jason had raised an eyebrow when he'd learned of Helm's decision, but was pleased. If Helm eventually passed Caroline as fit to upgrade to the ASV Echo, it would be high praise indeed.

"I will be fair to her," Helm had said.

Jason did not doubt it.

Helm was not a petty man and would be scrupulously fair, though ruthless, in his examination of her abiltities as the pilot of such a tremendously powerful fighter.

The wing commander would not have expected less. Standing on the balcony of the control tower, he now waited for the aircraft to take off.

In the front cockpit, Caroline slowed her breathing, disciplining herself to achieve the sort of calm that had served her well throughout her flying training. She was now sitting at the controls of an airplane which, though less powerful than the ASV Echo, was still a great deal more potent than the standard Tornado F.3 of the RAF's interceptor fleet.

"You are all right?" came Helm's voice in her ear.

She looked beyond the sleek nose of the superflick, to the great highway of tarmac that stretched towards the Moray Firth.

"I'm fine," she replied.

"Good. For this first takeoff we will do nothing fancy. A nice, easy, but well-controlled launch, and a direct climb to twenty-thousand feet. Yes?"

"Roger."

"Turtle Dove Two-Six," came the tower, sharp and fast on her headphones. "You are cleared for takeoff. Wind . . . one-five . . . three-six-zero . . ."

The wind was fifteen knots, coming from due north, on the nose, which was good. No cross-wind to make this, her first ASV takeoff, clumsy to behold. The headwind also meant a quick lift-off.

"Turtle Dove" for a callsign. Someone's idea of a joke, but she had decided to stick with it for this, her first ASV flight as pilot. It did not worry her. She was more interested in ensuring she flew the aircraft well.

"Roger, November," she heard Dieter Helm replying. "Wind is one-five at three-six-zero."

He fell silent.

He's waiting for me! Come on. Come *on*. Final check of immediate environs. All clear. Great expanse of runway. All the space in the world. Rudder pedals neutral. Brakes off. Ease throttles forwards. Smoothly. *Smoothly*. Don't jerk them. They're like a knife through hot butter. Speed building rapidly. Throttles right against the stop now, and into afterburner. *Hold* them there. Oh God, the *speed!* It's running away! The tarmac is a blur. Nose coming up. *Already?* Airborne! Unbelievable. The wheels, the *wheels!* Get them up or the hooter will start going ballistic and you'll know you've damaged them by exceeding gear-down speed. The lever. The *lever.* There . . . on the left. Spindly thing with little white wheel at the end. Push the catch on the top. Lift. Wheels coming up. Triple red lights blink, then go out. Gear's up and stowed safely away. Wings on auto sweep, moving back as speed rushes. Readout on HUD whirling. What altitude? *Fifteen thousand feet! Already?* Should be out of burner. Check that. Throttles already back. When done? All so quick. Twenty thousand. Level out. On course. Forehead damp. That felt like a ropey takeoff. What's Helm going to think?

"That was excellent, Caroline," came Helm's voice. "Very stylish and clean. Well controlled. I can tell you now that the boss was watching. He will be impressed. This is good flying. Keep it up, and you will be soon going to the ASV Echo."

Caroline felt a rush of relief. She had imagined herself taking off like a clumsy first-flight student. Instead, she had behaved instinctively on a totally different level where her skills, and discipline, had taken over.

Zero-One squadron, she thought. *Here I come.*

10

Bosnia, the small town in the mountains, 1800 hours.

MacAllister did not find any bones that day, but someone else did. One of the men, a Finn, working a hundred meters from where she had found what had later turned out to have been the still-living root of a long-felled tree, had made the first discovery, late in the day.

There was now little doubt that greater discoveries lay in wait. They marked the site with small, yellow flags and wondered about its security during the coming night. The IFOR captain was reluctant to split his forces. and leave a contingent on guard. He therefore called for immediate reinforcements and more diggers, and was told they'd be on their way in the morning.

However, two heavily armed Apache A-64 assault helicopters, with their anti-armor missiles, lethal chain guns, and night sights, would be dispatched to guard the area. The Apaches had arrived at 1700 hours and would take turns in patrolling the site throughout the hours of darkness.

The investigating crew had then returned to the hotel. MacAllister was sitting by herself, at one of the café's outside tables. There was still plenty of daylight left and even at this mountain altitude, it was pleasantly warm. On either side of the hotel, the captain's humvees were parked, his soldiers holding their weapons at the ready, in case of trouble. Now that the first evidence of a mass grave had been found, the very few locals who had previously been using the café had decided to take their custom elsewhere. The hotel manager complained the team was ruining his business.

The team leader, Hendrik van Petrus, came up to the table and sat down. His pale eyes mirrored the horror of the find.

"These people never cease to astonish me," he said in his excellent English. "Right outside this town is a horror in the making. But he complains that *we* are taking his business away. I wonder if he even bothers to think why we're here in the first place. Because of what his own people either did themselves, or condoned, we have come to this beautiful, rotten community."

Petrus shook his head in despair. "I have been in other war zones. But this . . . this is beginning to smell a little of Cambodia. Do you know what someone I once met in Africa said to me? Perhaps, this person said, the world needs a nuclear war to clean it out. We are pushing, pushing all the time, he said, like a child that wants to see how far he can go before he is punished. I was shocked, of course. How can you want a nuclear war, I asked him. He pointed at the bodies of children we were finding in the bush. Full of bullet holes. All of them. This is better? he asked.

"I could not answer. He was full of despair, of course. The murderers had over-run his country. It was the only way he could think of punishing them. Even they could not resist such a terrible power. In his mind, it was the ultimate sanction. And at that moment, I saw the nightmare. Imagine such a despairing man, in charge of a country, and someone sold him a cheap bomb. This man was no mad dictator. He was a doctor, and he felt useless in the face of such carnage. All he wanted to do was punish the perpetrators."

She touched his shoulder briefly, a sign of understanding. "Perhaps there are some people with real power who can see the nightmare, and will do something before it is too late." Her English sounded as it would have, had she been genuinely French.

"They were not of much use here, Jeanne. Were they?"

"You should not lose faith."

He looked at her, thinking he was seeing someone who was perhaps still much too naive to be in such a place. "There are no knights on white chargers. Only flawed people with a lot of self-interest to protect."

"You should not lose faith," she repeated.

"I hope you're not one of those who thinks she can see good in everyone," he said. "I've been to too many hell-holes to believe in that joke."

I know someone even more cynical than you are, she thought.

Petrus was looking about the square, studying the locals in the other cafés. One caught his attention.

"Look at that man over there," he said. "The one in

the pale suit and the shades, who looks as if he is in love with himself. This is a man with money. What is he doing here? I'll bet you some of the IFOR supplies, among other things, go through his hands, for a price. Perhaps these people are his customers. And look at the way he has just finished his cigarette. The man's arrogance is like a flag. He also thinks every woman in the world wants him. See the way he keeps reaching out to the waitress. But she doesn't seem to mind," Petrus added drily.

MacAllister turned to look, just in time to see the pinching of the cigarette, and the curving white arc as it was flicked away. She felt her pulses race.

Serenic.

"He's coming over!" Petrus said in disbelief.

They had been drinking coffee, freshly and reluctantly brought by one of the hotel staff, who'd turned out to be the owner/manager's daughter. Petrus had wryly commented that it was probably black market stuff, given the price. About fifteen minutes later, the man in the sunglasses had decided to come over.

They watched him cross the small square.

"Perhaps he is only coming to the hotel," MacAllister suggested. "Perhaps he is bored with that waitress and wants to try his luck with the manager's daughter."

"A man like that would not look at her twice."

MacAllister had also made a swift scan of the area, and had spotted each of the bodyguards, all pretending to be ordinary café customers. Even if she hadn't, their sudden alertness when their boss began to move, and their constant scrutiny of the soldiers, would have given them away to anyone who knew what to look for. They were good, but not good enough. The captain, she decided, would have been shocked to know who was walking within such easy range of his guns. However, the soldiers watched carefully as Serenic approached the hotel café.

He stopped by the table and smiled down at them. He kept the glasses on.

"Do you think those men will shoot me? Are their guns now pointing at my back because I am here with you?"

Petrus glanced to his right, and to his left. "Some are."

"They worry about what I might do. Do they really think I would be so stupid as to cause you harm? Right here, in front of everybody? In front of their guns? I am not foolish enough to commit such suicide."

"Soldiers are nervous people," Petrus said. "It is the nature of the job."

"You were once a soldier?"

"Weren't we all at some time?"

"Not all."

"Ah. I see. You do not like soldiering?"

"There are other . . . more lucrative ways of serving your country."

Petrus, a big, normally genial, man, turned his lips down briefly. "I can imagine."

"Please," Serenic said. The palpable antipathy from the Dutchman was of little consequence to him. "May I join you?" He looked from Petrus to MacAllister, remaining focused upon her.

She nodded at him, ignoring a puzzled glance from Petrus.

"Thank you. You are most gracious, madame." Serenic pulled a chair from another table, then sat down with the air of a man who was accustomed to having his own way. "I am Milan Pavlic. A . . . businessman."

Petrus gave MacAllister another glance. *I told you so*, it said.

"I'm . . ." he began.

"Hendrik van Petrus," Serenic cut in smoothly, "and this charming lady is Jeanne Beauleon. A strong name, madame."

"You are well informed," Petrus said shortly.

"You know how it is in such communities. People gossip."

"Yes," Petrus said, the chill in his voice increasing by the second. "They do. Unfortunately, they never seem to know anything when we ask them. They suddenly become ignorant of everything. They are all model citizens."

Serenic's head turned slowly towards him, an act that seemed very much like a snake about to strike.

"Then I must see if I can be of service. They will talk to me. I know these people."

"Your English is very good," MacAllister said to him, deliberately choosing to deflect Petrus.

He inclined his head slightly. "Thank you. I speak many of the European languages. In my business, it is necessary." He turned again to Petrus. "You do not like me, Mr. Petrus."

"I don't know you, Mr. Pavlic. How can I have any opinion?"

"You are obviously a diplomat. You know how to cover an insult with clever words."

"I did not . . ."

"Of course you did not. I am merely having a little fun. Come. Let us forget any possible unpleasantness. Will you please allow me to buy you both a drink? I have noticed that the people of this town are . . . not very welcoming to you. If they see I am drinking and laughing with you, they will be a little . . . less cold.

That may be of some help to you. As I have said, I know them." He looked at each, his glasses still on, giving the impression of a sightless, yet unnervingly menacing, creature, groping by sound to guide it on its way.

"You can help," Petrus said sceptically, ignoring the offer of the drink. "Find out if they know anything about what we discovered today."

"Ah," said the man who called himself Pavlic. "I believe you will *discover* collective . . . amnesia. Yes. Amnesia. That is the word."

"Such a surprise," Petrus said.

"A note of sarcasm."

"Life makes you sarcastic."

"Are you a philosopher, Mr. Petrus?"

"I thought you knew everything."

"You really do not like me. However, I am still not offended. You will have a drink?" Serenic was looking at MacAllister.

She nodded. Petrus looked aghast.

"Bravo!" Serenic exclaimed. "A woman who knows her mind. I like that. Mr. van Petrus?"

Petrus shook his head and stood up. "I have some reports to complete."

"I understand," Serenic said.

"I don't think you do, Mr. Pavlic."

"Please. Call me Milan."

"Good evening, Mr. Pavlic." Petrus turned to MacAllister. "Don't leave the hotel. You will be safe as long as you remain here where the soldiers can see you."

"I am not going anywhere," she assured him.

"Good." He nodded curtly at Serenic, and went inside.

Serenic watched him leave. "Humorless Dutchman, isn't he?"

"He has plenty on his mind."

"Yes. Perhaps I am being unkind."

Just then, the manager's daughter arrived, rather more quickly than when Petrus and MacAllister were waiting for service.

"Ah yes," Serenic said to her, beaming. "My friend would like a . . ." He waited for MacAllister to order.

"You choose," she said.

That pleased him. "There are many wines from this region, but also from other middle and Eastern European countries, even up here. For this evening, I would recommend a Hungarian Tokaji; the soft and spicy Hárslevel[a]. Yes?"

"I will go with your recommendation."

He grinned at her. "Good. Excellent." He gave the order to the girl, who dimpled at him and left. He glanced round at the soldiers. "They are watching me like hawks."

"Their job is to protect us."

"Of course. So. You are perhaps surprised this small hotel can have such a wine?"

"I wouldn't know," she replied. "I have never heard of Haarz . . . what did you call it?"

"Hárslevel[a]."

"Well I have never heard of it."

"A Frenchwoman, surely, is interested in wines?"

"If they are French." She smiled sheepishly.

"Spoken like a true Frenchwoman! Do you know, when you smile, I see a different woman. Please pardon me for saying so, and do not think me rude; but I believe you are not fair to yourself."

"No?"

"No! Any man of perception can see there is a great beauty in you."

"You mean my glasses, my . . . big body and my . . . my face which would not go on magazines?"

"Do you really believe those women in the magazines would look like that if they did not first cover their faces in make-up? We had a very famous singer when we were all one country, who was very beautiful. One day, I saw her walking in the street. No make-up. I tell you, you are much prettier. Ah," he went on before she could say anything. "Here is our wine. Now you must tell me what you think."

The girl made a song and dance of opening the wine, mainly for his benefit, before going away again.

He filled their glasses. "To the future," he toasted.

"To the innocent dead," she said.

He appeared to pause but recovered so quickly, there was the barest indication of it.

"Oh yes," she said after a mouthful. "This is very good."

"So you see? A new experience." Serenic had another drink, then continued, "I have a confession to make."

"Oh?"

"I have a room here, in this hotel. It is the one I use whenever I visit."

"So you do not belong to this town?"

"Oh no. I am not from here."

"You do not seem like a man who would stay in a place like this."

"Ah, but you see . . . my room is very special. Better a special room in a small hotel, than an anonymous one in a big, joyless place."

She gave a slight giggle. "Hendrik will not like to know you will be in the same hotel." She giggled again. "Your wine is very . . . very pleasant."

It was nearly another hour before she stood up. Serenic also rose to his feet.

Swaying slightly, MacAllister said, "An early . . . night for me. Much . . . much to do in the morning."

On his second cigarette since coming to the table,

Serenic removed it from his mouth before speaking. "It has been very pleasant speaking . . .

"And drinking . . ."

"And drinking with you. Are you sure you will not have a coffee with me?"

"Sorry, I can't. I think I need to be in my room. This place is . . . turning around. That wine was *very strong!* I will ask for a coffee to take to my room, if the girl finds the time to . . . take the order."

"Let me help," Serenic said quickly. "I will get it."

Without waiting for her to say anything about that, he hurried into the hotel.

Continuing to feign her drunkeness, MacAllister checked out the bodyguards. They were remaining where they were for the time being. It was clear they were at pains to keep as low a profile as possible. It was also clear they had no intention of initiating a confrontation with the IFOR soldiers.

MacAllister entered the hotel, to see Serenic smiling triumphantly at her. "It is done!" he told. "A coffee will be brought to your room."

"Thank you."

"The pleasure is mine. My room is number eleven, if you need me."

"What I need is sleep," she said.

"Of course," he acknowledged gracefully.

He pinched out his cigarette, went to the hotel entrance, and flicked it out into the square.

By the time she'd got to her room, MacAllister knew how she was going to do it. She had thought it through quite clinically.

"It will have to be tonight," she said to herself softly.

There was no sign of drunkenness about her.

●   ●   ●

Serenic came awake, knowing someone was in his room.

"Milan!" came an urgent whisper.

He relaxed, smiling to himself in the darkness. He was going to get a little action, after all. He had deliberately left the door unlocked.

He put away the gun he had taken from beneath his pillow and switched on the bedside light. He was expecting to see her in some form of nightwear. What he did see stunned him.

She was fully clothed, with her backpack on, and there was a very mean-looking automatic pointed unerringly at his head. Her glasses were gone, but the rest of her disguise remained.

He stared at her for the beat of a second, then a slow smile came to his lips.

"No glasses." He did not seem afraid.

"Get dressed, Serenic," she said coldly. "You're going on a trip."

His dark eyes widened briefly, but he did as she'd ordered.

"I didn't expect you," he began conversationally. He got out of the bed, naked, and began to put on his clothes. "No. That's not right. I expected you, but for . . . other purposes."

He lingered as he put on his trousers, giving her a sly look to gauge her reaction. The chill in her eyes shook him.

"That sort of crap doesn't work with me," she snapped. She looked round the room. It was almost luxurious. Her mouth turned down. "The best room in the house. Do you bring the daughter here?"

"Please. Do not insult me."

"So you thought a bottle of wine would do the trick, did you?"

"It has worked many times before."

"On airheads? I can drink you under the table."

But she wasn't really interested in slapping him down for boasting. Something far more disturbing was nagging at her. She couldn't understand why he was being so cooperative. It just didn't feel right.

"What a surprise you are, Jeanne. I was expecting Petrus," he added unexpectedly.

"Petrus?"

"Of course Petrus," he replied as he buttoned his shirt, then made a big show of zipping up his trousers, doing it loudly. "I thought the hostility with which he treated me earlier was just an act."

"Shows how wrong you can be. He really doesn't like you."

"He can't take a joke. I certainly didn't expect a woman," Serenic went on. "But you must be very good, if they sent you." He put on his jacket with a flourish. "Okay. I am finished."

"Sent me?"

"But of course. Why do you think I am here? You have come to take me to Britain. It has all been arranged." Serenic was now looking insufferably smug.

"What?"

"Ah, my poor Jeanne," he said condescendingly. "I am assuming, of course, that is not your real name."

"And Pavlic is yours? Or Serenic?"

He shrugged. "What is a name? If I may misquote. So . . . your masters did not trust you enough to tell you. Do not deny it. Your eyes tell me you are very angry. And now that I realize your glasses were false, let me tell you your eyes are beautiful; even when they are so angry. I was right about you. You are a beautiful woman, hiding under all . . . that."

"Get one thing straight, Serenic," she told him

harshly. "Your lounge lizard pose will not work on me. I'm highly pissed off and if you try to hit on me, you won't make it back. I'll shoot you right here in this miserable excuse for a hotel. This is not a threat."

"Do you know? I *like* you. Not a threat but a promise?" He wagged an admonishing finger at her. "You do not understand, my Jeanne."

"I am not your fucking Jeanne!"

Serenic gave one of his more feral smiles. "You even swear! Oh, oh. I really *do* like you. Yes. But you do not understand," he repeated in his smoothly infuriating way. "You will make some very powerful people very angry if you kill me. Do you really believe I would have been taken so easily, if arrangements had not already been made? I have been promised a very great deal of money, certainly . . . in seven figures . . ."

"*Money?* Is this some kind fantasy you're having?"

"Not a fantasy. Reality. I have information that will aid the international community," Serenic continued in a manner that was too confident for him to be faking it, "in a way they would never have dreamed of in a thousand years. I can give them all the answers they need. This, is *real politik.*"

MacAllister was staring at him. "You really are being paid? You're being given *money* and then, you'll go *free?*"

"Annoying, is it not?"

Her eyes riveted themselves upon him. *"Annoying? That's the strongest word you can find?"*

He pointed at the gun. "Your finger is looking tense. I would advise against shooting me here," he said conversationally. He kept a wary eye on the weapon. "Your soldiers would have to fight my bodyguards—who will be killed, of course—but then the entire town would turn on the IFOR troops. There are many guns here. You would all be killed, even if the soldiers called for the Apaches. It would be too late to save you." He stared challengingly back at her. "You need me to get past my bodyguards."

The gun did not waver. "So you're running out on them."

"Why should they share my good fortune?"

"They would risk their lives for you."

Though she would kill the bodyguards without compunction, Serenic's willingness to betray them so easily disgusted her. There was not even a vestige of honor among these thieves and murderers.

He shrugged. "Such people will die for any stupid cause. They are the cannon fodder of history. And please don't give me any of your high moral rubbish. Do you believe your masters . . ."

"I have no master."

"Have it your way. Your . . . principals. Do you think they care? I can give them what they want. They are happy to pay. It will still be cheaper than becoming tied down for years in this country. *Real politik.* The name of the game. Come, come, Miss Goodlion," he continued, translating her name into English in a weak attempt to humor her, "this cannot be news to you, considering the business you're in. You understand such things. You are not naive. We both know the world is a harsh place. There are two kinds of being: the prey, and the predator. From time to time, the roles are reversed; but essentially, nothing changes . . . except the face of the predator. So . . . shall we go? Or do we stand here all night, with your gun pointed at me?"

"There are people," she said quietly, "who actually

do things because they are right, and not because of any *'real politik.'* She spat the words back at him. "People like you are primitives. You are savages. You are dogshit."

MacAllister suddenly walked up to Serenic, taking him completely by surprise. He felt a sharp stab in his thigh.

"Wha . . . what?" His eyes widened at her, then he stared at his thigh. He could see nothing. *"What have you done?"*

"Flexible plan. I always have one. You're going to sleep. Don't worry. I haven't killed you. Your time will come. But first, I'm going to get some answers when we get back. Have a nice snooze."

She watched clinically as his mouth hung open and he crumpled slowly to the floor, desperately fighting to stay conscious. It was a one-sided battle. The ampoule with the needle-like snout and soft sides that she'd emptied into him would have knocked out someone twice his size. He'd be unconscious long enough for her to get well away from the town.

"And now, Jeanne," she said to herself, "let's see just how flexible you really are."

She took off the backpack and placed it on the floor next to the body, then left the room, locking the door behind her.

"Captain."

MacAllister's glasses were back on. She approached the hotel entrance, where the captain was in subdued conversation with the manager's daughter. The girl's father did not look pleased, but was content to glower from behind the tiny reception desk.

The IFOR captain politely asked the girl to excuse him, before looking round.

"Miss Beauleon. I thought you were gone for the night."

"I couldn't sleep." She stared hard at the girl, who flounced off. "I need your help, Captain," she said quickly, in a low whisper.

"Problems with that guy?" he asked, whispering in return.

"You could say that."

"What can I do to help?"

"You need to come upstairs. Make it sound as if you want to talk to me about tomorrow's search."

His eyes searched her face. "I guess you don't want Smilin' Jack over there by that desk, and his daughter, getting the townsfolk all worked up."

"Something like that."

"Okay. I'll just tell my sergeant. Sarge!" he called loudly.

"Yo, Captain!"

"Take over. I've got to talk with Miss Beauleon about tomorrow's digging."

"Roger that, sir."

"All right, miss," the captain said, lowering his voice once more. "Let's see to this guy."

He followed MacAllister up the stairs, while the manager stared with undisguised hostility.

The girl smiled shyly at the captain, and promptly earned herself a ferocious look from her father.

"*Jesus!*" the captain said, staring at the sleeping form on the floor in Serenic's room. "What did you do? Kill him?"

"He's just asleep."

"Just . . . hey. Wait a minute." The captain was suddenly alert. "You sound different. You sound *American*.

What's going on?" His hand rested on the pistol at his hip.

"There is no time to explain," MacAllister said, speaking quickly, "and even if we did have the time, I would not be authorized to tell you . . ."

"What the hell's this?" The captain eyes were distinctly unfriendly and suddenly distant.

MacAllister went for broke. "Captain," she began in a tone that suggested she was way above him in rank, "I'm assuming you've got secure communications?"

"Sure, but what's it to you . . . ?"

"Send a message immediately. It's to go to 'Thug.' Just that one word. The message is also one word. 'Hercules.' The reply will be one word. 'Twelve.' You will receive instructions."

"I can't just . . ."

"Better do it, Captain. You can become a private real fast."

He stared at her for long moments. "This had better be good."

"Or else?"

"I'll think of something."

"Just send that message, please."

"All right, miss, whoever you are. I'll be right back."

He was gone for less than five minutes. When he re-entered the room, his attitude had changed to one of respect for a superior.

"Ah . . . I've been told to ah . . . give you what you want."

"Thank you, Captain. I had not intended to involve you."

The captain looked down at Serenic. "So who is he?"

"Sorry."

"Ah . . . yeah. Okay."

"There are four bodyguards out there," MacAllister

said. "I'll show you where they've positioned themselves. We've got to get him past them and into one of
your vehicles. You're taking it on patrol, leaving the
other to guard the hotel. I'll be coming with you, ostensibly to look at a site. You will leave the two of us out
there. Anyone watching when you return must assume
I came back with you. So stop close to the hotel to give
the impression I got out, even if no one's seen me do
so. Then you'll forget you ever saw us." She stared
hard at him. "And I never talked to you. The people
who processed your message will say the same thing, if
asked."

The captain briefly raised a hand. "Hey. I know nothing from nothing. But what about Mr. Petrus? What do
I say to him? If you're missing, he'll want a search."

"Mr. Petrus will be given an explanation, eventually,
by others."

"He won't like it."

"He doesn't have to."

"No point worrying about if you're going to be okay
with that guy," the captain commented drily, glancing
down at the deeply slumbering Serenic.

"No point at all."

"Okay, miss . . . ah . . . do I call you 'sir'?"

"'Miss' is okay."

"Sure." The captain glanced about the room. "Some
place."

"He called it his special room," she said distastefully.
"I hate to think what he did in here."

"I can guess," the captain remarked drily.

In the end, it was a lot easier than expected.

The captain went down to the square and said loudly,
"Munro, you can draw, can't you?"

"I can join lines, sir," replied the laid-back soldier modestly. He was an art student who had joined the army to record conflict. He hoped to publish a portfolio one day.

"Over here, Munro. I want you to draw a site plan for Miss Beauleon."

"Isn't that for her own team to do, sir?"

"You arguing with me, Munro?"

"No, sir!"

"Then get your butt in here."

"Sir."

The captain took Munro to Serenic's room, where MacAllister was waiting.

"Oh shit," Munro said when he saw Serenic on the floor. "Sir, we got a problem."

"Thank you for that observation, Munro, but we got there before you."

"Sir."

"Now get out of your gear."

"Sir!" Munro stared at his captain. "If the Captain doesn't mind, *sir!*"

"The captain minds. Off!"

"The lady, sir!"

"The lady will turn round, if you feel so shy."

Hiding a smile, MacAllister turned her back on Munro.

"Now hurry it, Munro," the captain ordered. "Your clothes are going on him."

"On a *stiff*, sir? *My gear?*" Munro was aghast. "They won't fit," he added, in a last-ditch attempt to avoid the inevitable.

"Quit stalling, soldier. He's not dead. He's close to your size. That's why I picked you. Now c'mon. We don't have all night."

Munro reluctantly began to remove his combat gear.

They undressed Serenic, then re-clothed him in Munro's.

"Now what do I do?" Munro asked reasonably.

"You wait till we get back. You don't move out of this room."

"Do I have to wear this outfit again, sir? After *he's* been in them?"

"Do I look like I carry a supply store with me, Munro? Of course you wear them."

"I keep my gun."

"You keep your weapon. Any more questions?"

"No, sir," Munro replied miserably. "The guys will give me hell when they find out."

"You'll say nothing to anyone, soldier," the captain ordered sharply, "unless you hear differently from me, or a superior. You got that?"

"Yessir."

Then there was a knock on the door.

Both the captain's and Munro's eyes widened when they saw MacAllister pull the big automatic out of a pocket. She flattened herself against a wall near the door and held the gun ready, muzzle pointing upwards. She indicated with a hand that they should take up alert positions, then raised a finger to her lips.

They moved swiftly, a barefoot Munro pinching out his underwear to indicate his embarrassment. The captain waved a censorious hand at him, then nodded to MacAllister.

The knock came again.

A few moments of silence, then, "This is Petrus. Jeanne! Are you in there?"

They looked at each other, then the soldiers focused on Mac. Your play, the eyes were saying.

She reached a swift decision. She yanked the door

open, hauled a startled Petrus inside, then shut the door quickly and softly.

Petrus saw the soldiers, the guns, the comatose Serenic, and turned shocked eyes upon MacAllister.

"I went down to see that you were all right," he began in a numbed voice. The words seemed to be tumbling out of their own accord. "You . . . you were not there and neither was this man . . ." He pointed at Serenic without looking. "The girl told me you were up here with the captain, but that you had also gone up with him." Petrus jerked a finger at the man on the floor. "She seemed to think you were . . ." He paused. "I wondered if you were okay." He stared at her gun. "But now . . . What are you doing with a gun, Jeanne? Did this man attack you?" Then he looked at Serenic, in the IFOR combat gear, then at Munro, and finally gave up. "Perhaps one of you should tell me what is going on."

"I'm sorry you had to see this, Hendrik . . ."

"Your accent! It is now American! What . . ."

"No time to explain. All I can tell you . . ." She paused, thinking how best she could explain the unexplainable to this modest and good man. "What I am doing here is worthwhile. It will make up for the terrible things you have seen."

Petrus said nothing for long, tense moments. They all stared at him, waiting.

"It will look better if two men took this . . . drunken soldier downstairs," he said at last, indicating Serenic. He glanced at Munro. "*He* can't do it in his underpants."

They all heaved a sigh of relief.

MacAllister smiled at Petrus, and gave him a quick kiss on the cheek. "Thank you, Hendrik. And thanks for coming to find me, even if I wished you hadn't."

"You can't put back the clock."

"No."

"Then please, do this well," he told her seriously.

"I will," she promised.

"Okay. Let us get this man out of here before that inquisitive girl, or her miserable father, comes to check."

Mac shoved Serenic's clothes into her backpack, then slung it back on. Petrus and the captain heaved Serenic up between them. Munro clamped his helmet onto Serenic's head, tilting it so that the face was mainly hidden. With the head slumped in supposed drunkeness, or illness, only a very close inspection would betray them.

"Don't get blood on my clothes," Munro said to no one in particular.

"There's not going to be any blood, Munro," Mac said.

"Okay. Just checking."

"Munro," the captain said.

"Sir?"

"Close it."

"Sir."

"All right, miss," the captain said to MacAllister. "Your game. We're as ready as we'll ever be."

She nodded, and opened the door.

November base, that same evening, 2130 hours.

Caroline Hamilton-Jones was carrying out a ground-controlled approach, in the standard ASV of Zero-Two squadron. This was her second flight and the GCA was part of a series of approach tests selected by Helm, who was again occupying the backseat.

The procedure had begun with an overhead approach, which required her to make her initial call above the approach radar cover. Contact and identification had been established, and the approach director had taken over as she'd descended into the radar cover. She was now into the training circuit, having requested a monitored approach, and was coming in at low level, on the downwind leg. She turned onto the base leg at ten miles from the runway threshold and began the last part of her descent as she curved onto the final leg.

"Roger, Turtle Dove," the controller was saying, "you are at ten miles. Maintain descent."

She held the stick in a relaxed grip, left hand on the throttles. She checked her angle of attack, checked that her wings were at twenty-five degrees full spread. Everything was okay. The aircraft flew steadily; descent nicely controlled.

In the backseat, Helm monitored her progress but remained silent, letting her get on with it.

"Seven miles," came the controller's voice. "On the centerline, on the glidepath. Maintain. Four-point-five miles. Check gear."

She glanced to her left, at the gear warning lights. Three greens.

"Gear down, and locked," she acknowledged.

She flew the ASV unerringly towards the runway.

"Two miles," said the controller. As the two-mile range was passed, the controller went on, calling out the range every quarter mile. "On the centerline, on the glidepath. One-point-seven-five miles. One-point-five miles. One-point-two-five miles. One mile. Point-seven-five miles. Point-five. Decision altitude."

And when Caroline had given no indication of any intention to carry out a missed approach and thus go round once more, the controller continued, "Point-two five miles . . ."

She brought the nose up slightly as the ASV crossed the runway threshold. The touchdown was smooth. The nose came down. The thrust-reversers, already primed, clamped themselves over the nozzles. The engines roared thunderously as she briefly pushed the throttles forward. The aircraft decelerated dramatically. She trod hard on the toe-brakes, then brought the throttles back, rocking them inwards to de-select the reversers.

She eased off the brakes and began to taxi off the runway.

"That," Helm began, deciding to speak at last, "was a perfect touchdown. I hope the boss was watching. He will be impressed. I am."

Her mask moved infinitesimally as she permitted herself a tiny smile of satisfaction.

While Caroline was taxiing back to her designated hardened aircraft shelter, Hohendorf and Selby were making phone calls from two of the four enclosed, soundproofed booths in Mess. The special briefing had just ended. They'd been informed that a coded message had been received, and that takeoff for Italy was within two hours. There would be a rendezvous with a tanker, en route.

Hohendorf was on the line to Morven Selby's number in Aberdeen. The phone had barely rung twice before she picked it up.

"This is Morven."

"And how is my marine biologist?"

"Hullo, darling."

Her voice had gone from polite friendliness to several degrees of warmth in an instant. Just hearing her speak sent a thrill of pleasure through him.

He shut his eyes briefly, to bring an image of her into his mind. He chose his favorite. He'd once caught her unawares, standing naked before a full-length mirror, stretching on tip-toe as she tried to find some non-existent trace of fat on her stomach. The fact that he was always telling her he loved her just as she was, while pleasing her enormously, did not prevent this periodic inspection.

It had been the first time he'd caught her in that

pose. He'd been driven crazy with desire as he'd looked on. The twin indentations behind each of her knees and just above the rising curve of each calf; the glorious swelling of her thighs as they rose to her buttocks; the stretching of her calves; all these things about her were, to him, pulse-pounding turn-ons. He had stood there savoring the view, until she'd spotted his reflection in the mirror. She had looked for something to throw at him, and had grabbed at a pillow; but he'd reached her before she could even raise it.

She had squealed with delight and mock fear as he'd got hold of her, turning her round to press her body against his. Feeling the heat of her body, the smoothness of her skin, the soft flattening of her breasts against his chest, had driven his desire to even greater heights on an afternoon made sullen by heavy rain. Their bodies had collapsed onto the bed even as he was entering her, forcing a shuddering sigh out of her slightly opened mouth. They hadn't made it off the bed for a long time afterwards, lost in their own erotic world, as outside, the rain had pounded itself into a fury against the windows.

From then on, and at every available opportunity, she would display the back of her legs to him, rising on her toes to enhance this. Each time, it had the desired effect.

"I like the sound of heavy rain," he now told her.

"Just a minute," she said. "I'm changing phones." A short while later, she was back on. "I'm in the bedroom. There's no rain down here," she continued, "but guess what I'm doing."

The suggestion in her voice was unmistakable and he felt the sudden, electrifying charge go through him.

"This is torture!" he protested.

"I'm in front of the mirror, and I'm taking off all my clothes . . . slowly."

"Aaah!"

"That's a strange sound. Of course, you'll be quite uncontrollable by the time I see you. You know how I like that." Her voice had now gone several frequencies lower. "Tomorrow? As we arranged?"

"No . . ." he said gently.

They had planned to spend some days together, and had it not been for the mission, he'd have been making his way to Aberdeen in the morning. She did not demand to know the reason for this sudden change, though it must have caused her severe disappointment. It was one of the many things he loved so much about her. She never questioned nor complained, having the intelligence, and the trust in him, to understand that only a mission of some importance would cause him to alter their plans so abruptly. He knew, however, this would then cause her to worry for his safety. If her brother Mark had also become unavailable, she would put it all together and understand the sensitivity of whatever they were engaged upon.

Then she'd worry about both of them.

But she would never ask for any details, now would she ever voice her fears over the phone.

How very different, Hohendorf had very early come to realize, from the attitude of the estranged wife who had walked out on him, long before he'd been selected for the November program.

The devastatingly elegant and blond Anne-Marie, Gräfin von Ettlingen und Hohendorf who, before marriage, was a von Ettlingen and a countess in her own right, had not taken at all well to being a service wife. She would have complained bitterly about his frequent selection for such missions.

Upon marrying Hohendorf, the initial thrill of capturing the fighter pilot, who had looked so dashing in his full ceremonial dress, had soon waned. Anne-Marie had declared that the service wives in their immediate circle were ennervatingly boring and had almost immediately begun to try and persuade Hohendorf to leave the *Marineflieger*. She had wanted him to join her father's highly successful domestic airline as its vice-president and senior pilot. The job, specially created for him, had virtually been waiting for his acquiescence.

He had refused, shocking both his wife and her father.

He was a fighter pilot. It was what he wanted to do, and she'd known that when she had married him. It was what had attracted her in the first place. There had never been any plans to switch professions. There had been no indication that this would happen. It had never been on the agenda; but the woman who had been the picture of excitement on their wedding day had begun to change. Then Hohendorf had swiftly come to realize that it was the *idea* that had excited her, not the reality. She'd got her fighter pilot, but she didn't want to be a fighter pilot's wife.

Before long, she had commenced taking long absences from the marital home to spend time at Schloss Drakenflüss, as they privately called the Ettlingen family castle, in Bavaria. These absences had inevitably culminated in an on-going affair with the airline's chief pilot, Gerhard Linden.

Then she'd walked out.

Hohendorf's great good fortune at finding Morven, when he'd come to November One, had suddenly rekindled Anne-Marie's ardor for the husband she'd once betrayed. It was Gerhard Linden, airline pilot, who had now become boring.

Anne-Marie had since put in unexpected and unwelcome appearances, usually when Hohendorf was accompanied by Morven. She had even once turned up at the gates of November One, demanding to see her husband. To limit his embarrassment, he'd been forced to meet her outside the perimeter and, after angry exchanges in her car, had persuaded her to leave.

Morven had been his salvation, Hohendorf knew, and he treasured her, notwithstanding her brother's continuing antipathy towards the relationship. Selby's ostensible reason was that he did not like the idea of his only sister being a married man's lover, despite the fact that Hohendorf was clearly deeply in love with Morven and had no intention of ever returning to Anne-Marie. Hohendorf, for his part, harbored the nagging suspicion that Selby's *real* reason was the fact that he was German. Selby would never admit to it, he well knew—even if asked directly—and would almost certainly appear to be horrified by the question. But the suspicion remained in Hohendorf's mind.

People who didn't know Morven at all well tended to call her untamed. While there was definitely an undercurrent of controlled wildness hidden deep within her, there was no overt sign of this; but it was one of the things about her which called so strongly to him.

She was disciplined and very clever, and understood the goals she had set herself. The wildness could indeed, sometimes, be seen in her eyes; but mostly during the most intimate of times, and was a look which he felt himself privileged to be able to observe.

The body that constantly drove him wild was sensuously curved, but fit and strong. The nature of her job showed in her physique. An expert diver, she had promised to teach him the finer points of using scuba gear, so that they would one day make love deep underwater.

"In a *wetsuit?*" he'd asked.

"I've found a cave," she'd replied. "No one else, as far as I know, is aware of it. It's deep down, but there's a ledge that's out of the water, and there's plenty of air. Plenty of room on the ledge too. The wetsuits and the equipment can come off. I want to be really, really loud." She'd grinned wickedly at him, then had slowly and unconsciously licked at her lips.

She'd not yet told him the location of the cave. Thus, their subaqua, subterranean bout of lovemaking was a feast to be looked forward to, with great anticipation.

The difference between her and Anne-Marie could not have been greater. Though at nearly five-foot-nine she was almost as tall, her more solid frame appeared shorter than Anne-Marie's slimmer, fashion-model shape.

Morven's hair was dark and lustrous, falling thickly past her shoulders like a rich, gleaming curtain. Her eyes, a vivid, luminous green topped with thick, dark eyebrows, were in sharp contrast to Anne-Marie's of diamond-bright blue. She possessed a heart-shaped face with a firm chin and a high, curving forehead. Her nose was strong; yet amidst all those strong features, her mouth was soft and vulnerable to look at. By comparison, Anne-Marie's patrician features carried a distinct hauteur when she looked upon anyone she considered rather less than herself, which was pretty close to being the rest of the world. She had once, with deliberate and malicious unfairness, described Morven to Hohendorf as a fat peasant girl.

When Morven smiled, light seemed to shine from the very depths of those vivid eyes. Hohendorf had looked into them, and was now lost forever. Anne-Marie knew this, and couldn't stand the thought of being vanquished by someone she openly considered her social inferior.

"We'll fix another time," Morven was now saying.

"Yes," he said.

They hung on to their phones, their mutual silence saying much more than any words they might have spoken.

"I love you," she said at last.

"And I love you."

They hung up slowly, together.

In his booth, Selby was coming to the end of his conversation with Kim Mannon, who was at the Chelsea flat in London. Like Morven, she had not asked him questions he could not, for reasons of security, have answered.

"I'll be up in Scotland next week," she said. "I'm having a dinner party. Friday. Can you make it to Princes Street?"

"I'll be there." He'd been to the big Edinburgh house on many occasions. "Who's coming?"

"You," she replied, with additional meaning.

"What's on the menu?"

"Me. Knickers are off."

"Sounds like my favorite kind of dinner party."

"I know," she said and hung up.

He stared at the phone for some moments. It had been her way of letting him know she was worried about him.

The smoldering beauty of her small, neat body had ensnared him as completely as his own sister's had entranced Hohendorf. Though when thinking of his German colleague, he hated to admit that.

He felt for the pocket in his flying overalls where he kept Kim's red knickers and stepped out of the booth, a reflective smile on his face.

And saw Hohendorf.

The booths were arranged along one wall. Each had entered the outer cubicle at different times, and had thus been unaware of the other's presence.

"Hullo, Axel," Selby began pleasantly. He nodded in the direction of the booth Hohendorf had been using. "Morven?"

"Yes."

"She make a fuss?"

Hohendorf shook his head. "You know how she is. She would never do that."

"No. She wouldn't. Same with Kim."

"They are good women, and we are very lucky men."

"I suppose we are," Selby agreed cautiously.

Ever since Jason had hauled him over hot coals for his attitude regarding the subject of Hohendorf and Morven, he had made a supreme effort to control his feelings. While he would certainly never knowingly jeopardize Hohendorf's life in the air, nor that of any other member of the unit for that matter, he had also greatly improved his reaction to the affair when on the ground. In addition to Jason, he also had Morven herself to contend with. She had warned him in no uncertain terms that if he ever forced her to choose between Hohendorf and himself, he would lose. He had taken that warning seriously to heart. Kim Mannon had also gone to work on him.

The changes these various influences had wrought had prevented him from blaming Hohendorf for what had happened to McCann. The old Selby, despite having a great respect for Hohendorf's astonishing air combat skills, would have seized the opportunity to discredit his colleague, so great had been his hostility.

Among their other differences, there was a telling physical one between the blond German and the dark-haired Englishman. Compact of frame, Selby was just under six feet tall. His closely trimmed hair seemed of the right cut to set off a squarish face, whose design appeared to have been halted just before it had become too exaggerated. The well-defined jawline had been pushed to the limits but again and just in time, had been saved from over-prominence. This all helped to give his features a precision that was neatly complemented by piercing, but distant, blue eyes.

A neatly barbered, thinnish moustache sat on his upper lip. His strong hands were broad in a manner that would have had Anne-Marie contemptuously describing them as peasant-like. But those very hands could fly the complex, high-tech Tornado ASV Echo with all the exactitude of a master surgeon and the delicacy of a loving caress. It was this superb talent that had made him, with Hohendorf, one of the two top combat pilots of the unit.

"One day," Hohendorf was saying, "I will be your brother-in-law."

Selby stared at him. "If your wife ever agrees to a divorce."

"Soon, she will not have a choice in the matter. I will initiate the action. She will not fight it, unless she wants to be publicly embarrassed."

"And what about Morven? Won't your wife drag her into it? I don't want this for my sister." Knowing about Anne-Marie's momentous visit to the base, Selby had no doubt she would use every dirty trick in the book.

"Morven will not be brought into it. I will *not* allow it. Do not forget, my wife betrayed me long before I was ever selected to come here. I did not even know of Morven's existence. I will make very sure she is not hurt, or brought into the action. If you think you know anything about me, believe this."

Despite himself, Selby had to agree. He nodded

slowly. "If you pull it off, I'll wish you both the best. I know I've been rough on you in the past, to the point of coming close to being dangerous to myself, and others, in the air. I don't know if I will ever completely lose my . . . uncertainty about this. I just didn't want my sister to be a married man's plaything . . ."

"*No, no!* She was never a plaything . . . !"

"Calm down, Axel. I'm not saying you treated her like that. What I'm doing a rather bad job of getting across is that despite my own reservations, if you manage it, good luck to you both. Although," Selby added, "given the way marriages are crashing and burning these days like kites with double flame-outs, you'll probably need all the luck you can get."

˙ Hohendorf gave a brief, rueful smile. "And despite that caveat, I shall take this as a form of acceptance. Thank you."

"Don't mention it, old boy. Now let's go and see what our backseaters are up to."

Bosnia, a mountain road, ten kilometers west of the town.

It was 2300 hours local time when the humvee stopped at the side of the road. It was fully dark on the ground, with only the barest hint of gray still in the sky to show that twilight was not long gone. A waning moon hung palely over the mountains.

Mac climbed out of the front of the vehicle. The captain and Petrus got out of the back. Petrus had insisted on coming, declaring it would look more natural if he accompanied her on her supposed search. It also meant his backpack would be available for the return of Munro's clothes.

Getting Serenic down from the room and into the humvee had gone off smoothly. The captain had pretended to be railing against Munro for being drunk on duty.

"Dammit, Munro!" he'd said loudly as they had passed both the girl and her sour-faced father. "I've warned you about carrying liquor in your water bottle! Your butt's in the sling for this. You're on report!"

The sergeant had approached as they'd been shoving Serenic into the humvee.

"Help me here with Munro, Sergeant," the captain had ordered.

"Yes, sir!" the puzzled senior NCO had responded, moving closer. He had put a hand on Serenic's shoulder, just as the helmet had moved slightly. "That's not . . ."

"Just do it!" the captain had whispered sharply. "I'll explain later."

"Sir!" the sergeant had whispered back quickly in a voice full of uncertainty as he'd glanced at both Mac and Petrus.

The captain had once again left him in charge in the town. Now Petrus and the IFOR soldier began to haul the still-unconscious Serenic out of the vehicle. During the journey, the two men had changed Serenic back into his own clothes by the light of the humvee crew's low-light torches. They had also applied camouflage stain to Serenic's attire.

"He's sure not going to like what we've done to his fancy clothes," the captain now said with dry humor.

"There's plenty he's not going to like," MacAllister told him grimly. "This is only the beginning."

"You will be all right?" Petrus asked worriedly. He was still seeing her as Jeanne Beauleon. "This man . . ."

"He has more to fear from me," she told Petrus gently.

Still confused by the change in her, he said, "You are so different . . ."

"I always was."

"I guess you don't need me to tell you to be careful," the captain said.

"No. But thanks for the thought."

"Your pack's got some supplies," he went on gruffly, "and there's a second one for . . ." he glanced to where Serenic lay in the gloom, ". . . him to carry. You'll also need these." He thrust two guns into her hands. "Never can have too many." One was another automatic to go with the one she already possessed. The other was a cut-down M16 with a grenade launcher attached. It also had an infrared scope. "His pack's got the food. You've got the ammo."

She shook his hand. "Thanks for all the help, Captain."

"I guess I'll never know your real name."

"I'm afraid not." MacAllister turned to Petrus. "Hendrik. Keep digging. People must never forget what was done to this country."

He gave her an impulsive hug. "I'll make sure. You watch that snake you are traveling with."

"As I've said . . . *he'll* have to watch *me*. I kill snakes before they strike. Thank you, gentlemen," she added to the humvee's crew.

"Sir," they acknowledged. Like soldiers everywhere, they knew when not to be too curious.

"Captain . . ." she began, to their commander.

"They know," he said. "They saw nothing."

"Thank you," she repeated. "Now you'd better get back while I wait for the baby to wake up. He's got a tough time ahead of him."

She stood in the gloom by the side of the mountain

road, her night-accustomed eyes watching as their silhouettes climbed back aboard the vehicle. She put a hand across her eyes as the humvee switched on its lights and began to cautiously turn around, in order to head back the way it had come. It crunched through undergrowth as it did so until, eventually, it was pointing away from her. The lights blinked once in farewell, then it made its way back towards the town. Soon, she was standing by herself in the dark and the silence of the night, with the unconscious Serenic for company.

Presently, the night-time creatures, once again confident now that the noise of the intruders had faded, resumed their foraging. She listened to them and waited for Serenic to wake up. She hoped this would not take too long. They had to be on their way before the girl in the hotel took it into her head to go into Serenic's room for her usual frolic and raise the alarm when she saw who was waiting in there.

She hoped Munro was up to the situation if he got a further surprise. At least it would be a relatively more pleasant one.

"Hope you're up to it, Munro," MacAllister said into the night with some humor.

At that moment, Serenic groaned.

"Ah," she said. "The babe awakes."

She cocked the rifle and move back out of his reach.

High above the Alps, 0100 hours.

Hohendorf listened to the subdued noises of the ASV Echo as they cruised at fifty thousand feet. It never ceased to amaze him just how many of these different, subtle noises there were in the jet, all vying for attention. Even his breathing, as he inhaled the life-sustaining oxygen, was part of this airborne orchestra. He looked out upon his high domain and loved it all.

In the clear air the moon shone palely, bringing a bright twilight to the scene. He looked about him and could clearly see the other four aircraft. The five ASVs were transiting, with four in a close double-pair combat formation and the fifth—Morton's aircraft—staggered slightly to the left, behind the lead pair.

Hohendorf had the lead, with the Double-C on his wing. Selby led the second pair, with Bagni as his wingman. Callsign was Tasker; Hohendorf's aircraft, Tasker Zero-One. The others followed in order.

"Waypoint Delta," came Flacht's voice, "five miles. Waypoint Echo five-two miles, one-five-four."

"Roger," Hohendorf confirmed as Flacht copied the new nav display to the front cockpit.

He banked smoothly to the right onto the new heading as Waypoint Delta was passed and the display changed accordingly. Waypoint Echo glowed brightly, signifying it was now the active heading.

The other aircraft followed suit with precision, as if attached to Tasker Zero-One by lengths of rope.

Hohendorf settled on the new course and listened to his airplane.

Moscow, 0300 hours.

The knock came briskly on the door to Kurinin's office. Though he had a small bedroom attached, he was currently at his desk.

"Come!"

Levchuk entered, still looking as smartly turned out as ever. He carried the inevitable folder under an arm.

"Do you ever sleep, Gregor?" Kurinin demanded, looking up from the papers he'd been dealing with.

"Do you?" Levchuk countered.

The general gave a reflective smile that vanished almost as soon as it had appeared. "The barbarians are not only at the gate, they're inside. A guardian must be even more alert."

"Then a guardian needs a deputy to watch with him through the dark and hostile hours."

"I hope the nation will one day understand what we're doing," Kurinin said.

"And how many people in history have had those same thoughts? Or spoken those same words?"

"Too many," Kurinin replied with a sigh. "And frequently, the nation did not understand, forcing the need for extreme measures, before stability could be resumed."

Levchuk passed him the folder. "We may have something. Yesterday evening, a burst of randomly encrypted code went from Bosnia to London and Washington. It was very short, possibly one word, between four and twelve letters long. *Each* letter appears to have been encrypted, hence the uncertainty of the actual word itself. The addressee was also one word. The reply, again one word. At first, we wondered whether the three words were not in themselves all part of the message . . ."

Kurinin had been studying the report as Levchuk spoke. "And?" He did not look up.

"We can't be sure. We don't know what the words are. I doubt that we could break the encryption in time, if at all. But we do know where the first message originated. One of our Bosnian listening posts identified it as a field vehicle, located in this mountain town." Levchuk leaned across, to briefly place a forefinger beneath a name in the report. "One of the burial teams is currently based there."

"And you believe *she* may be with them?"

"Why else would such a high priority message come from such an insignificant little place and go not to IFOR Headquarters to be dealt with, but to the Pentagon, *and* London? And there's more."

"There's more?"

"Next page," Levchuk said. He waited for Kurinin to read what had been set down.

"'Copied to Scotland,'" Kurinin read softly. He looked up. "That could only mean our friends on the Moray coast."

"My considered opinion, General."

"But how are they planning to act upon it?" Kurinin was almost talking to himself. "If she *is* there, I'm assuming she has gone in for a specific reason, and she has now completed that task. It must be of great importance, or she would not have risked a return to this theater. But why that town in particular? The message also has to mean she is now on her way out. So what was she doing out there?"

"Next page," Levchuk suggested and waited for the general to study it.

Kurinin stiffened as he read, then slowly closed the thin file when he'd finished. He looked up at Levchuk, who had remained standing.

"You are absolutely sure of this?"

"Our information suggests that's what she is there for."

"To capture the leader of the Black Lynxes, and take him to the West?"

"Not capture, General. He is giving himself up."

"Giving himself up? *Surrendering?*"

"The information is quite specific. Its source is on the last page."

Kurinin re-opened the file and read the last page. He made no comment about the source, but his expression showed he believed it.

"In return for a vast sum of capitalist dollars, for the betrayal of his friends, no doubt," he now said, mouth turned down in distaste. "Do not misunderstand me. I have no love for that animal and others like him out there; but it is despicable that a commander can be bought like that."

"Most people have a price."

"No one can pay ours," Kurinin said. His eyes held Levchuk's. "At least, I sincerely hope so."

"No one can pay mine, General," Levchuk said calmly. His eyes did not waver.

Kurinin broke into a tension-relieving smile. "Which is what I would expect of you, Gregor. Now we must move quickly before that woman escapes," he went on briskly. "The Black Lynxes would be most annoyed to hear of their commander's betrayal, don't you think?"

"They most certainly would. We have some influence with the deputy commander. I am certain we can motivate him to give chase."

"I agree. Our friends at that special NATO unit will, of course, give her cover while she's being pulled out. That means a transport aircraft of some kind; fixed-wing, or helicopter. It will naturally require an escort."

"Naturally."

Kurinin nodded thoughtfully. "So let us cover our bets. Send word to Lieutenant-Colonel Asnayev. He is to mount combat air patrols with his 'goodwill' Su-27Ks, near the border closest to this town. The transport aircraft and its escort will be in his area soon. These patrols should commence at first light after receiving the signal. If they find that transport, it must be destroyed. Send that immediately."

Levchuk raised an eyebrow.

"Don't worry, Gregor," Kurinin said. "Our Western friends will not make a fuss. Their mission is as clandestine as ours. It will not have happened. We *must* have that woman, and spoil their game into the bargain. If she's not caught on the ground, her flight out must *not* make it back. Go on. Get those signals off, Gregor."

"On my way," Levchuk said.

When he'd returned to his own office, Levchuk did a curious thing. He drafted the necessary signals, sent them to be encrypted, but had them routed in such a way that there would be a substantial delay before they reached their respective destinations. The route he used would not be subsequently questioned, as it was one that was normally utilized for enhanced security. But he had shortcuts at his disposal.

He had chosen not to use them.

12

The Bosnian mountains, 0500 hours.

Serenic's groan had been a false alarm. He had not come out his drugged sleep and MacAllister had been compelled to drag him into the undergrowth, to await his eventual return to consciousness.

But she had not wasted the time. She had checked every weapon, even in the dark—as she had long been trained to do—and her supply of ammunition. There were enough 40mm grenades for the launcher. The captain, she noted with satisfaction, had given her a mix of rounds: some phosphorous, some smoke, but most were high explosive. He had also given her a pair of powerful day/night vision binoculars.

There was also plenty of ammo for the two automatic pistols and the M16. She was an arsenal on legs, she thought with grim humor.

"Bless you, Captain," she murmured gratefully.

She also had Serenic's pistol; but that was precious evidence, which was being taken back with her so that it could be put through stringent forensic tests. She had no doubt at all that quite a few bodies would turn up all over Bosnia with bullets from that gun. It was safely hidden in her backpack.

The automatics were now in shoulder holsters. Two ammo hip belts with pouches crossed her waist. They held a mixture of magazines and grenades. The cut-down rifle/launcher with its folding stock—now extended—was secured by its sling, across her body. Her big knife was in its sheath, strapped to her upper thigh. She had also checked the pack already strapped to Serenic's back. There was more than enough food and water to last till the pick-up and beyond; but she hoped to be out of Bosnia long before that. Not having to forage would save valuable time.

She was sitting on the ground with her back against a tree and well in cover, waiting for Serenic to come awake. The rifle was held across her chest, ready for action.

It was precisely 0510 hours when he at last opened his eyes. He found MacAllister's cold gaze fixed upon him, and noted in the early light how she was dressed. He took a hard look at the weapons.

"What . . ." he began hoarsely. He licked his lips. "What did you put into me?"

"You're not dead. That's all you need to know."

He'd been lying on his side and now tried to get up, eventually realizing he was attached to something.

"There's something on my back!" He inspected himself as he rose groggily to a sitting position. "My clothes! *What have you done to my clothes?*"

"Dirty clothes are the least of your problems. Now

you're awake, *on your feet!* Too much time has already been wasted." MacAllister glanced upwards. "It was not my plan to travel in daylight, but your little snooze leaves us no choice. Your tolerance is weak. The shot I gave you would only have put me out for three hours or so, which is what I expected of you. You've been down for *seven.* You've clearly not been leading a healthy life, Serenic. Now come on. On those feet! We've got a lot of time to make up, and you're about to make the forced march of your life. Many of your victims must have been made to do it. Now you can share the experience."

"I'm thirsty!" Serenic protested.

"I wonder how many people have said that to you in the past, and how many you actually gave water to, instead of a bullet."

"You cannot treat me like this!" Serenic objected arrogantly. "I told you I am worth plenty of money to some powerful people. They will not be happy if . . ."

"They're not here. I am. So you'd just better do as I say. I *can* make you walk. I've got something else in my pack, which if administered causes intense pain unless you use your muscles. In this case, those in your legs. Walking helps to dissipate the effect. You can only rest when it's gone completely. How long it takes depends on your physical condition. To judge by your recent experience, that could take a long, long time."

"This is torture!"

"Of course it is. But I won't feel a thing. I promise you."

For the first time, real hatred sparked in Serenic's eyes. This was no longer a woman to be chased and made to yield to his advances. This was an adversary; an enemy.

He smiled. "You will not always have it your own way. I will get my chance."

"Hell will freeze over first." She indicated with the rifle that he should get to his feet. "Start walking, damn you! Or I use that fucking needle. I'm not bluffing."

Serenic got to his feet.

Lieutenant-Colonel Ilnukahmed Ilnukahmedovich Asnayev was an unusual commander to be in charge of the six spanking new Su-27K Flankers on the "goodwill" visit; unusual in that he was a Kazakh and all his pilots were Russian.

But Asnayev was an unusual man. Far from being a supporter of Kazakh independence, he was a fervent believer in the Soviet system, and could barely wait for its eventual return, which, he was positive, was inevitable. The evidence was all around. The nation was spiraling into chaos. Only firm control could halt this decline and bring it back to the world stage—feared and respected—as was its proper position.

The West not only had worked assiduously to destabilize the Soviet state and finally destroy it; but it was now actively seeking to make Russia its vassal. Asnayev firmly believed that this should be resisted on all fronts and at all times, with force, if necessary. He had therefore looked forward immensely to leading his flight of potent fighters this far west.

When he had first received indications that there might also be some action, he had barely been able to contain his excitement; but he'd successfully hidden it behind the impassive expression that he habitually showed the world.

Asnayev's pilots greatly respected him, despite the

fact that he was not an ethnic Russian. Though they were an elite group, none were as good as he, and they knew it. They obeyed him without hesitation. They trusted his expertise and his instincts in the air. He had served with friendly air forces round the globe and legend had it that he had a personal kill tally of thirty-five. Many pilots had met an untimely death at his hands, without realizing that the man flying the aircraft that had killed them had not been a citizen of the country to which it had belonged.

His aircrew looked upon him both as sound politically and as a fighter pilot. He was a small, neat man; but to his pilots, he was a colossus.

"Can we stop now?"

"No. Move it."

"It is nearly mid-day! We have been walking for over six hours!"

"Stop whining. We've got a long way to go."

She was taking a random zig-zag route, using all available cover, to throw off any intended pursuit. This meant a greater distance to the pick-up point; but it was also safer. Six hours without hostile contact was a bonus to be cherished.

It was also a bonus that the Black Lynxes had no aircraft at their disposal, in order to carry out an aerial search; but even if they did have spotter planes, they would need to brave the NATO no-fly cover to get through. Spotter aircraft were therefore not a worry. The real problem was whether there were teams of Lynxes already in the mountains who could be reached by radio.

"My legs feel strange," Serenic muttered, as he trudged on ahead of her.

"For a man who brought so much terror to so many people," MacAllister said with contempt, "you're not very strong, are you? But that's par for the course. Bullies are always weak."

"I am not weak," Serenic retorted, pride wounded. "You pumped me full of that stuff. It is still affecting me. It makes me thirsty. I need a rest, or you'll be taking a corpse to London."

"That's okay by me," she said unfeelingly. "Keep going."

"You're a ball-breaking bitch!" he screamed at her suddenly. He stopped and turned round, dark eyes glaring.

"I've been called that before. It's not news." The rifle pointed unerringly at him. "I will shoot you, if you don't move. Not to kill. Not just yet, anyway. And you'll still have to walk. Your choice."

He continued to glare at her, but he was already backing down. "You will not be so sure of yourself," he snarled, an angry rictus of a smile distorting his features, "when the Lynxes catch up with you." He turned round and continued walking. "There are teams of them in these mountains."

"I thought there might be. But I have this feeling you would not like that to happen. They will surely not greet you with brotherly love."

"I will say you kidnapped me. You have the guns. They will believe *me*, not you. Remember, my body-guards saw me talking with you."

"Do you seriously believe that the people who arranged this little ballgame did not take out insurance? I would be very surprised if someone has not already whispered to your ex-comrades. Perhaps to one with a grudge, who would like to take over from you. It's a classic move."

An abrupt silence from Serenic indicated he had given that possibility some serious thought.

"I also had the feeling you might agree with my prognosis," MacAllister remarked drily.

Serenic said nothing and kept walking.

"Nobody loves you, when you're down and out," Mac said.

She smiled thinly as Serenic walked on ahead of her, back stiff with anger.

She called a halt two hours later.

Serenic greeted this with a relieved expression, though he would not admit to it. Keeping up with her had now become a matter of what honor he still possessed. During the two hours, he had not once complained. The effects of the drug had clearly at last worn off, for though he was obviously tired, his strides had become more purposeful.

They had made no contact with anyone. This, MacAllister decided, was either due to the fact that none of the Black Lynx teams were in their immediate area or that the alarm had not yet been given. She wondered why.

Unless a pursuit team was even now already on its way.

"Take off your pack," she commanded as they sat down near the bank of a small stream. "We'll have some cold rations."

They were on high ground, and there was plenty of cover. From their vantage point, they had a clear view of the terrain that any approaching pursuer would have to use. Behind them was an almost perpendicular rock face. There was a small cave in it, through which they had come, which was their fast exit back to the other side, should any of the Lynxes turn up at the front door. Mindful that others could also follow them in,

MacAllister had laid a booby trap at the far entrance. Anyone coming through there would get a very nasty explosive surprise.

Serenic had removed the backpack and had put his water bottle into the stream. He then drank out of it sparingly, before topping it up and sealing it.

"You realize," he said to her, "I know these mountains like the back of my hand? So do my men."

"I am well aware of it. But I also have a pretty good idea of this place," she told him. "I know my way around."

"So I have noticed. You have clearly worked here in Bosnia before."

She made no comment about that.

He looked about him. "A good position, and it was clever of you to booby-trap the other entrance. But what if we are attacked from both directions? The booby trap will block our exit with a rockfall, even if you have managed to kill those trying to get in."

She said nothing, and pointed to the stream. It led away from the area, and was always in good cover. It was shallow enough to allow fording. It would also leave no tracks to be followed.

There was a supercilious smile about his lips. "You're not bad," he said.

"For a woman?"

"I did not say that."

"You didn't have to. This woman will still shoot you if she has to. Now get out those rations. Let's eat and have a rest. We're going to walk for the remainder of the day and all night, to the rendezvous. It's in friendly territory; friendly for *me*, that is. None of your posturing there."

"My men will follow. The Black Lynxes go everywhere."

"That depends on how many are still alive. And try to get it into your head they are no longer *your* men. Pickup is at 0500 hours," MacAllister went on. "The plane won't wait. If we miss it, that's it."

"Then what happens?"

"Shit does. I shoot you and make my own way out."

He paused in the act of getting a ration out of the pack and stared at her. "I do not believe you."

"Then hope we make it in time. Your life depends on it."

"All right, Serenic. Pack up. We're moving."

He'd been lying on his side facing her, eyes closed. He roused himself and began to get ready.

MacAllister had been leaning against the rockface, the rifle ready for immediate action.

"You did not sleep," he said as he stood up and slung the backpack on. "I was watching. You will be tired soon."

"In your dreams." Her own pack was already in place. "I know you were watching. You're not going to get the chance to take this rifle; so forget it. And I'm not tired. But I've rested. I can go on for days yet."

The supercilious smile twitched on briefly. "Who goes through the cave first?"

"Nobody. We're using the stream."

This clearly took him by surprise, but he was determined not to say so.

"Why bother waste time disarming the trap?" she said, knowing exactly what he'd been thinking and hoping for. "Or did you think I'd be stupid enough to go in first to neutralize it and give you a chance to get at the gun? And even if I had been that stupid, where would you go? I'm your only ticket out of here, buster."

"I would have made you tell me the way to the rendezvous. There are many ways to make a woman talk. Some are quite . . . exciting."

"You could have died trying. Now *move!*"

They set off down the stream.

They had traveled for about an hour in the shallow water, staying in the middle of the stream, when a distant ripple of explosions sounded in the mountain air.

"Ah," MacAllister said calmly. "My alarm bell."

Serenic paused and looked round at her. "You *knew* they would come!"

"If you want to cut down the opposition, you must lead them into your traps."

"You *led* them?"

"Of course. I left enough clues that any reasonably competent Boy Scout could have followed."

"Now they know where we are!"

"And here I was thinking you wanted to see your comrades again. They don't know where we are. That explosion will keep them busy for a while. They may have to dig some of their pals out. I rigged the trap so that a few would get inside the cave first. Nice touch, huh? *They're* getting buried for a change."

He stared at her. "You are *evil!*"

"A *compliment*. From you, of all people! How nice. Time to leave the water. Take the left bank. Do it. *Now.*"

"Bitch," Serenic muttered through gritted teeth.

But he obeyed.

The cave in the mountains.

Six of the pursuing party were down: three wounded outside the cave by the staggered explosions and three buried inside. The remaining six of the original twelve were unhurt.

Their leader, Milos Vanic, was one of them. He was also the Black Lynx deputy commander Levchuk and Kurinin had discussed. As MacAllister had guessed, he did have a grudge against Serenic. Serenic had once stolen a woman from him. Vanic had never forgotten the humiliation. In the mountains, such insults tended to be repaid bloodily; but while Serenic was still in command, he would not have dared move against him. All was now different, whether the information he'd received was true or not. Vanic was in a foul temper, and was not taking the sudden decimation of his pursuit group with equanimity.

"Dammit!" he said furiously, staring at his wounded men and at the effectively blocked entrance. "We'll have to go on."

"What?" one of the others exclaimed. "We can't! We've got to see to the wounded, and get the others out."

Vanic glared balefully at him. "Take a look at that entrance!" he snarled. "How long do you think it would take us to clear it? An hour? A day? *Two* days? We don't have the time! We have got to find Serenic and that woman. If they get away, he's got plenty on the whole Black Lynx force to put each of us away for the rest of our lives. It's *our* necks. Besides, maybe the others are okay in the cave. There is an exit."

"I still don't believe the commandant has betrayed us. The West has kidnapped him, and it's putting out those stories . . ."

Vanic continued to stare at the man. "Perhaps. But are you willing to gamble with your neck? You are not clean, you know, Tranovic. You're just like the rest of us . . . swimming in blood." He looked up at the high rampart of stone. "Now we're going to have to go around this damned thing. It will take a few kilometers, at least. It's almost as if we were led to this spot," he went on, his voice laced with anger. "Deliberately. I'll have to warn the second team. Let's have that radio."

"You won't get much of a transmission out of here," Tranovic commented. "Except perhaps to a snooping NATO listening post, or plane."

Vanic glared frustratedly at his comrade. "Don't get smart with me!"

But he didn't use the radio.

The Bosnian mountains, 2000 hours local.

"So far so good," MacAllister said. "Your friends appear to have come to a halt for the time being."

"Don't count your chickens . . ."

"I never do. I always expect the unexpected. I won't think we're out of this until I've delivered you. We won't necessarily be safe in the air either, even if we make the rendezvous. But don't worry, Serenic. We'll have a fighter escort."

"You see?" he began smugly. "I told you I was important. Fighter escort! They really want my information."

"Can you stop loving yourself for a few seconds?"

"Why? I know my worth."

"And *I* know it," she said grimly. "But I count your tally in dead bodies, not currency. Stop!"

He kept moving.

"Stop, dammit!"

He stopped and turned slowly, the supercilious smile getting ready to be switched on. Then he saw her expression. She was tense and alert, and unmoving.

"What?" he began nervously. "What do you hear?"

"I didn't hear anything. I *saw*. Get down! Flat! *Now!*"

He did so with practiced agility.

They were on the spine of a hill, about to work down towards a wooded valley. MacAllister thought she'd seen movement far below, among the trees. She hoped they had not themselves been spotted. They'd been traveling in a manner that would have prevented their silhouettes from showing up against the skyline; but you never knew. There was still sufficient daylight, and keen eyes behind binoculars might have tagged them.

She had deliberately kept out of areas that might have been patrolled by the IFOR troops. The rendezvous point had been chosen with that in mind; but there were other armies around, and they respected no rules.

They stayed flattened against the crest, looking down upon the valley. A minute passed.

Five. Then ten.

"Probably some animal . . ." Serenic began.

"Don't fucking move!" she snapped at him. "I saw an animal, all right. It was on two legs and walked upright."

"How can you be sure? And this far?"

"I'm sure."

Serenic was not ready to accept that. "I think . . ."

"*Don't* think! Just do as I tell you, and you'll make it to the rendezvous in one piece."

He bristled. "You seem to forget that I am the commander of the most successful special unit . . ."

"Were."

"What?"

"You *were* the commander. Your men are now hunting you. It's a bit different from hunting frightened old men, women, and children. *You* are facing those special troops you're boasting so much about. You're in a different ballpark now, mister."

Fifteen minutes, and still she waited.

"Look . . ." Serenic began.

"Shut up!"

"I don't have to . . ."

MacAllister turned her head towards him. "It's a very bad idea to mess with me. I told you to shut up, so do it. I told you to lie flat. You do it. And stay flat till I tell you to move out."

Serenic looked into her eyes and kept his mouth shut.

She turned once more to look down the slope and into the valley.

Movement. One, then two figures came out of a screen of trees. They ducked immediately for cover and were once more hidden. There could be any number of them in there, she thought.

She carefully got out the binoculars and had a long scrutiny of the area; but they had moved well into cover. She saw nothing more.

"They don't know we're up here," she said, putting the binoculars away. "But they're taking no chances. Whoever trained them taught them reasonably well. Did you?"

Serenic took an appreciably long time before answering.

"An old friend," he replied at last. "Almost old enough to be my grandfather, if he'd started at twelve. That was his age when he was a partisan in the war against the Nazis. He was an instructor in guerrilla warfare with my reserve unit. He seemed a lot younger than his real age. When things went crazy, many of us got together to form a special unit, operating freely behind the lines. Then we formed the Black Lynxes."

"Guns for hire."

"Isn't that what you are?"

"I'm very, very different from you."

"Are you?"

"Oh yes. I am. We have very different perspectives. I suppose," Mac continued, "your defense is that you were obeying orders."

"But yes." He had either missed, or had chosen to ignore, the irony in her voice.

"But yes," she mimicked.

"That is what you are doing here," he said. "Obeying orders."

"Let me tell you something about me and obeying orders," she said, not looking at him. "I know why I do what I do, and I take responsibility for it. I don't hide behind the obeying orders bullshit. Cowards do that."

"I am not a coward!"

She remained contemptuously silent.

"*You* kill," he accused.

"I kill people like you." She rolled away from him and began to crawl towards the slope, away from the men in the valley. "Now let's leave your friends to chase their own shadows." She paused, rifle pointing. "Get moving."

He obeyed.

They hurried down the slope, putting as much distance as possible between them and the men in the distant trees.

An airbase in former Yugoslavia, 2140 hours.

Lieutenant-Colonel Asnayev stood before his pilots of the "goodwill" air detachment, in a small room on the base.

"I have received," he began, "a signal from a very sensitive source. We have been ordered to mount combat air patrols in an area you will find marked on your maps. I have to tell you that we may see some action . . ." He paused as they began to grin. "I have also to tell you," he continued, "that this action is clandestine. I have always taught you to fly with a greater degree of autonomy than the old way. I still expect strict discipline, but I also expect you to show some individual initiative.

"This signal has come from people with the best interests of our country at heart. They do not like what they see. They do not like the way the West has put our faces in the dirt, and they desire what we all desire: a return to the great status of the Soviet Union. I expect each of you to follow me into battle, if we must do battle, and destroy the enemy. However . . ." Asnayev paused once more, his hard little eyes raking each man in turn. "I want no one with me who is not committed to this. You all know me. I am a man of my word. If any of you would prefer not to fly on this mission, you can say so without fear of any reprisal upon your future career."

Asnayev stopped, and awaited their reaction.

They came smartly to their feet as one. "We are with you!" the five pilots said together.

Asnayev's normally impassive face actually softened as he regarded them.

"Get some sleep," he told them gruffly. "We take off at 0430, with a full weapon load."

The Bosnian mountains, midnight.

The burst of firing, when it came, was as shocking in its suddenness as its starkly brief illumination of the night.

Nothing came within life-threatening distance of them.

MacAllister and Serenic were deep in undergrowth cover, on the edge of a small clearing with a huge rock jutting out of the middle, like a volcanic island rising out of the depths of the sea. The shape of the rock could just be seen in the moonlit gloom. The firing had come from there.

"Whoever it is hasn't seen us," she whispered. "That was just a probing burst."

"He heard us moving."

"Perhaps. Perhaps not." MacAllister always moved silently.

"You're saying I made the noise?"

She didn't reply. Instead, she had brought the M16 up and was traversing it across the clearing, looking through the infrared scope. She made out four blooms of heat, all man-sized.

"Four of them," she said. "Two behind that rock, and two more in the bushes behind it."

"What are you going to do?"

"Wait. Let them make their moves. They've first got to find us. That means they've got to move out of cover. They're your men. Call out to them, if you like. Perhaps they won't shoot."

"That was not funny," he hissed at her.

"I thought it was."

He said nothing.

She looked through the scope again. One of the men behind the rock was moving, leaving cover at an angle, and heading for some bushes at the edge of the clearing. If he made it, he would be too close to their hiding place.

She sighted on him and fired. A single shot.

The infrared image seemed to leap into the air like a

frightened stag, to fall back to earth and lie still. Immediately, a sustained burst of firing raked the bushes. The firing was getting closer.

"Move!" she ordered sharply.

She flattened herself against the ground and worked her way against the travel of the fusillade. It was risky, but it also meant that once the stream of tracer had passed above, it would continue beyond them. Shattered leaves and bark spattered down. Though some bullets came close enough to be heard zipping past, none struck home.

The firing stopped.

The sudden silence was unnerving, but she was already looking through the scope, searching out the remaining Lynxes.

She found one, still behind the rock, but too far in cover for a clear shot. It took her a few moments to find another, this time lying flat down, right at the opposite edge of the clearing.

The third was climbing a tree.

As she followed the climbing man with the scope, she knew just how she was going to get them. She had already loaded the attached grenade launcher. The man in the tree was positioning himself almost directly above his companion. She could see his bloom in the scope and aimed the launcher at him.

She fired.

The 40mm round exploded in a starburst of phosphorous against the red bloom. There was a sudden high scream that was abruptly cut short. Then all was drowned by the sound of the explosion. The man seemed to have disappeared. Branches came off the trees, cascading in all directions. The man on the ground looked above him and saw that a great chunk of shattered wood, seemingly etched in the light of the grenade, was tumbling towards him. He leapt to his feet to run.

MacAllister watched all this through a scope that now seemed to have too much light in it. But she could still make out the man. She fired again. A single rifle shot. The man was stopped in mid-run, his body jerking marionette-like in the searing phosphorescent glow as he staggered back to the ground. The residue of the grenade hissed and crackled. The smells attacked the nostrils. It was a scene from hell.

She swung the rifle, hunting out the man behind the rock. He was on his feet, staring at his fallen comrade. Then he swung round, unsure of the direction the attack had come from, assault rifle coming up. She shot him before he had completed his swing.

"Time to go," she said to Serenic. "This will bring more of them round here like hornets. Come on! *Move, move, move!*"

They hurried through the gloom, the only noises the rush of their passage and the sounds of their breathing.

It was a good twenty minutes before Mac decided to slow down. Then she began to double back.

Serenic was stunned. "You're going *back?*"

"Not precisely. We're back-tracking, but still moving away. Their comrades will expect us to go *from* the location; not *towards* it. They won't think anyone would be so crazy."

"*I* don't believe anyone would be so crazy."

"I've made my point."

They walked on in silence, then Serenic said, "I can't believe I just watched you take out four of my Lynxes. This has never happened to them before."

"Always a first time. They'll also have lost some at the cave. And they're no longer yours. It's two hours to friendly territory. We'll see if what's left of your old friends choose to follow."

They walked on.

"Just who the hell are you?" Serenic demanded after a while.

"Your nightmare," she said. "Keep moving!"

13

NATO airbase, northeastern Italy, 0300 hours.

The November squadron detachment had been allo-cated their own facilities at a section of the airbase well away from curious eyes. They did not mix with any of the many IFOR aircrews stationed there. No one, apart from those involved, knew of the reasons for their presence.

They were now grouped, in full kit, in the room that had been set up for the final pre-mission brief. Jason had surprised them by choosing at the last moment to invite himself along as detachment commander, flying in an hour after their arrival in a sixth ASV Echo. His navigator was *Capitaine* Yves Voisin, a former Mirage 2000N backseater with the French Air Force. Voisin, from Zero-Two squadron, was known to be an excellent man in the back pocket, with quality time on the ASV Echo.

The crews suspected Jason was hoping for some action.

"Gentlemen," he began, "takeoff is at 0345 hours. The C130 is already on its way and will arrive at the rendezvous airstrip at precisely the same time as you. It will have flown directly from the UK, and will return without diverting here. Your escort role will end when it is once more safely in Italian airspace.

"The reason for your not overtly escorting it during ingress is to avoid undue interest in its presence until the very last moment. However, you will surreptitiously scan for hostile aircraft while you catch up with it. An AWACS aircraft will also keep you updated, via secure datalink. That will be its only interest in the affair. Its role is to pass and receive information. It will not direct the air battle, should you become involved in one.

"As you all realize, it is a high-value target and will not risk getting too involved in a combat that's not supposed to be happening. You are therefore essentially on your own. Morton and Carlizzi are on standby, as previously designated." Jason paused. "I'm sure you're all saying to yourselves that the boss would like to get into the action. I won't deny I wish I were going with you. But there it is.

"However, as you are in the lead, Mr. Hohendorf, remember you've got two of the most formidable aircraft in existence at your disposal. Reserves are there to be used when needed. Should you need assistance, do not hesitate to call for it. Do *not* risk yourself, or your aircraft and crews, by playing the hero. Your sole consideration is to ensure that the C130 makes it back.

"Therefore, you will use every means at your disposal, including calling out the standby aircraft. Inform AWACS, who will in turn give the call. We shall already be airborne. If you do call us out, you will still have command in the air. Use us as you think fit."

"Yes, sir," Hohendorf said, slightly overwhelmed by the fact that he may be put in a position to command the wing commander.

"Good show. That is all, gentlemen. Good luck."

The Bosnian mountains, 0400 hours.

"Well," MacAllister said, "we seem to have made it. We're well into friendly territory, and the airstrip is only half an hour away at this speed. All we'll then have to do is wait for our pick-up. You can ease back a little. We've got a safety margin."

Serenic was breathing harshly. They had been traveling at a punishing pace, but MacAllister appeared to be totally unaffected.

"How . . . how the hell can you keep this up with all the stuff you are carrying?" he asked between gulps for air.

"I told you, you weren't fit. Riding around in an armored car chasing refugees is not quite an exhausting exercise, I guess."

"You . . ."

But Serenic's intended retort was rudely interrupted.

The burst of fire came almost at the instant that she shoved powerfully at his back. He stumbled and fell.

"Stay down!" she commanded. She had dropped to the ground in virtually the same moment. *"Shit!"* she muttered savagely.

"I told you they would come across."

"And I thought those were butterflies that just went past our heads."

She was looking about her, assessing her options. Now they were down, they were in good cover. Though the sky would be lightening soon, the valley they were traveling in was steep-sided and the darkness was still unrelieved. She assumed whoever had fired had done so by sound. If they'd had nightscopes, they would certainly have scored at least one hit.

But firing acoustically meant they had to be close. Too close. She was annoyed with herself for allowing that to happen. Hadn't she told Serenic she would not consider them safe until the aircraft was well out of the area?

You're never safe, until it is safe, she reminded herself silently.

"Stay here," she said to him.

"Where are you going?" he whispered sharply.

"Hunting. We're not going to get out of here until I've neutralized them."

"Then leave me a weapon to defend myself!"

"Not a chance."

"You can't do that . . ."

But he was talking to the empty darkness.

"Damn you, woman!" he snarled softly, and tried to remain as still as possible.

She had been moving for about ten minutes, pausing to scan the area with the infrared scope. She made sure she did not betray her own whereabouts by leaving the scope exposed. Its red eye would be a beacon in the darkness a good aiming point. So far, she had counted three pursuers. That seemed to be all of them; but she was taking no chances.

One was very close.

She lay in wait as he moved, taking her eye away

from the scope to allow full night vision to return. She put the rifle down quietly, then drew her knife.

The man came *towards* her position, pausing to listen, every so often.

MacAllister remained as still as a big cat awaiting the approach of a prey it had selected.

The man came on.

He was a foot from her and still did not realize it.

Then she moved.

It was a swift and awesome strike. Her left hand went to cover the mouth as the right slammed the knife in and upwards. The fearsomely sharp blade drove in deeply, doing fatal damage. The man gasped softly in surprise and mind-stunning pain. By the time she had released him, he was dead.

She wiped the knife clean on his clothes, resheathed it, then picked up the rifle and moved on.

Seconds only had passed.

She had found a new target.

She lay flat within tufts of shrubbery, the rifle held almost along the ground, the red eye of its scope well screened. The man was standing, pressed against the trunk of a tree about forty meters away. No distance at all. Only a tiny portion of shoulder and head was within the scope. It was not a perfect view of the target, but it was enough. She knew she wouldn't miss.

She fired.

The single shot echoed through the fading night. She kept the scope on target, in case a second was necessary.

It wasn't.

The man was hurled sideways, his assault rifle flying out of his hands. She followed him down until the scope zeroed in on twitching feet. Then they were still. The head shot had been sufficient.

Still she waited, in case he hadn't been hit seriously and was faking it. She doubted that; but decided not to take any chances. After a while, she carefully made her way to where he lay. He was never going to move again.

It was time to find the last of them.

Despite the noise of the shot, no further shooting had followed in response. This one, she decided, was not going to be easy. But she had to find him, and quickly. Time was running out, and the safety margin she'd told Serenic about rapidly eroding.

She traversed the scope, looking for the tell-tale bloom. Nothing.

She moved the scope to where she'd left Serenic. He had been in a depression, which would have positioned him well below ground level within a heavy screen of shrubbery; but there should be a slight heat trace at the edges.

Nothing.

She intensified the heat-amplification of the scope and waited for it to increase its heat-gathering properties. The intensification should pick up even a minute trace.

Still nothing.

"Why the hell did you move?" she muttered tightly.

That was all she needed so close to pick-up time. A missing Serenic, after all she'd gone through.

And where was the last man?

The last man was very close to Serenic.

Milos Vanic had crept upon Serenic while he was still lying flat in the depression.

"Who would have believed it?" Vanic had said gloatingly in the dialect of the mountains, pressing the snout of his automatic pistol against the back of Serenic's head. "The great Serenic hiding out like a frightened Ottoman bitch. Lost your balls? Turn around. Slowly! We're moving out of here. I'll wait for more light. I want to see your face properly." He glanced up at the perceptibly lightening sky. "It won't be long. I want to see that damned face of yours when I put a bullet in your brain. Thought you could sell us out, did you? Crawl out of there, traitor! The Western money won't do you any good now. Come on! Move!"

But Serenic had not lost his arrogance. "I am tired of people telling me to move!"

"If you don't get out of there," Vanic said in a hard voice, "I'll give you one in the knee, then drag you out myself. So where's the woman? Have you screwed her yet? That's your real pastime, isn't it?"

"Still thinking about losing out to me with that girl, are you, Vanic? Still eating your guts out over it? I had a great time. She loved it any way I wanted. She liked to feel me in there, filling her up. She loved it when I pumped hard inside her. You should have heard how she screamed. *More, more, more!* For a girl you treated like a precious jewel, she was rampant for it. I rode her like a . . ."

"Shut up!"

Vanic brought his gun hand up as if to smash the pistol against Serenic's head. Then he stopped.

"I can wait," he said. "That trick of yours won't work on me. You get people to lose their temper, then you strike when they're out of control. I've watched you do that for too long to too many people. I've waited for this moment, and I'll take my time. Now get out of there!"

They began to move. When they had reached sloping ground away from the depression, MacAllister's single shot rang out.

Vanic froze, listening.

"That was the woman," Serenic remarked with satisfaction. "You're one down, at the very least. When she's finished out there, she'll be coming for you next. And no, I didn't screw her. That one has barbed wire between her legs."

Vanic seemed uncertain of what to do next. His desire for revenge was being tempered by the need for survival. Then he made a decision. Without warning, he swung the pistol. It happened too quickly for Serenic to avoid the blow, which was hard enough to knock him cold. His unconscious body tumbled down the hundred-foot incline, to come to a rest near a trickling ravine.

"I'll come back for you," Vanic uttered with soft anticipation, then went in search of MacAllister.

She saw the bloom creeping some distance ahead of her.

Serenic? Or the last man?

She moved closer. She had to identify him positively before she fired. It took her another five minutes before she felt she was closer enough to risk what she was about to do. She had no choice. There just wasn't the time for a long stalk. They had to get to the pick-up point, and time was becoming an increasingly scarce commodity.

She sighted on the crouching figure.

"Serenic?" she called softly and rolled even as she spoke.

The answering fire that shredded her previous location gave her all the reply she needed. She had stabilized into a firing position on one kneee, at a new location. The man, standing now as he fired in the wrong direction, was squarely in the scope.

She fired, twice to make quite sure.

The man jerked backwards, gun stabbing upwards, firing its tracers uselessly into the air. Then the gun stopped. The man continued standing, swaying with increasingly desperate urgency as he stubbornly fought to stay alive.

She watched it all in the scope, waiting to see if she would need a third shot.

She didn't.

Vanic abruptly stiffened, then fell forwards with a slamming sound, as if a plank of wood had been dropped from a great height. He didn't move again.

MacAllister slowly got to her feet, then hurried to where she'd seen the man come from. After the briefest of searches, she found the incline. The light had improved sufficiently to allow her to see a shape at the bottom. She knew it was Serenic.

Was he dead? she wondered,

"Shit!" she said and began to clamber down.

He was groaning when she got there.

"Serenic!" She grabbed at him. "We've got to move on, or we'll miss the plane!" She reached for his water bottle and emptied it over him.

He gasped. "That fucking bastard!" he swore, gingerly feeling his head as she helped him up. "Where is he?"

"Dead."

He tried to stare at her in the gloom of the ravine. Above, the light was getting better by the second. "You got them all?"

"All."

"My Black Lynxes."

"Will you quit going on about that?" MacAllister sounded exasperated. "They're not your goddamned Black Lynxes anymore. And don't sound so surprised. They never came up against some *real* competition before. They were too sure of themselves. Even though your partisan gave them some good training, they still made mistakes.

"Now we've got to get out of here. Or that plane goes. Remember what I told you. We miss that C130, and you stay. Permanently. I don't care who the hell's waiting for you, or how important they are. I won't put myself in further jeopardy. So if you want to continue living, get moving!"

He glanced up at the incline. "My head. It feels as if someone is inside playing drums on my temples. I can't climb up there fast enough. My head *hurts!*"

She didn't waste time arguing. "This ravine," she said quickly. "It seems to slope upwards. We'll go along it. Might save us some time. Come on!"

She prodded him with the rifle.

"Come on, come on!" he grumbled. "Get moving, get moving! That's all I get from you."

"You could get a lot worse," she told him shortly. "Believe me." She prodded him again with the M16.

He made no further protest and moved forward, staggering slightly.

Lieutenant-Colonel Asnayev led his six Su-27Ks into a steep climb from the airfield.

They maintained the ascent until they reached forty thousand feet, where they leveled out. They then went into a ladder formation. This positioned the aircraft in a stepped configuration, with Asnayev in the lead at twelve thousand feet above the last man, who brought up the rear four nautical miles behind the leader. Attacking a ladder gave problems, in that it was easy to miss the full extent of the formation until too late; a fact that Asnayev well knew.

They remained well within their airspace.

● ● ●

The Hercules C130 crossed the coast right on time. It headed at ultra low level for the rendezvous. In half an hour, it would be there.

"Do you hear something?" MacAllister enquired.

"No. Nothing."

They had found a gentle slope out of the ravine and had in fact made some good time. The almost dry watercourse had curved towards their destination. There was plenty of light now, to enable them to see the hard-packed grass airstrip clearly.

It must have once belonged to a flying club, she decided, when such pursuits had been a more normal activity. The few buildings that were still standing could barely be described as such. The war had come, had ravaged them, and had gone on. The strip itself, however, was remarkably intact. Its far end terminated in a precipitous drop.

There was no one around. It was as if the world of people had never been to this place, so isolated did it feel, high up there in the mountains.

As they drew closer, Mac revised her opinion. It looked less like a flying club and more like a diversionary airfield for the military. Perhaps that was why the strip was itself in such good condition. It would explain why it had been picked for the rendezvous.

She paused. "Definitely a sound. Come on! That's our ticket out of here, and right on time. We've got to be *on* that strip."

"I still hear nothing," Serenic protested as he hurried. Vanic's blow had left an ugly weal on the side of his head.

"You'll hear it soon enough. Now come on! I'll be in a very bad mood if I miss this plane."

"You mean you have a good mood?"

"Not where you're concerned, I don't."

Hohendorf had deployed his four aircraft into two combat pairs, five miles apart. Selby had the lead of the second one, with Bagni and Stockmann on his wing, while Hohendorf had the Double-C for company.

"Interesting if we call out the boss," Flacht said in German. "We'll have command."

"It will be a strange feeling," Hohendorf agreed in the same language. "I hope it won't be necessary. I'm not sure I like the idea of having to worry about the boss remaining alive, if we do have to mix it with those Flankers. Can you imagine what would happen if he got shot down, under *my* command? It also doesn't help that I keep thinking he's out there assessing me. I wish he had stayed back at November base."

"Too late now."

"Yes."

"Anyway, bosses are like that. Permanent assessing machines. Remember Wüsterhausen?" Flacht added. Wüsterhausen had been their old *Marineflieger* boss in Schleswig Holstein.

"Who can forget the Sea Eagle himself? He could spot a mistake at a thousand miles."

"A slight exaggeration, but close enough. I have the C130 at twenty miles," Flacht continued briskly, reverting to English.

They'd snagged the Hercules on the radar for some time now, although Flacht had "painted" it only once. As its course was already known, all the updating was done without the need for a further sweep. The radar was thus on standby.

"If anything is going to happen," Flacht continued, "it will be soon."

"Tasker, Tasker!" came from the AWACS suddenly. "You have six bogeys, repeat six bogeys at seven-five miles. Static."

"You were saying?" Hohendorf said drily.

"At least they're static. That means they're staying well inside the border."

"It also means they're twenty miles closer to the Hercules. We're going in." As he eased the throttles forward to increase speed, he went on to the other aircraft, "Tasker Zero-Two and Zero-Four, altitude one-four-zero. Six-zero-zero knots."

"Roger," came Selby's acknowledgement. "One-four-zero. Six-zero-zero- knots."

Over to their right, the distant pair of Tornados rolled onto their backs and plunged through cloud to descend to the new altitude of fourteen thousand feet and increased speed.

"Wolfie," Hohendorf continued to his backseater, "get the AWACS picture patched over. Let's see what we might have to deal with. Leave the radars on standby. No point letting our pals across the border know where we are."

"Doing it," Flacht confirmed, and spoke to the AWACS.

Instantly, a swift datalink transfer gave him a radar picture of the Su-27Ks. It was a two-dimensional view from above, with the aircraft depicted as solid green squares. The overhead view gave the formation a close, line astern pattern. Speed, altitude, and heading were also coming in. Flacht manipulated the picture to give him various three-dimensional views. The extent of the ladder formation, with correct spacing, differential altitudes, and course, were neatly displayed.

"Exciting formation," Flacht said. "Copying to you. Of course, now that the AWACS had painted them, they may decide not to keep that formation for long."

Hohendorf glanced at his central MFD, where Flacht had patched the copy. "That's a big ladder," he said. "I don't think they're on parade. Do you?"

"I don't think so either. The others should have this."

"Do it. Give it also to the boss and Zero-Six."

"Doing it."

Flacht patched the display over to all the remaining November aircraft, using the AWACS to transfer the modified picture to Jason's and Morton's aircraft far to the rear.

"If those Flankers do come across the border, I'm going to call in the boss. I think we'll need everybody for this."

"What happened to not wanting to put him in danger?"

"Would you like to face him if I didn't, and because of that, lost the C130?"

"I think it would be safer to take up residence on Mars."

"*I* was thinking of the next galaxy."

"Oo-bee-doo-bee-do," McCann said.

"Put your dummy away and talk properly, McCann," Selby cut in sharply. "What have you got?"

"Pacifier."

"What?"

"Pacifier. What you call dummy, we call pacifier."

"Of course you do, and I'm very happy for you all. Now can we please get down to business?"

"Sure. Take a look at this nice present I got for you." McCann patched over the Su-27K formation he'd received from Flacht. "They look a real mean bunch, don't they?"

Selby was silent for some moments. "I see what you mean," he commented gravely.

In the other November aircraft, a variation on the same theme of sentiments was being expressed.

"This looks promising, sir," *Capitaine* Voisin remarked from the backseat of Jason's ASV(E).

"I'd describe the situation rather differently," Jason responded drily. "But yes. It has possibilities."

"Do you think Zero-One will call us out?"

"That, we shall have to wait and see. Get your systems ready for combat, just in case."

"They're ready."

And you, Mr. Hohendorf, Jason thought. *Make the right decision. Do not be inhibited by my presence.*

Seconds later, Hohendorf's voice came on the headphones. "Tasker Zero-Five."

"Zero-Five," Jason acknowledged.

"On my call, close escort with Zero-Six on Tasker Charlie-One-Three-Zero."

Hohendorf was warning him to prepare to give very tight escort to the Hercules C130, if the need arose.

"Roger," Jason acknowledged briskly. "On your call, close escort Tasker Charlie."

"We'll keep them occupied up top, if the situation warrants. Any get through, splash them."

"Roger. We copy."

"On my call only," came Hohendorf's voice, this time very firmly.

"Roger. Your call."

Good move, Jason thought approvingly. A tiny twitch creased his face briefly in his mask as he remembered the no-nonsense tone in Hohendorf's voice. *You're learning to command.*

"Looks as if we're invited to the party, after all," he said to Voisin.

"Yes, sir," Voisin said calmly. "Let's hope we can take the cake home in one piece."

"You're mixing a few things in there, Yves, but I get the message. Alert Zero-Six."

"Doing it."

Across the border.

As soon as the warning of the AWACS search radar had sounded in his cockpit, Asnayev had ordered a change of positioning. They were now in an extended wall formation.

If viewed from above, they would appear to be superficially in line—abreast, spread out over fifteen miles. However, a front view would show a very different picture. Each pair was at staggered altitudes with the top aircraft—Asnayev's—being twelve thousand feet above the lowest. The Wall, requiring a very high level of discipline to be flown properly, would give a very effective radar coverage when all six aircraft combined for a long-range, wide-angle search. As yet, they were not doing so.

"Each time their AWACS paints us," Asnayev was saying to his pilots, "I will call a change of formation. We'll keep them guessing. The AWACS is a nice, fat target, but it is staying well out of range. We are forbidden to go after it, unless it gets close enough to mistake its course for a border violation."

"What about the escorts?" someone asked.

"We'll find them soon enough, Blue Four. Not long now."

But the AWACS had also been scanning them in infrared.

The Bosnian mountains.

MacAllister soon had proof of her acute sense of hearing. She had arrived at the airstrip itself, with a clearly wilting Serenic stumbling on ahead. They were three-quarters of the way along, heading for the far end near the precipitous drop, when the characteristic "whisper" of the Lockheed Hercules's four engines suddenly grew to a humming crescendo and the big, high-winged, unmarked aircraft seemed to leap up the cliff face to pop over the lip of the airfield.

Serenic stared disbelievingly at the antics of the airplane as it rose above the strip, to dive sickeningly. He fully expected it to slam into the ground, effectively ending his hopes of escape and access to instant wealth. But it didn't crash. Instead, its steep descent was suddenly halted as its accomplished flight-deck crew flared the aircraft for a perfect touch-down.

MacAllister was waving energetically at the airplane. It began to slow until just above trotting pace. Already, the huge loading ramp was being lowered. The crew had seen them.

"I saw your face," she told Serenic as she pushed him into a run. "You thought it was going to crash, didn't you? That dive was the Sarajevo Approach; intended to expose itself to your comrades' nasty surprises for the shortest possible time, during the 'semi-official' shooting war. I told you I'd heard it. Count yourself lucky, Serenic. You've actually made it. Now for the last time, *move!*"

She thought she could hear the sound of jets, but did not look up to check.

The presence of his means of escape, plus the thought of all that money, suddenly gave impetus to Serenic's legs. He ran strongly after the Hercules.

MacAllister kept up with him easily. Soon, buffeted by the slipstream from the props but sheltered by the aircraft's fuselage as they drew closer, they were nearing the lowered, moving ramp. One man was at its center, urging them on. Two more stood further inside the aircraft, on either side of the ramp. They were armed. Their attention was on Serenic.

Briefly, his pace slackened.

"For God's sake!" Mac shouted at him. *"Don't slow down!* They're not there to shoot you! They're checking that no one's chasing us. Come on! You're nearly there!"

Serenic leapt onto the ramp, stumbled, was grabbed by the crewman, then directed into the cavernous body of the C130. MacAllister leapt on, agile as a cat, and hurried through.

The crewman spoke to the pilots and the Hercules began to gather speed. The ramp began to rise.

Then the aircraft was leaping into the air, even before the ramp was fully closed. It had been mere seconds on the ground, and had never slowed to a stop.

"When this lands," MacAllister said to Serenic as she strapped herself into a sideways-facing, hammock-like seat, "my association with you comes to an end. We don't see each other again."

"I shall miss you," he told her, as the crewman secured his straps.

She stared at him. "Why?"

"I would like to have seen you in something other than these ... unflattering clothes, more suitable for tracking across the mountains, or combat."

The crewman looked from one to the other. "Coffee?" he suggested diplomatically. "It's nice, hot, and sweet if you take sugar. Or would you prefer something cold?"

"Coffee, please," Mac said. "Black with sugar. Thank you."

The crewman looked at Serenic. "Sir?"

"A cold beer would be very good, even at this hour. The running has made me hot."

"Sorry, sir. No alchohol."

"Then white coffee, without sugar. Thank you."

The crewman inclined his head. "Our pleasure. Anything to eat?"

Serenic shook his head.

"I'm fine," MacAllister said.

"He called me 'sir,'" Serenic remarked, as the man went off to get the coffee.

"That's the British for you. Polite to anybody."

"Well?" Serenic persisted.

"Well what?"

"Will I get to see you in better clothes?"

She again stared at him. "Do you have to hit on every woman you meet? No matter what?"

"Only those I find sensuous."

"You mean anything with tits." She began to shake her head at the sheer brazen amorality of his behavior, when the returning presence of the crewman prevented her from adding the more poisonous comment she'd been about to deliver.

The crewman handed them their mugs of coffee. They were indeed hot.

"Better drink your coffee," she went on, as the man went back to his duties, "and quit trying your worn-out routine on me . . . unless you want my coffee all over you."

He gave a smile of irredeemable smugness. He was feeling important again. He was going to people who would pay him handsomely for the information he possessed. He was away from the vengeance of Milos Vanic, forever. It didn't matter what she did, or said now. He was untouchable.

Then the C130 was flung over in a series of violent evasive maneuvers. Coffee rose into the air, to splash hotly. Serenic yelped.

"Oh dear," MacAllister said calmly in a loud voice to make herself heard as the aircraft again tilted over, its engines howling. She stared at Serenic's suddenly pallid face. "It seems as if you got coffee all over you, after all."

![14]

Flacht looked at the one-word datalink message:
HERCULES.

"First part of mission complete," he said to Hohendorf. "The pick-up was successful."

"Now comes the really hard stuff. Give the others the message."

"On its way."

"Now to see what our friends across the border intend to do," Hohendorf said. "Tasker Zero-Two, Zero-Four," he continued to Selby and Bagni's ASVs.

"Zero-Two."

"Zero-Four."

"You have the successful pick-up message. Let's get between the bogeys and Tasker Charlie. Watch those bogeys. If they come over, it's a free-fire zone."

"Roger," they both acknowledged and began moving into position.

Hohendorf's instructions meant that Selby could work his combat pair independently.

"Zero-Three, follow me."

"We're on it," Cottingham acknowledged, and his Tornado banked hard to follow precisely Hohendorf's maneuver.

"Zero-Five," Hohendorf called to Jason.

"Zero-Five."

"Stand by. Anything can happen from now on. Tasker Charlie heading back, low altitude."

"Roger. Understood."

"Well, Wolfie," Hohendorf said to Flacht as they took up position to block any incursion by the Flankers. He activated his helmet sight. "Now we find out."

In Zero-Two, Selby said, "Are you okay back there, Elmer Lee?"

"Sure. Shouldn't I be?"

"You know what I mean."

"Hey, man. If there's a fight coming, just make sure we don't lose. That's all I ask."

"I'll see what I can do."

"And just remember, I only fly with pilots who win. Second place can give you a terminal illness . . . if you see what I mean."

"I see what you mean, Elmer Lee. I have an aversion to second place."

"Now that's the kind of pilot talk I like."

The C130 was still twisting and turning.

Serenic was looking decidedly unwell in the subdued aircraft lighting.

"Are we . . . are we under attack?" he asked MacAllister weakly.

"No . . ."

"Then why . . ."

"Precautions. The pilots are taking no chances. They're weaving between the mountains. More difficult for any fighters that might try to shoot us down. As we're over friendly territory, there should be no surface-to-air missiles or anti-aircraft guns to worry about. But things can happen."

"That crewman must have known the airplane would be doing this. Why bring us coffee?" Serenic looked peeved.

Mac showed him her mug. "I've still got mine." She grinned without humor at him.

"That was not funny," he said.

"It wasn't mean to be."

Moscow, 0705 hours local.

Levchuk knocked on Kurinin's door and entered. The general was at his desk. He looked up.

"I can tell by your eyes," Kurinin said steadily.

"Vanic failed. Our outposts can get no reply from him. It is to be assumed he is dead, and that the pick-up was successful. They are airborne."

Kurinin's lips tightened. "Send word to Lieutenant-Colonel Asnayev. Stop them at all costs. Whatever the organization that woman's really working for, it is inimical to our interests. She is obviously one of their prime assets. Losing her would be a severe blow. As for that pychopath she taking out with her, he could also hurt us with his information.

"Connections we would rather keep hidden, could be exposed to the light of day. Both dead, Gregor. That's the bottom line, as the Americans would say," he added, looking amused. "You see? I don't mind using their phrases."

Levchuk hesitated.

"What is it, Gregor?" Kurinin stared at his subordinate and friend. "I see. You believe we should not unleash Asnayev."

"It could get out of hand. Asnayev is still fighting the Cold War."

"*We* are still fighting the Cold War."

"Not in the same way. Our methods are rather more subtle. We have a long-term goal."

"So does he. I know the man's record. I respect his motives. True, he may not have our long-term vision. But people like us sometimes need people like him. Empires are built by people like Asnayev. They man our legions. Send that message, Gregor."

"As you wish, General."

"I do wish."

"*Go!*"

Asnayev stiffened slightly in his cockpit as the message came on his headphones. That was all he received. Just the one word; but it was enough. He already knew the purpose of the mission.

"To all aircraft," he began. "We are active! Primary target is the transport aircraft. It *must* be destroyed. Destroy any escorts only if they stand in your way. Do not waste time with them while the target escapes. They are of secondary interest only. We can and will take care of them later . . . if there are any of them left. Formation V-ladder, ten thousand meters, pairs. Let's go!"

The formation Asnayev had called was his own modification of the standard ladder. The ten-thousand-meter—about thirty-three thousand feet—separation he had indicated meant this altitude would be the space between the leader of the top pair and the wingman of the bottom pair. This particular ladder formation would mean that if viewed head-on, it would look like a huge V tipped onto its side with the top and bottom pair positioned at the tips and the central pair marking the base. Distance horizontally between the leader and the sixth aircraft was ten nautical miles.

The lateral spread was thus a huge one, giving an attacker a serious problem in deciding which pair to attack first. It also meant that in a normal radar sweep from an opposing fighter, two of the pairs would invariably be missed. Very bad news indeed.

But the ASV Echo was no ordinary fighter. Its crews were no ordinary crews, and they never did things by the book.

"Tasker, Tasker!" came from the AWACS. "Situation going hot! I repeat . . . *hot!* Here's the latest picture." The AWACS sent in the most recent configuration for the attacking Su-27Ks. "Going out of area. Will maintain coverage within limits." The voice sounded regretful at having to leave.

Hohendorf understood. It was not really their fight. The downing of an AWACS would be more difficult to conceal. News of combat between fighters could be selectively drip-fed until confusion reigned.

"Roger," Hohendorf acknowledged, feeling a tightening in his stomach. It was all in his lap now. "Thanks for your help."

"You guys take care, little brother," the voice said.

"We will. Zero-One out. Zero-Two," Hohendorf went on to Selby's aircraft.

"Zero-Two."

"We are hot. Free-fire."

"Roger."

Hohendorf now called Jason. "Zero-Five."

"Zero-Five," came the crisp reply.

"Go!"

"Roger." Jason's voice betrayed no emotion. "On our way."

"Zero-Three."

"Zero-Three," Cottingham acknowledged.

"Combat spread. We're going high."

"Roger. Going high. Combat spread."

The Double-C Tornado moved further outwards as they went into a rapid climb for altitude.

"Hope I've done this right, Wolfie," Hohendorf said to Flacht.

"I have every faith."

"Say that to me when it's all over. I'm taking no chances," Hohendorf went on. "Those people flying those things out there could be tough. So we're not going to let them get close before we have seriously damaged them. Arming Skyray B. As soon as they're over the border, I'm shooting."

"What if they have the same idea?"

"They do, but they'll go for Tasker Charlie first. This could be the only chance we get to catch them out. The boss's and Selby's pair puts four defenders on the C130, while we sort out any high boys."

"What if they've got *four* up here?"

"Those are good odds."

"Just what I wanted to know."

"Wolfie . . ."

"Yes."

"You're beginning to sound like McCann. Are we all going to have to put up with half-crazy back-seaters?"

"We've got to be fully crazy. We fly with you pilots."

Hohendorf smiled in his mask. Wolfie was taking it all in his stride.

As they raced towards the Hercules C130 at low level, Morton felt his pulses race. *He was going into combat at last, and with the boss himself.*

Morton was astonished to find that he was not feeling elated. He'd thought his nerves would have been pinging with suppressed anticipation. Instead, he'd found that though his pulses were indeed racing, an almost detached calm had descended upon him. He stared ahead at the barely visible shape of Jason's aircraft as it hurtled between the high walls of a valley. Voisin, Jason's backseater, was clearly employing the Chameleon. Every so often, Zero-Five would seem to vanish. Then an indistinct shape would leap over a mountain range.

He glanced to his left to check his own wing. It was a really weird sensation to watch as the wing changed color. Carlizzi was himself wasting no time in employing this quite startling offensive/defensive aid.

"How're you feeling?" came the voice of the Italian major with the New York accent.

"I'm okay."

"Remember *the* air combat lesson. Don't rush. Do it fast, but don't rush."

"Got it."

"Okay."

"The way to do this is hard and fast," Selby was saying to McCann as they rushed towards the approaching Su-27Ks. "A zap in the teeth at long range will make them think twice. They won't be expecting it."

His helmet sight was already activated, its designator arrow hunting about, waiting for sensor coupling. They were still keeping all sensors on standby, to delay the warning as long as was effectively possible.

"The last picture from the AWACS," McCann said, "shows a V-shaped ladder formation." Flacht had relayed the last AWACS update to all the November aircraft. "Only, they've done it sideways. I'm patching it over. Center MFD."

Selby glanced at the display and saw Asnayev's modified ladder.

"Axel and the Double-C will handle the top boys," he said. "We'll take the ones in the middle, and the boss and Chuck Morton can attend to the low pair."

"You realize that may not be their formation right now? They'll have changed as soon as the AWACS painted them."

"Very likely. But they're still out there, and coming. Time to flash our radar at them. Very quick, very short."

"You got it."

McCann carried out two rapid sweeps, in look-up and look-down modes, before selecting standby once more. He'd also used extreme long range, to ensure there were no surprises *behind* the six Flankers. The radar had caught all six, displaying them as solid green squares that had now split into independent pairs. Then it began to give historical positions for each pair, with all the attendant information of course, speed, and altitude.

"They'll be changing position like fish surprised in a barrel," McCann said, "but I've got the suckers. They're well inside the border. Our meat. Got you a priority target. Four-five miles. Easy-peasy range. Go to Skyray Beta at any time. It will get there before they know it."

A seventh square, much closer, was moving down the screen. This one was blue. The C130.

"Skyray armed," Selby confirmed. "Helmet sight linked."

Immediately, the designator arrow on the helmet sight pointed to his right. Half of the targeting box peeped from the peripheral edge of the helmet.

Selby banked into it, and the box became whole as it moved towards the center, in concert with the turning of his head. The flashing diamond appeared within the box, then froze. The lock-on tone sounded in his helmet. He squeezed the release.

"One off the rail!" he announced as the Skyray B hurled itself explosively off the launcher and, trailing a bright white plume, rocketed into the distance. He immediately broke away, reversing direction and leaving the missile to independently guide itself towards the target.

Almost on cue, and over to his left as he turned, another streak had appeared, heading towards the Flankers.

"Looks like Nico and Hank got themselves a pigeon too," McCann observed. He glanced upwards. Two more streaks etched themselves on the high blue. "Oh wow. We got two more hot trails. The guys had the same idea. Beautiful. Four Flankers are going to go totally defensive and . . ."

Beep, beep, beep, beep, beep, beep . . . !

"Holy shit!" he exclaimed. *"Incoming! Ugh!"*

McCann's grunt came as Selby wrenched the ASV into a tight climbing turn, then was again reversing direction, to head back down towards the mountains.

McCann's systems had identified the missile as radar-guided, and he released a decoy that proceeded to give off a rich signature in the location they had recently vacated. The ASV's already low radar return meant that it was now being effectively screened by the broadcasts from the decoy. The incoming missile should thus be seduced into taking the decoy instead.

Beep, beep, beep, beep, beep, beep . . .

"Hell," McCann said tensely. "The sucker's still hunting us out. The seeker must be a smart one and decided it didn't like our spoof. Here's another decoy," he said to the missile. "Have *that* for breakfast. Hey, Mark. Do some hot shit pilot stuff, buddy." He was turning in his seat, trying to visually locate the tell-tale plume. But he could see nothing trailing them.

Then he felt a giant hand press at his body as Selby pulled into a high-G turn close to what seemed like the biggest high-rise building in the world, which blotted out the sky. The building turned out to be the side of a mountain flashing past. Then they were in clear air once more, heading upwards.

There was no sound from the missile warner. Then something flamed against the now-receding mountain.

"Good stuff, Mark. Good stuff! That mountain just cut short the incoming's career." McCann glanced down at the attack display. A small sunburst had appeared where the target aircraft's solid diamond had been. "But *we* got our pigeon! And then there were five. Good kill."

"Why thank you, kind sir."

"Hey. You're not done yet. Go git 'em, boy!"

"McCann . . ."

"I'm still here."

"Never mind. Zero-Four," Selby went on to Bagni and Stockmann's aircraft.

"Zero-Four," came Bagni's voice.

"Status."

"We're fine. But no score."

McCann glanced over his right shoulder. The indistinct shape of the other ASV flitted through a strip of cloud.

"Got them," he said. "Four o'clock. What the hell happened?" he went on. "Skyrays don't miss."

"This one did," Selby remarked.

"Those guys will be pissed off."

"I think that's putting it mildly."

"I'll give another flash to check how many bogeys are still alive. Go right, one-zero-five."

"Right, one-zero-five."

McCann again glanced over his right shoulder as Selby turned onto the new heading. Zero-Four was following, covering them, but in position to act independently if necessary.

"Okay," McCann said, more to his multi-function display than to his pilot. "Here goes."

He did a quick scan. Two small green squares were caught, both heading for the C130.

"I got just two," he said. "They're making for Tasker Charlie. Hope the boss is on them. Now we have four missile trails. We scored, but Zero-Four didn't. Even if Axel and the Double-C scored, there should still be one extra guy floating around. But he sure ain't on my little screen. Zero-Four," he called.

"Zero-Four," came Stockmann's reply.

"I got just two bogeys on my space invader kit. You?"

"Ditto."

"What the hell's going on?" McCann said to Selby. "There could still be *five* of them out there!"

"Check with Wolfie Flacht," the pilot suggested, head turning this way and that as he tried to acquire another target with the helmet sight. But the two McCann had spotted were not tagged by the designator arrow.

"Zero-One," McCann called.

"Zero-One," came Flacht's voice.

"You guys scored?"

"No." The way Flacht said it spoke volumes.

"What the . . . the Double-C?"

"Negative."

"Zero-Two out. Shit," McCann went on to Selby. "I don't believe it. *Three* no goes? This mean *five* of the suckers really are still out there. Mark, Skyrays don't miss, dammit."

"These did somehow. We may have a fight on our hands."

"Jeez! This could get dangerous. But danger's my game."

Asnayev was furious.

When he'd realized that four missiles were on the way to his formation, he had at first assumed that the opposing fighters were flown by over-eager pilots who had launched too early. He had swiftly revised his opinion when the phenomenal speed of the hostile rounds soon had the entire formation breaking in all directions to evade. Gordiev, in Blue Four, had left it too late and had paid the price. For what had seemed a never-ending time, the remainder had careered across the sky, trying to avoid the seemingly implacable missiles.

Asnyaev had himself got off one shot, but had been forced—like the others—to practically skim the ground in a bid to escape. But escape he did, when the westerner's missile had impacted in some woods. His own missile had not properly achieved a lock and he'd not really expected a kill. He was annoyed with himself for being hustled into the quick shoot.

The others had literally flown for their lives and only their piloting skills had enabled them to come through unscathed. Less gifted pilots would have been shot down. But the evasive maneuvers had cost valuable time. The C130 was getting farther and farther away.

Asnayev had thus ordered that all effort be made to find and destroy it. The fighters had to be left alone until that task was complete, and were to be engaged only if vitally necessary.

Asnayev was also furious because he'd lost Gordiev, and because he was restricted by the demands of the mission. Until the C130 was destroyed, he would have to remain essentially defensive. It was clearly obvious they were not dealing with over-eager pilots, but with people who were employing a clever tactic. Their opening gambit had been deliberately early, establishing the parameters of the combat.

They were, in effect, calling the shots.

It was not a situation that Asnayev liked to be forced into. It was also obvious that the opposing pilots did not intend to mix it up in a close-in fight, unless forced to by developments in the battle. Their long-range missiles would be used to decimate his formation, so that if a close-in tangle did evolve, he would be at a serious disadvantage. The initiative had been taken from him, and he didn't like that at all.

He had been forced to take his formation low down, where they were not at their most effective.

These pressures would make Asnayev perform at less than he was normally capable of.

Despite the failure of three of the Skyway Betas to score, Hohendorf's battle plan was in fact already bearing good fruit. The C130 was still flying at ultra low level, threading its way to safety between the mountains.

MacAllister was observing Serenic's pallid expression

with some amusement, when the crewman returned. He glanced at the erstwhile leader of the Black Lynxes. He too found Serenic's pallor amusing. Then he turned to Mac.

"You'll be pleased to know we've got fighter cover up top," he said. "Anything coming after us would have to go through them first. Someone, somewhere, also thinks very highly of you," he went on. "We received a strange message. 'Have no fear, Chuck's here.' That make any sense?"

She beamed suddenly, transforming her face.

"Wooo!" the crewman said. "There's light coming from your face, and if you'll pardon the impertinence, there's a certain look in your eye. I can see the message does make sense." He grinned. "Now I do feel safe. Whoever Chuck is, I know he's not going to let anything happen to us, if he can possibly help it."

She simply carried on beaming.

The crewman nodded his head understandingly and went away, still grinning.

"So who is this Chuck?" Serenic asked weakly.

She didn't answer.

When Jason's combat pair had made contact with the Hercules, they had gone into a series of weaving turns above their charge, covering a full three hundred sixty degrees, guarding against threats from any quarter.

Then Jason had received warning from Hohendorf that only one Flanker was known to be down, and that all remaining five might be heading his way, at low level.

He had immediately warned Morton.

Jason now considered the options. If all the remaining Su-27Ks were making a beeline for Tasker Charlie, it could only mean the destruction of the C130 took precedence over all else. This meant the commander of the Flanker force was prepared to commit everything to that objective. That, Jason reasoned, left the 27Ks at a serious disadvantage.

In his opponent's place, he would have carried out a series of attacks by pairs, always leaving a force to fend off the incoming fighters. The way the planned attack on the Hercules was evolving meant that all the attack assets were down somewhere among the mountains, inhibiting radar search and seriously losing coordination. This would give Hohendorf—now closing in from the rear with his four aircraft, attack radars on standby and thus not emitting—the chance to launch before the target aircraft could successfully evade. The proximity of the mountains would seriously inhibit any widely divergent maneuvers.

The Flanker commander had allowed his obsession with the target aircraft to lead his force into a trap of his own making.

Jason was not one of those people who rubbished his adversaries and their equipment. He considered the Su-27K to be one of the finest fighter aircraft in the world, and it almost pained him to see them being so wasted, even though this was good news for him.

He chose not to interfere with Hohendorf's tactics,and concentrated upon his own part within them.

"Zero-Six," he called to Morton.

"Zero-Six."

"Eyes peeled."

"Roger."

"How do you feel now?" Carlizzi asked.

"Will you quit worrying about me, Carlo?" Morton said.

"I'm not worried."

"Think they gave her my message?" Morton asked, after a while.

He banked into a steep turn, carrying out the defensive pattern that Jason had instructed him to. Just above him, Jason's aircraft flashed past in the opposite direction. Their weaving, circular track moved across the sky on the general heading of the C130, a shifting, protective umbrella.

"Love of your life, is she?" Carlizzi asked mildly.

"To tell you the truth, Carlo, I don't know. I mean, I really care about her. A lot. She's ... well ... she's kind of hard to pin down ..."

"A woman who owns herself."

"Yeah. Something like that."

"The best kind. Not easily caught, but not easily distracted once you do get her. Is she very attractive?"

"Very, but in a very special way. I think a lot of guys try to hit on her; but she's no bimbo."

"I wouldn't expect her to be."

"She's tough too. Can lay you out as look at you. But she doesn't look tough when you see her for the first time."

"A woman like that is worth her weight in gold. Treasure her, and thank your lucky stars."

"I do," Morton remarked simply.

He banked once more, to reverse his pattern. Right on cue, Jason's aircraft shot past, going the other way.

Hohendorf was not too disappointed about having missed with his first shot. Now that he had a good idea of the Flankers' strategy, he knew just how to close the trap. He'd instructed Selby and Bagni to drop down among the mountains in pursuit, while he and the

Double-C remained up top to take on anyone who tried climb out. With Jason primed and waiting with Morton farther west, the jaws of the trap were closing.

Hohendorf was astonished to realize that the Flanker leader was so intent on killing the C130, he appeared to have forgotten to protect his team.

"All the better for us," he said to himself.

"Speaking to me?" Flacht asked.

"Thinking aloud."

"You were doing plenty of that," Flacht said. "The Flanker leader, even if he has a fantastic airplane, is still fighting the old way. The target's the main objective. All else is secondary."

"I didn't realize I had spoken."

"Not exactly speaking. Ruminating."

"*Ruminating?* Cows do that. Okay, Wolfie. Time to wake them up. Tasker aircraft . . . go hot."

Flacht immediately switched the radar from standby, knowing all the other November ASVs would be doing the same. Instantly, five solid squares appeared among the mountains. Working swiftly, he designated a target and that turned into a diamond. They had lock.

"On the HUD and your helmet sight," he said to Hohendorf.

"I have it."

The arrow pointed. The box drew into the center of the missile steering circle. The diamond appeared within the box, pulsed, then froze.

He squeezed the release.

"One off the rail!" he said.

He watched as the Skyray etched its trail of death, heading for its target below.

"There goes one from Zero-Three," Flacht said. Then he was studying the moving trail on the screen as it shortened, the closer it got to the target.

Then a sunburst appeared where the target had been.

"We got him!" Flacht exclaimed. "Two down!"

"Elmer Lee would call this shooting fish in a barrel."

"I'm not complaining."

"Neither am I. Our objective is to get Tasker Charlie to safety."

"And theirs is to kill it."

"Which we're not going to let them do."

One of the remaining squares on Flacht's MFD suddenly winked out. "Either he's managed to hide from my artificial eye," he said to Hohendorf, "or we just got another."

"That's a splash," they heard from Cottingham.

"Three down," Flacht said. "He's only got three left now. What's he going to do? I don't how good he is, or his plane. He's two-to-one, and down there among the mountains. We can sniff him out. He should just leave it and go home."

"I would let him go," Hohendorf said, "but I don't think we're dealing with a man who would take the opportunity. Even if he's left with one plane, he'll still go for it. He has to. He can't go back as a failure."

"His pride will kill him."

"That's his problem."

Asnayev was not contemplating failure. The target *had* to be taken down, fighter screen or not. He would not let his men down by giving up. They had come with him, and three were gone. Not to kill the target would be an insult to them.

He rose briefly to skim a mountain range and did a fast scan with his radar, coupling it to the infrared tracking ball. He blanked out all other returns until he got the one he wanted.

There! That was it. The C130 at twenty miles.

He would close the range inexorably and gun it down, if necessary.

He had a lock. He fired and dropped down into a valley. The missile would make its own way to target.

"Missile incoming!" Voisin said to Jason urgently. "Not to us. To Tasker Charlie."

"Warn them!"

"Tasker Charlie, Tasker Charlie."

"Tasker Charlie."

"You have incoming. Repeat incoming! Radar. Deploy chaff. Go *left*, one-two-zero. *Left*, one-two-zero. *Now!*"

"Roger. Left, one-two-zero. Deploying chaff."

While the Hercules was heaving over onto a left wing to defeat the missile tracking, Jason headed towards the C130's nemesis.

"I'm going to tempt that missile to come after us," he said to Voisin. "Eject a decoy, and give us plenty of chaff as well."

"Attending to it."

Jason turned towards Asnayev's missile, then flashed across its path. It wavered just as the little decoy canister popped into space and began transmitting. A cloud of chaff followed.

Jason headed for the mountains.

The missile wavered some more, decided the decoy was a better meal, and fused explosively with it.

In the Hercules, everyone grabbed something for support as the big aircraft seemed to be turning onto its back as the pilots heaved it over some high ground to drop into the next valley.

Then it was wings level once more, and it continued to fly serenely on.

MacAllister glanced at her companion.

Serenic's eyes were staring into an emptiness only he could see.

Asnayev knew he'd missed. He was determined to get closer. A close-range, infrared dogfight missile would not miss. An R-73 should do it.

He pressed on, tipped on a wing as he skimmed the high wall of a mountain pass.

Behind him, his remaining three aircraft followed. The mission had already become too expensive.

But he had passed the point of no return.

"This one could be yours," Carlizzi said to Morton.

On his MFD he'd spotted a lone square rising from the remaining three. Its altitude was well above that of the others.

"This guy may be thinking of engaging," he went on. "He's left his buddies." He copied the display to Morton. "See? Two of them in different valleys, and the third climbing. Perhaps he's had it with the low-level stuff. It's not very comfortable down there with a wing like his. Great turner, bad ride way down, even in a neat ship like that. I've got him locked up. Now's your chance."

Morton had selected the medium-range Skyray Alpha. "I'm on him. Target locked in the box."

He squeezed the release button, and the ASV gave a slight tremor as the missile blazed its way off the launcher.

"This one's going all the way to target," Carlizzi said. "God knows why he climbed out. Perhaps he really wanted to fight. Too late now."

The other pilot had begun to evade. The readouts whirled into blurs as the systems constantly undated the position and speed of the target aircraft. The missile trail on the screen followed inexorably.

Then suddenly, the locked diamond had turned into a sunburst on the MFD.

"Yes!" Carlizzi exclaimed. *"You got him!* Congratulations, Major! You just made your first kill with the November squadron."

"Thank you, Major."

"Anytime."

But Morton was not feeling elated. He'd thought he would have been. A man had died so easily.

And it could just as easily happen to him.

He returned to the pattern, keeping a more urgent look-out for hostile aircraft.

"Well done, Zero-Four," he heard Jason say. "That was a classic missile engagement. Good look-out too."

"Zero-Four says thanks."

"Eyes peeled. There's still more out there."

"Roger."

Bagni had slipped into a valley behind one of the two remaining Flankers. Like his colleagues, he had found it hard to understand why the flight leader had allowed his assets to be boxed in like that. Again, like the others, he was not going to look a gift horse in the mouth.

Air combat was crazy at the best of times. People did things you never expected. Sometimes they gave you a serious fright and maybe killed you, at other times it worked for you. That was the nature of the game. No two engagements were ever alike. What worked the first time was not guaranteed to work the second. Tactics were constantly evolving, even during the engagement. Even the slightest modification of a well-known maneuver could mean the difference between life and death. The slightest alteration, a change of speed, an extra angle of bank, a thousand-foot difference in altitude, plenty of excess power, or the lack of it, airbrakes out at the right moment—or the wrong one; each time was different.

This one was more different than most.

Then the Flanker pilot spotted him. Immediately, it hauled into a steep climb and rocketed out of the valley, afterburners blazing.

Bagni was ready for that. He followed.

The ASV stood on its tail and chased after the fleeing aircraft. He knew he had to be quick if he was to make the most of this chance. He was determined not to allow the Flanker to gain the initiative. Life could become very problematic if that happened, and he had no intention of finding out just how problematic.

Less than a second had passed. The Flanker pilot would soon be cutting the burners, rolling in the climb, then dropping the nose and hauling round tightly, to try and catch the ASV as it shot past, still going up.

Not today, Bagni thought. *Look for some other sparrow.*

The trick was to take the shot while the boy upstairs was still sitting on the fires. No point wasting such an opportunity, when everything had so neatly come together. In air combat, *every* piece of good fortune had to be exploited. There were no points for second best. Being second best meant being dead.

Bagni had switched to the agile, infrared Krait and had the Sukhoi nicely locked on the helmet sight. The blazing afterburners gave the missile a massive heat source to lock on to. It had begun the characteristic modulated slavering that made it sound almost like a live animal.

It was ready, and wanted to go.

Bagni pressed the release button. The Krait shot off the rail with a kind of *paff* sound and streaked towards its still-climbing target. Belatedly, the Flanker pilot canceled his burners and was about to begin his roll; but that was of little avail against the superfast Krait. It could switch spectrums in flight and home-in on the heat source of the friction against the skin of an aircraft, caused by its passage through the air. It didn't really need the lure of the burners, but their afterglow, trailing in the wake of the Sukhoi, was a nice, fat bonus. It couldn't miss.

It caught the fleeing aircraft just as the pilot was breaking out of the climb to roll away and head back down, entering a tail pipe and erupting in a great darting, fiery cloud. Pieces of the aircraft began tumbling down and Bagni had to take violent evasive action to escape being hit by one, or be showered with burning fuel.

"Hey, Nico," Stockmann said, watching as a flaming piece of wreckage sliced past, too close for comfort. "Next time you want a firebath, warn me, huh? I'll bring my fireman's outfit."

It was only when he came to reply that Bagni realized his lips were drawn tightly across his teeth. He had to exercise the muscles briefly, before he could say anything.

"Next time . . . I will."

Stockmann frowned. "You okay there, Nico?"

"I am . . . okay. It was just . . . close . . . that . . . that's all." Bagni breathed deeply, relieved he had got the 27K before its pilot had fully realized what was happening.

"You can say that again," Stockmann commented drily. "One of those two monster sails of a fin came right past my head. If you'd broken away a moment later, it would have been in my lap . . . or what would have been left of my lap. Some kill, huh?"

"Yes. Some kill."

They're gone! Asnayev was thinking. *My boys are all gone, and all because of one wretched transport aircraft. I have failed. The aircraft still flies, and my flight is gone!*

Suddenly, he rose out of the valley and into the open. Almost immediately he got an infrared lock on the Hercules, which, in the process of changing valleys, had become well exposed.

This time. This time he would get it. Whether it had been worth the terrible sacrifice hardly mattered now. He *wanted* to get that C130. He was determined. It had become inescapably personal.

But at that very moment, Asnayev heard an ominous sound. His threat-warner was telling him that a missile was on its way.

The distraction cost him the opportunity. He could still try to retrieve it but the Hercules, forewarned by its escort, was laying down a veritable curtain of flares. These had been joined by those of the escorts. Added to all that, a missile had selected him as its next meal.

Asnayev broke his mission imperative and reverted in an instant to what he really was: a fighter pilot.

He rolled away from the target aircraft, cursing the circumstances that had led him here, and headed back down, trailing flares. The superb agility of the Su-27K aided him. He was able to turn impossibly tightly, close to the ground, before pulling steeply into a climb. The

chasing missile, determined to follow, had actually leveled out, prior to climbing after him. But momentum
and gravity had taken its toll on its turning circle. It
skimmed along the ground and, incredibly, attempted
to get into the air once more, to continue the chase of
its target. Then it hit a rock and exploded in what
seemed like thwarted, maniacal fury.

"What kind of missile was that?" Asnayev muttered.
"It didn't want to let go." It was, he thought, as if it had
been keyed to his own body signature.

But other things were now on his mind. The aircraft
that had fired the missile was waiting for him, somewhere. His head moved continuously, looking for his
attacker.

Then he glanced down into the cockpit to his right
and saw, on the radar warning display with the aircraft
silhouette on its face, that his adversary was close
behind him. He cranked his head round and saw, fleetingly, an aircraft that seemed indistinct, its shape losing definition even as he looked.

A quick check of the threat display showed it was
still there, remaining behind him, no matter what he
did. He toyed with the idea of temporarily switching off
the fly-by-wire control system to enable him to haul
the Su-27K into a high-alpha yank, then slice the nose
downwards as speed dropped, to escape; but doing
that while still in front was committing suicide. In any
case, he was not one of those who believed this was a
serious combat maneuver, even when in a position of
advantage. The resulting sudden deceleration left you
hanging in the air, just nicely ripe for an alert wingman
to chew you to pieces.

Asnayev rolled the Flanker onto its back, pulled into
a steep dive, rolled ninety degrees, then hauled tightly
into another bone-crushing race for altitude.

The other aircraft was still behind him.

He couldn't believe it. This was a maneuver he'd employed constantly during many combat sorties, in various parts of the world. He'd always got away, and had always converted the maneuver into an offensive one that had subsequently resulted in a kill. In the Su-27K, it was like carrying out a reversal of heading on the face of a coin. No opposing aircraft should have been able to cope.

But this time it didn't work.

The other pilot was staying with him all the way, anticipating, always ready, whatever he did. Grudgingly, Asnayev began to admit to himself that he was up against one of the masters of the art of air combat, who was flying an aircraft that was a very serious problem indeed. The way his flight had been devastated had comprehensively proved it.

The Su-27K was a big, curvy, beautiful aircraft. It made the needle-sleek, super-superflick ASV Echo look almost tiny by comparison; though this was relative.

Jason swiftly ran through his mind what he knew about the Sukhoi. The "K" version, developed as a carrier-borne fighter, was also designated the Su-33. The dedicated naval version had folding wings. He wasn't sure about the one he was now fighting.

There were many variants, each with its own special suite of equipment. The "K" had canard foreplanes, which enabled the already highly agile aircraft to be even more so. Further developments of the aircraft—the Su-35 and Su–37—were vastly enchanced versions, the Su-37 having thrust-vectoring; but both were still in the prototype stage, supposedly strapped by lack of funding. The big, wide-apart Lyulka engines were the secret of its phenomenal power, because for an aircraft its size, it was a relative lightweight. With everything else it had going, the whole set-up combined to give it its astonishing agility.

Jason was determined to practice what he had preached, time again, to his own crews.

"*Never* give an opposing aircraft an even chance," he would drum into the minds of the newly arrived crews during his welcoming speech. "If you're unfortunate enough to find yourselves in a turning fight with the various models of either the MIG-29 or the Su-27, *always* start from a position of advantage, and *keep* it. You're exceptionally fortunate to be coming to an aircraft that is not only agile, but is fitted with superb systems, and lethal weaponry. *Make them work for you.*

"You're of no use to me if you can't, and the aircraft are too precious to lose. I am not interested in kill ratios of one-to-one, or five-to-one. I become interested when the figure *ten*-to-one heaves into view. There are no passengers here. You will find it tough; but you will also feel you have accomplished something very special when you join your designated squadron, a fully operational pilot on the ASV.

"But exceptional as these aircraft are, do not take them for granted. Do not believe you've only got to be in the same piece of sky as an adversary and he'll simply tumble away, dead meat, before you've even breathed at him. When facing something like a MIG-29, or an Su-27, irrespective of the quality of the pilot you're facing, those aircraft will *kill* you, if you give them half the chance. *Keep* the advantage . . . *always.* It's either that, or get roasted."

Now he had to follow his own words. That man out there would certainly make toast of him, if allowed the most minute of advantages.

"But you're not going to get it," he grunted as he hauled the ASV Echo tightly into another pulverizing left turn, after the Sukhoi.

In a surreal leap, his mind found itself admiring the beauty of the other aircraft's planform as it pulled ever tighter, streaming great vortices of tortured air. Death in seductive curves.

Then Voisin's almost faint voice was cutting into the fleeting reverie. "You said something?"

"Uh . . . talking . . . to . . . my . . . self."

Jason's voice was punctuated by his straining against the constricting G-forces as he reversed the turn to keep the ASV glued to the Flanker's tail. He knew that neither aircraft could now dare extend into missile range. It was now down to guns; but as yet, there was no solution for a good shoot. The designator arrow on the helmet sight was all over the place, trying to keep up with the big, dancing aircraft. The gun "snake"—the dotted line that predicted the fall of shells—was weaving in seeming desperation. But the 27K would not oblige.

It pulled into a rapid climb from practically ground level, and almost immediately had flipped into a quarter-roll and was scorching away at ninety degrees to its original path.

But Jason had read the signals and was on to it. He was not going to let go.

Asnayev could not believe it.

The strangely insubstantial aircraft was still with him. Where were the others? It was almost as if they had retired from the combat, to become spectators in this deadly contest.

He briefly took the Sukhoi low once more between

the high sides of a narrow valley, then flipped out of it over the razor edge of rising ground and into a short climb, before suddenly pulling into a painfully tight turn, intending to come back at his pursuer for a head-to-head gun shoot.

But the other aircraft was nowhere to be seen. It appeared to have vanished. Asnayev was momentarily puzzled as he flew through strips of cloud. It was odd how the aircraft that fought him so tenaciously had stopped giving him the pre-lock tone. It had simply followed in ominous silence, as if its pilot had decided to unnerve him, knowing that he was now all alone in a hostile sky. But where was it now?

The helmet sighting system was still confirming its presence. Too close for even a close-range missile shot, even if it had been within the parameters.

Then something white flashed directly above him, going from right to left.

Asnayev gave an involountary shudder and a little yelp of astonishment, as he instinctively went into a vicious avoidance break.

What was that? his mind screamed.

Then he checked the threat display. His nemesis was again behind him.

For five astonishing minutes, the ASV Echo and the Flanker danced across the sky. Hohendorf had sent Bagni and Selby to shepherd the C130 home. The remaining ASVs would easily catch up later.

Asnayev had been correct about what had happened to the rest of them. Giving the combat a wide berth, their crews watched as Jason defeated everything the Flanker tried to do, time and again. When the battle went out of sight, they followed it on their displays as their sensors picked up every maneuver performed in the fatal dance by the furiously cavorting aircraft.

It was then that they began to realize that Jason did not actually want to destroy the magnificently beautiful Sukhoi, after all, and so kill the man who was piloting it with such consummate skill. Jason, they believed, was hoping the other pilot would call it a day.

The man, whoever he was, was very brave and highly capable. Jason clearly had no desire to end the conflict in death. They found that they too, were hoping the other pilot would give up.

But he didn't. He kept on fighting.

Then abruptly, he broke off. Jason hung back, waiting, but ready to rejoin and keep the initiative, if need be.

What happened next shocked everyone.

Without warning, the Flanker pointed its nose towards the ground and kept going.

They watched it get smaller and smaller as it plummeted down, everyone mentally willing their unknown adversary to pull out.

It did not stop until it hit the ground.

The last Su-27K exploded in a great ball of flame, a huge pillar of smoke boiling upwards to mark its end. They had followed it down and now circled over the spot.

It was almost as if they had lost a friend.

"My God," a shocked Flacht said to Hohendorf in German. "He killed himself! Why?"

Hohendorf was silent for long moments.

"I think," he said at last, in the same language, "he was ashamed. Or perhaps it was G-lock. Those were some tight turns."

"*Ashamed?* But you can't know . . ."

"And I think the boss knows it too. Let's go home, Wolfie. We have done what we came to do. Zero-Five," he called to Jason, reverting to English.

"Zero-Five."

"A good kill?"

"No," Jason said. "Not a good kill."

Even allowing for the effects of his mask and the transmission, the wing commander did not sound triumphant. There was a strange catch in his voice too.

"Tasker aircraft," Hohendorf called briskly. "Let's go home. Cruise formation."

They closed up on him, and flew on to join the others.

EPILOGUE

The Algarve, Portugal, near the fishing village of Alvor.

She walked barefoot along the beach, her sandals in one hand.

The beach itself was nearly empty and when she came upon the man who looked like a bedraggled beachcomber, she stopped. His hair was long and matted, his face hidden by an overgrown beard.

It was a hot August day, and there was not even a cooling breeze off the sea. The water was calm, its surface twinkling like a huge quilt of diamonds. A coastal fishing boat lay out beyond the headland to the right, and in the distance the white sails of small yachts seemed fixed upon the bright horizon.

The section of the beach where the man sat was devoid of other people. Footprints came and went past him, but a great loop on either side showed that their owners had moved well away when passing. He was by himself, in an island of sand. Next to him was an old sack of hessian. There were bottles of red wine within it and it was clear by the stench that came from him, he had been making good use of their contents, and not only on this day. There was a bottle in his hand and he drank from it, even as she watched.

He belched. Loudly.

She went closer and stopped again, remaining outside the rough circle of footprints. Neither said anything for at least five minutes.

At last, he spoke, without looking at her. "I spotted you a long way off. You can disguise yourself, but not your walk. I know that walk." It was a voice marked by long alchoholic abuse. The language was not English.

"I deliberately used the walk I knew you would recognize."

He laughed hoarsely. "Why? Did you think I would shoot you? Out here on this wide beach?"

"Who knows. I've seen you shoot in more public places. Are you carrying a gun?"

"Are *you?*"

"Yes."

"I've got one on me somewhere."

"Don't give me that absent-minded crap. Remember the person you're talking to. Even drunk out of your brain, you could shoot straight."

He still hadn't looked at her. "How did you find me? I made sure no one could."

"No one can . . . except someone you once taught the business, and treated like a little sister."

He chuckled. "I should have known. I taught you too well." He held out the bottle in his left hand. "Drink? Or if you don't want to touch this one, there are three full bottles in there."

"No," she said.

"So what are you calling yourself today?"

"Mac."

"You can call me Max. The old name."

He had still not looked at her. Another five minutes drifted by. She entered the footprint circle and sat down, cross-legged.

He took a deep rasping breath. "She broke my heart, Mac," he began suddenly. "Tore it out of me and left me empty. I thought I had found just what I was looking for. Someone who had nothing to do with the mendacious, conniving world we moved in. I was fooled, because she was more scheming than anyone I had come up against. I was fooled because I did not expect her to be.

"She was having affairs, Mac. Can you believe that? I got *fooled. Me.* The great cynic himself gets felled. I sometimes ask myself whether what we do—*did* in my case—is ever worth it. She's the kind of people we do it for. And I'll tell you something. Her kind are more conniving than some of the bastards we've had to deal with. Know why? We expect it from the bastards; but not from the honeymouths. That's . . . that's why we get caught by them. We become vulnerable."

His self-imposed exile appeared to have released a desire to talk about what happened, to the one person in whom he felt he could safely confide. She let him.

He belched again. "Sure you won't have a one?"

"I'm sure."

He tipped the bottle and took a long, noisy drink.

"I went on a screwing spree. I tried to screw her out of my system. Didn't work. I traveled. It just got worse. I *missed* her, dammit. I missed getting up in the mornings and feeling her next to me. I missed hearing her voice. I missed . . ."

His voice broke and faded suddenly, as he remembered. Another silence fell between them. He took another drink. The bottle made a popping sound as he drew it away from his mouth.

He drew in his breath, cleared his throat. "This still haunts me. I sometimes dream of her, even now. I used to think of other men going where I have been . . . doing what we had done together. . . . It's a killer, having such thoughts. I began to hate seeing couples together. I realized I was going out of my skull. I quit, and came here. I chose this place because anybody we've dealt with who has a grudge won't know where to find me. I'm not exactly recognizable either. So I've come here with my bottles. I have enough money to keep me going till my brain gets pickled for the last time. What's left over is yours. You would have found yourself with a big bank balance one day. I've already made the arrangements."

"I don't want your money . . ."

"You don't have a choice. It's already there. So why are you here?" Max went on. "I know it's not just to see what I've done to myself. And don't try to tell me differently. Remember whom *you're* talking to."

She told him about Serenic.

He listened quietly, drinking, while she told him about the girl from the café. When she'd finished, he said nothing for a while.

"Why did you come to me?" he asked at last. "I don't think you need my advice. I think you already know your answer. Or have you come to me for absolution, because you let him go? Or is it absolution for something else?"

In all the time she had been there, he had not once looked at her.

"*Look* at me, damn you!" she said.

He turned to look at her then, and she understood

why he hadn't before. The pain in his eyes was so shocking, she felt as if she had violated him by looking into them.

"I'm . . . I'm sorry, Max. I had no right."

"If anyone has the right," he said, looking away again, "you do. I have lost something I never thought I could have. That is far worse than never having it at all. Is there someone who means as much to you?"

She hesitated.

"So," he remarked softly. "I hope he's worthy of you."

"You should have kept the faith," she said after another pause. "What we do is important."

He waved a hand vaguely. "Do you really think they care? These people out there? Since the New World Order collapsed before it was even born, we have more surveillance of citizens than ever before. Spy cameras everywhere. They'll be behind the mirrors in homes next. Orwell only got the decade wrong. Is this what we really worked for? To have a *western*-style soviet? *Keep what fucking faith?*" He stopped suddenly to take another drink and gave another of his loud belches. "I've looked up the asshole of the world, and guess what? Shit comes out."

She got slowly to her feet, wanting to say something that would shock him out of his self-pitying, alchohol-induced stupor.

"I'm leaving now."

"Good."

She felt a heat behind her eyes. "You used to be a good man, once."

She left the circle of footprints. She did not look round. He did not look at her.

He belched. "Used . . . man," he said to himself, repeating just two of her words. "On the beach."

He took another drink.

The sails of the yachts remained painted upon the bright horizon.

The mansion in a southwest corner of England was in beautiful, landscaped grounds. The car drew up at the gated entrance. The armed guard inspected the U.S. Air Force major's credentials, saluted, and let the car through.

The car pulled up before the building. The dark-haired major got out. The two armed soldiers looked on appreciatively, as she walked towards them. She showed her ID.

They saluted and opened the door for her.

"Bloody hell," one of them said when she was out of earshot. "Just looking at her gives me a right hard-on. See those legs? What's the regs for trying to date an American major?"

"Same as ours, mate. Trouble."

"God. She's so tasty." The soldier made a fist and brought his forearm up sharply, in a well-known gesture.

"Look and dream, mate, and weep. That's as far as you'll get. You need to be a general. At the very least. And if it's her legs that've got you all worked up, like I said, the only thing *you'll* get into . . . is trouble. Big, big trouble."

She was shown to a door by one of the people in the house. The man knocked on it, then opened it for her.

"Thank you," she said, smiling prettily at him. "I'll take it from here."

"Pleasure, Major."

The man left. She entered, shutting the door softly behind her by leaning against it.

Serenic stared uncomprehendingly at her. "And you are?"

"Major Lane Holroyd. G6. What's the matter? Have you forgotten your ride in the Hercules?"

He beamed, eyes widening. "It *is* you! So you are really an Air Force major. You are so beautiful out of those terrible clothes, even in uniform. I always knew. Did I not tell you?"

"You told me." She went closer.

"So. You have come to see me? It is so boring here. Questions, questions, *questions. Always* questions. They treat me well, of course. But I would like to go out and enjoy myself a little."

"They must prepare a new identity for you," she said. "Remember, there will be people looking for you. They have to be very careful."

"I know all this. But it is still boring. You will have dinner with me tonight? Here? This is the only place in the house where they do not have cameras. I insisted. I always check every day, in case they break their word. As you can see, there are no mirrors either. We will be quite private."

"Do you ever stop?"

"With a beautiful woman? *Never!*"

She moved closer still, hands behind her back.

He watched her with open admiration. "Such a beautiful walk. I did not see this in Bosnia, although I knew you had a real woman underneath all the guns and the grenades. Aah." He nodded to himself. "Very, very nice."

It was the last thing he said.

She was close enough and one of her hands moved swiftly. In it was a small ampoule, similar to the one with which she had knocked him out in Bosnia. The contents of this one were very different.

The needle-sharp point struck him through his shirt, just beneath the heart. She squeezed it empty, then withdrew it.

Serenic's mouth opened wide, but no sound came out.

"The pain is too great," she said coldly. "That's why you can't cry out. But it won't last long. *You* won't last long. This is personal. It's for a young girl in a café whom you probably don't even remember."

She turned away and went into the bathroom, drawing on some cotton gloves as she did so. She wrapped the used ampoule in toilet paper then dropped it into the toilet. She flushed it away, then went back to where she'd left Serenic.

He had collapsed to the floor. She did not touch him. She let herself out, then put the gloves away.

She met no one until she had again reached the front door. The same man who had shown her to Serenic's door was there.

"Everything all right, Major?"

"Perfect. He's agreed to see me and my colleague tomorrow. Say, 1200?"

"That will be fine."

"Thank you."

"Thank you, Major. Good day."

"And you have a nice one." She shook his hand, then walked past the soldiers to her car.

The excited one watched her legs as she got in. "That's a great view, Major," he said boldly, ignoring protocol.

She gave him her best smile. "Down, boy!"

"See?" the soldier said eagerly to his companion as the car went down the drive. "She's game."

"Dream on, mate."

The Pentagon, a month later.

General Abraham Bowmaker had no idea how the card in the envelope had got on his desk. He opened it carefully and took out a card of the Norwegian fjords. The message was a simple one.

For a girl in a café, he read silently. There was no signature.

There was no need for one.

November base, the Grampians, Scotland.

Jason and the air vice-marshal were at the far end of the airfield, looking out over the Moray Firth.

"Damnedest thing," the AVM was saying. "The way that man you helped bring back popped it just like that. Last person to see him was an American major. Air Force, by all accounts. Some mysterious intelligence department."

"Do they think she had anything to do with it?" Jason asked cautiously.

Thurson glanced at him sideways. "I never said she was a woman."

"No, sir. You didn't."

"Less said the better."

"I agree."

"And I haven't forgotten, you put yourself in harm's way. Good God, man! You're in command here. Can't have you going off on jaunts."

"No, sir."

"Good mission, though. Very successful, in fact. Huge feather in the unit's cap. Mark you, in your place I'd have been fascinated to go up against a Flanker . . ." Thurson stopped. "Less said about *that*, the better."

"Yes, sir." Jason contained the smile he felt coming.

Just then, the swelling roar of an ASV on takeoff made them pause to look round.

The sleek aircraft came towards them, wheels

already up, keeping low. Then it reefed into a vertical climb, almost directly above their heads, afterburners blazing. It shot upwards on its tail of fire, wings sweeping as it went.

"Impressive," Thurson said looking up at it. "Who is it?"

"Caroline, sir. This is her slot."

Thurson stared at the diminishing aircraft until it had vanished.

"Women fighter pilots," he said at last, looking back at Jason. "Good God. Don't know what the world's coming to."

"Less said about it, sir?"

"My thoughts precisely."

ABOUT THE AUTHOR

Born in Dominica, **Julian Jay Savarin** was educated in Britain and took a degree in history before serving in the Royal Air Force. Mr. Savarin lives in England and is the author of *Lynx, Hammerhead, Warhawk, Trophy, Target Down!, Wolf Run, Windshear, Naja, The Quiraing List, Villiger, Water Hole, Pale Flyer,* and *MacAllister's Run.*

DON'T TAKE OUR WORD FOR IT.

When you grab one of these HarperPaperbacks, you won't be able to put it down.

THE PARDON
James Grippando

"Move over John Grisham! The legal thriller of the year!"
—PAUL LEVINE, AUTHOR OF *MORTAL SIN*

"One of the best novels I've read in a long time. I was unable to put it down."
—F. LEE BAILEY

BAD MEDICINE
Eileen Dreyer

"Eileen Dreyer writes top-notch, page-turning suspense with a perfect twist of wry, quirky humor. A winner every time."—TAMI HOAG, AUTHOR OF *NIGHT SINS*

DREAMBOAT
Doug J. Swanson

"Gruesomely funny...In this sort of company, you don't so much follow the plot as trot alongside, giggling in horror, while it sniffs its way home."
—*THE NEW YORK TIMES BOOK REVIEW*

ORIGIN & CAUSE
Shelly Reuben

"Fascinating...delightfully written...a story I couldn't put down."
—STUART KAMINSKY, EDGAR AWARD-WINNING AUTHOR OF *LIEBERMAN'S DAY*